LETTERS *to a* STRANGER

BOOKS BY SARAH MITCHELL

The Lost Letters

The Couple

The English Girl

LETTERS *to a* STRANGER

SARAH
MITCHELL

bookouture

Published by Bookouture in 2023

An imprint of Storyfire Ltd.
Carmelite House
50 Victoria Embankment
London EC4Y 0DZ

www.bookouture.com

ISBN: 978-1-80314-954-7
eBook ISBN: 978-1-80314-953-0

This book is dedicated to the Glaven Community Caring Centre and the members of care homes everywhere – especially the ones whose own stories will never be told.

More than kisses, letters mingle souls.

– John Donne

Behold me going to write you as handsome a letter as I can. Wish me good luck.

– Jane Austen

PROLOGUE

Letter Ruby to Edmondo

25 August 1942

Dearest Edmondo

We're spending our third night in the shelter of the cellar this week. Mother has brought down blankets and pillows as makeshift beds together with a large thermos of vegetable soup and a box of candles. Nobody wants any soup though. Father is sipping whisky from his hip flask whereas my stomach is so tied in knots I couldn't even keep down water. The shelling is louder than ever tonight. Although the anti-aircraft guns never seem to stop, five minutes ago two explosions in quick succession rocked the walls and made dust rise from the floor like desert sand. Still, I'm trying hard not to listen to the raids and to focus on the page in front of me, even though I know that at any second the house could come down on top of us…

Just now Mother asked me what I was doing. 'Writing a letter to Edmondo,' I replied matter-of-factly. Her face froze in shock. Then she exchanged a quick, panicked glance with Father. My hand paused. I waited for them to say something. Anything. But neither of them said a word. What *could* they say? That I was mad or deluded? That I couldn't send a letter to someone who no longer exists? But you do exist, Edmondo, at least to me. In my head you're still as alive and as dazzling as ever. I can see you sitting beside me right this minute. Taking my hand amidst the crack and thunder of the bombs to stop me from shaking, whispering something funny in my ear, so that even now, when any instant could be our last, I find myself smiling, my breath calming.

Or perhaps not.

Maybe you're crouched in the furthest corner of the cellar? Sullen and angry and as far away from me as possible. After all, there's been enough time now for you to work out what I did. For the incredulity and disbelief to fade away and for you to finally understand that me, Ruby, the person you loved most in all the world betrayed you.

Another blast, it feels as if the earth is being torn apart and all the candles Mother lit earlier have sputtered and gone out. Except for mine. Only my small puddle of light remains – at least for now. If tonight turns out to be the end, it's no more than I deserve.

I love you, Edmondo.

I always will.

Ruby

PART ONE

Note Cassie to Mrs Amanda Gibbons

30 March 2020

Dear Mandy,

I so badly wanted to talk before I went. I've been wanting to talk to you for so long, ever since that awful night before Christmas, but if I don't go now I might lose my nerve completely and not manage to leave at all.

Noah is in the car. He has Elephant (obviously) and a box of tiny cars concealed by a folded-up Lion King sweatshirt. All I'm taking are three Tesco carriers stuffed with clothes and Noah's medicines covered up with packets of cereal and tins of tomato soup. Hopefully they look like bags of shopping. If anyone sticks their head in the window to ask where we're going, I'll say that Noah couldn't sleep so we did a dash to a 24-hour supermarket. They won't though, will they? Ask us where we're going, I mean. Not in the small hours of the morning. A parking ticket is enough to make me come out in a rash, and I'm not even kidding. Surely the world hasn't become so mad that I'm turning into an actual criminal for taking my son out of London, for keeping him safe. To be honest, it seems years since I booked the holiday, before anyone knew the word Covid, so I didn't even remember where we were going until I googled it an hour ago. Mainly east, by the looks of things. About one hour north, then *three hours* east. A kind of bottom-shaped hump with an awful lot of coastline. And practically empty by the look of the photos on the web. When the advert said 'beach', I imagined rows of pink umbrellas and sunbeds, maybe some kind of bar and paddleboats for hire, like the resorts in France or Spain. But Norfolk seems nothing like that at all. The beach is just big...

enormous. And empty. Even though the pictures were taken well before this wretched virus arrived, when presumably the place was actually busy. I'm not even certain I'll find the right caravan. In his email the owner simply said to head for the green one at the far end of the holiday park next to a tree!

I'm prevaricating, aren't I? Noah and I need to be on our way. Any minute Stuart will come down the stairs and start to list the reasons I shouldn't go, all over again....

I can see Noah's face squashed against the car window. He's wondering why on earth I'm leaning on the bonnet, scribbling so furiously on a notebook. Normally I would have messaged you, but it's 2am right now. Maybe not so late for a Saturday night, but this isn't an ordinary Saturday night. Nothing is ordinary any longer, is it? Everything is closed. Silent. Still. Everyone has gone to bed, and you wouldn't want to be woken up by your phone.

Besides, you would have ignored me. I know you would have done because I've tried calling you nineteen times over the last three months. Twenty-eight, if you include the texts and WhatsApps, which I do – I did – I added them all up because I wanted to check I wasn't actually going mad. And that's not even counting the times I've rung the doorbell knowing you're inside, then stood on the step for ages waiting... It's just I have to explain what happened. Even if you never forgive me, we've been friends for so many years I need at least to try to make you understand. Especially now, Mands. When I'm scared. Scared for me. Scared for Noah. And scared because I'm about to break the law to hide away in what seems like the flattest, most desolate place you can possibly imagine where I don't know a soul.

Anyhow I've been standing here for ages and this note is by far the longest thing I've written in the last 20 years (so make the most of it!).

Please call me. Or if you don't want to talk, send me a

text. Or an email. Anything. You're the only one who would understand exactly why I have to do this.

Cassie

PS Don't let anyone cut those gorgeous curls of yours but me. OK, nobody can cut anyone's hair at the moment, but still... I'm the only hairdresser you trust, remember? You must have told me that fifty times at least.

Email Cassie to Mr Stuart Rowlands 07.15

30 March 2020

We made it. Me, Noah & Elephant more or less in one piece, apart from Noah being sick halfway down the A11 and a burst bag of self-raising flour (messy *and* tragic since flour is so scarce). I was worried the park might be locked up (actually that was worry number three – number one being I'd forgotten one of Noah's medicines, number two that the police would stop us) but the fob the owner had sent me opened the gate and the caravan was easy to find because it's the only one the colour of a tennis ball.

Anyway, I'm standing on top of a dune, balanced on tiptoe, waving my right arm in the air and hoping this will SEND. How huge is this beach!! Though the sea must be out there somewhere all I can see is sand stretching a million miles to a blurry blue horizon. It's like the desert, just not as hot. Not nearly as hot. And no camels. Nothing at all actually – except a solitary seagull pecking at something that's hopefully a heap of seaweed rather than a dead body. The light is sort of *spangly* and there's so much of it, I feel quite dizzy.

Can light make you dizzy? Maybe it's lack of sleep. Where the hell am I, Stu? And what am I doing here?

Email Cassie to Austin Davy 09.38

30 March 2020

Hi Mr Davy

I'm sorry to bother you so soon, but I need some urgent information regarding the caravan and there doesn't seem to be anyone else here to ask. (Actually there isn't anyone else here at all.)

Most importantly, is there any Wi-Fi? I'm sure your Airbnb advert said Wi-Fi was available, but I can't see a code. I'm crossing my fingers there is one – crossing everything, to be honest, because the phone signal is patchy to say the least. The only place I get any bars is on the beach, which doesn't really work as I can't leave my six-year-old son on his own every time I need to make a call. Plus, I absolutely need to be able to access the internet to be able to teach him. Noah (my son) has already missed so much school I can't possibly let him fall any further behind.

My other queries are the bins – where are they? The big ones, I mean. I've only found a very small one under the sink. And the gas hob – which I can't seem to light – is there a particular knack? I've only used a microwave or an electric oven before.

I'd be very grateful If you could reply as soon as possible. I really do need that Wi-Fi.

Thanks so much

Cassandra Ross

PS You were right, I had no trouble finding the caravan. The green is very striking.

PPS What's the tiny bronze key for? Nothing apart from the outside door seems to have a lock.

Email Austin to Cassie 10.27

30 March 2020

Dear Ms Ross

I do hope you are enjoying the beach. I expect the scenery is quite a change from London, especially at the moment. Normally the caravan park is full of visitors, but the travel ban has stopped all the tourists and second homeowners from coming here – apart from you, that is.

The Wi-Fi Code is written on the back of a postcard tucked into the mirror. If you can't see anything sticking out, it must have fallen behind the glass. In that case, you'll have to use the metal spatula in the drawer under the hob to fish it out. A slow sweep of the blade along the underside of the mirror should do the trick. Let me know if it doesn't, I wouldn't want your son to miss any more school on account of being away from home.

Concerning your other questions, the community bins are on the opposite side of the park from the caravan, which is good news from the smell perspective, though it does mean further to take the rubbish. To light the gas, you must press the knob and turn it at the same time as you hold a lighted match beside the burner. The right-hand ring can be a little temperamental so best to use the left one when you can. No need to bother with the little key, it's for the postbox. There's a row of them on the wall outside the campsite gate, one for each caravan. I don't suppose you'll be getting any letters, but in case I'm wrong the number of my box is 17.

Sincerely

Austin Davy

PS I trust my reply was speedy enough. I'm out and about at work, and as you've already noticed the phone signal in these parts isn't the most reliable.

Email Austin to Cassie 10.29

30 March 2020

Dear Ms Ross

I've just reread my previous text. I do hope my comment about the travel ban stopping everyone except you didn't cause offence. None was intended. I'm sure you have your reasons.

Sincerely

Austin Davy

Text Cassie to Austin 11.13

30 March 2020

I am on the Wi-Fi! The spatula worked a treat. I haven't yet tested out the gas ring or the bins as I'm too busy unpacking and trying to persuade Noah to label a diagram of a castle (ramparts, battlements, and something called a murder hole...) Anyhow I wanted to let you know the Wi-Fi problem has been solved in case my previous text sounded a bit stressed. And we are enjoying the beach, thank you for asking. At least, I hope we will once we adjust to the space. Noah and I are used to pavements, parks with pigeons and over-fed ducks, and snatches of sky between rooftops.

Cassie (from the caravan)

PS 'Out and about at work'? I thought everyone (except me) was abiding by lockdown?

PPS No offence taken, by the way. I do have my reasons.

Text Austin to Cassie 11.23

30 March 2020

I'm a farmer, Ms Ross, and your message makes me glad I am. It's not the kind of work you can do from home, however much the government might wish otherwise. Our lives sound very different from each other's. I'm used to a sky full of geese, grazing deer, and air that nobody but me is breathing.

Austin Davy

Text Stuart to Cassie 13.40

30 March 2020

Glad to hear all (but flour) arrived safely.

Why are you in Norfolk, Cassie? Because you wanted to go there, remember?

Email Cassie to Stuart 16.10

30 March 2020

Hooray, finally I'm not having to balance on a dune to get a phone signal. I'm sitting on the step with my laptop while watching a huge yellow sun hover above the pine trees that guard the approach to the beach. Thanks to the guy who owns the caravan, I finally found the code for the Wi-Fi (a spatula and a mirror were also involved but you probably don't need that level of detail). The good news means I can access emails. The bad news means I can access emails... Nine today from school with 13 links and 5 assignments on top of a project on knights and trying to help Noah master his five times tables (anything above 5 x 5 = hit and miss). Trouble is, Noah's far more interested in the beach than staring at a screen. When I told him we had to stay inside and work because it was a school day he went very quiet. Then after a moment he said seriously, 'Why can't school just be on the weekend days and the rest of the week be for interesting things?' It made me smile so much that since the weather was less grey this afternoon, I relented and took him to the beach after all. The sea was all churn and white frills, crashing on the sand with a roar and sliding back with a sigh like the waves were trying to haul their way to the pine trees. I'd been planning to do some sandcastle stuff until a man with a dog appeared in the distance and began to wave a stick at us. I told Noah it was the friendly kind of waving, but actually the man was scowling, and the dog looked thin and unpredictable, so we hurried back to the caravan to learn about jousting instead. Noah and I can't hide away for ever though, can we? We'll have to face locals and the supermarket soon. Maybe you were right. Perhaps I should have cancelled my booking like everyone else. The location would be idyllic for a normal holiday, one with cafes and queues, and the sound of other people shouting and laughing. Instead, it's like being on a film set, a scary one where the inhabitants of a town have been abducted by aliens. (If this is my last message, you'll know what's happened... ha ha.)

Is the emergency dentistry hub up and running yet? I hate the thought of you being so exposed to the virus. Presumably you'll be wearing a Darth Vader outfit or similar but the news gets scarier by the hour and nobody seems to be certain how to avoid becoming infected... I know, I know, you're too busy to call me during the day, but phone me tonight the minute you get home. You can tell me I'm worrying over nothing. Or not.

Love you

Cassie xxx

Text Cassie to Austin 18.37

30 March 2020

Really sorry to trouble you again but none of the lights seem to be working and the torch I used when we arrived last night is starting to look tired.

Text Austin to Cassie 18.45

30 March 2020

Dear Ms Ross

There's a master switch on the panel beside the main door. Unless that's turned on nothing will work.

Austin

PS It might need a little jiggle.

Text Cassie to Austin 19.02

30 March 2020

Help, the sink!! How do I get the water to come out?!! I've tried every kind of combination of tap movement – forwards, backwards, side to side. Is there a switch on the panel somewhere for that too? Or am I supposed to sing and stamp out a tune with my left foot at same time...?! Sorry, I don't mean to sound rude. I'm just beginning to doubt whether caravan life is for me.

Cassie

Email Cassie to Stuart 21.32

30 March 2020

There was no reply when I called earlier. Was it a horribly long day at the hub? I don't dare phone you now as Noah is finally asleep, and the caravan is basically one room (apart from a tiny loo). I suppose it's cute really, in a retro sort of way. All the cushions and curtains are covered in an orange and brown tartan check. Noah likes to drive his cars along the sofa and arrange them in different squares depending on the size and colour (of car, that is, not fabric) which is fine until we want to sit down or go to sleep, and I have to persuade him to park them somewhere else. Although it's going to be a little weird being here by ourselves – today the *only* other person we saw was the man on the beach – I know a lot of people are on their own right now and I'm sure we'll be fine. (Ignore my panicky message earlier. Why would aliens trek all the way from Mars to Norfolk and the man was probably waving his stick at the birds or his dog or something.) After all, who wouldn't want to be where I am now? A huge beach. The sea. And by the looks of it about a thousand pine trees.

I wish we could have talked tonight, though. I know you didn't want me to come here, Stu, but I had to, for Noah's sake. The risk of you catching Covid from a patient and giving it to Noah made me shake every time I thought about it. He just can't get sick again, he simply can't, and I have to keep him as safe as I can, even if that means you and I being apart for a while. You do understand, don't you?

Masses of love

Cassie

Email Cassie to Mandy 22.15

30 March 2020

Hey Mandy

I really don't know why I'm writing again so soon. Perhaps it's because there's literally nothing else to do, except email you or Stu (or my mother?!) and if I say any more to Stuart, he'll work out how I'm really feeling and then try to persuade me to come home. Anyway, perched here, tapping away, I could almost believe we're back at the White Hart, two large glasses of Pinot Grigio, a tube of cheese & onion Pringles and that bonkers nineties playlist making us shout across the table. I've got the Pinot anyway. Third glass already, which is probably why the words are pouring out of me like they're escaping, but there's no soundtrack, not unless you count the owls. Even a city girl can recognise owls. Every low-budget scary film has an owl or two, and now I know why. They remind us how outnumbered we are. Each time I hear one I feel as if someone is dripping water down my spine. And it's dark here, properly dark. I'm writing by the light of a torch so I don't wake Noah and if I opened the door and went outside it would be like walking into a solid black wall. I guess that's what happens when there aren't any streetlamps, or cars, or crappy illuminated shop signs missing half of their letters. Although the park probably has about thirty caravans I can't see a light on in a single one of them. I think Noah and I must be the only humans in the whole place. That's an incredibly creepy idea because our location is pretty remote. I realise the whole point of bringing Noah here was to avoid other people but until now I hadn't considered what remote would actually feel like. The beach and caravan park are at the end of a long sea wall that runs out of town along the edge of the harbour. On one side of the road is water, with boats – proper fishing boats, with masts, and crates and soggy nets – and on the other side is marsh, with grass and reeds and the occasional cow. To get to the beach from the camping site you follow a path through pinewoods that smell damp and green. There's a quiet, watchful sensation, similar to being inside an empty church, until you step from the zigzag shadows of all the trunks and suddenly you're on an expanse of sand so vast that there aren't any edges. It's how I'd imagine Africa or the Outback. There's literally nothing to stop the wind and the colours all seem to blur into one another so the horizon is smudgy like a kind of liquid eyeliner which makes it impossible to see where the sea stops and the sky starts.

On top of that I can't make anything in this wretched caravan work. I'm so rubbish at all things electrical (half the time I don't even know whether the problem *is* electrical, or plumbing, or just a question of turning a knob or kicking something hard) and I've already tested the patience of the man who owns the caravan so much, that he hasn't even replied to my last plea for help. His name is Austin and he's a farmer. I picture him about sixty with a handlebar moustache, chugging along in a tractor, high up on a ridge with lots of white birds following the line of the plough. Not that I have any idea whether farmers plough this time of year, and apparently there are no ridges in Norfolk because the land is too flat.

To be honest, I can't believe why anyone would come here when they can fly to Spain for thirty quid. The main appeal of the countryside must be the pubs (if only they were open... sigh...), especially the ones with saggy armchairs and fireplaces. Not caravans, and certainly not this caravan. Apart from being a ridiculous shade of yellowy green, when the sofas convert to beds the cushions are so close to each other you can lie in them holding hands. Everything else either folds up or down, apart from the sink which is so small the only way to wash plates is to hold them sideways. Only I can't wash them (or myself for that matter) because for now there isn't any water coming out of the taps.... You're right, you're right... being alone somewhere strange is a small price to pay for keeping Noah safe. They say the virus doesn't affect most children. But Noah isn't most children, is he? He's been so ill, so brave. I've almost lost him once and we're not out of the woods yet. I would never forgive myself if the reason he got sick again was because of a virus that *I* could have prevented him from catching.

He's finally asleep. Despite the night-time journey and the exhausting newness of everything he took ages to settle down. He doesn't understand why we're here. He must know this isn't an ordinary holiday because he keeps asking, 'When are we going home?' And I don't know what to tell him. How on earth do you explain what's going on to a six-year-old, for heaven's sake? All I could say was this might be our home for a little while. When he queried why Stuart hadn't come with us, I simply said. 'Because he has to work,' and thankfully that was the only Stuart question he posed. We've always been a team, me and Noah. Us against the world, with dads optional, which is probably a good thing if we end up staying longer than our holiday week.

Well, I've finished my wine, and you're not here to pour me another so I'm going to bed. My baby looks beautiful tonight, Mands, yet so pale and fragile. Maybe it's the torch-light, that makes him seem whiter, more helpless, than normal. I can notice how each individual eyelash curls against his skin and when I gaze at his thin little arm I can still see the hospital drips and needles... If I have to stay here for weeks, months, to keep him safe, I will, but please call or message me. Tell me what happened next, what you both decided to do. Don't let me lose my closest friend. Not now, when I'm alone, when we're going to need each other more than ever over the next few months. When I still don't know how I could have done things differently.

Love

Cassie

Text Cassie to Austin 22.41

30 March 2020

The sink....? Still no water... Lever? Button? Special whistle?

Text Austin to Cassie 23.02

30 March 2020

My apologies, Ms Ross, I've been occupied all evening with a difficult lambing. When did the taps stop working?

Text Cassie to Austin 23.05

30 March 2020

Now I feel awful. Awful and ashamed. I actually only tried to use the taps for the first time this evening, so I'm not sure when they stopped. To be honest washing hasn't seemed much of a priority today. I've been using sanitiser for our hands and – well – nothing for the dishes. Can I ask what happened to the lamb?

Text Austin to Cassie 23.06

30 March 2020

He pulled through but the mum wasn't so lucky, I'm afraid. Have you found the lever in the cupboard under the sink?

Text Cassie to Austin 23.07

30 March 2020

How stupid of me. I haven't so much as glanced under the sink, but I will now.

Text Cassie to Austin 23.07

30 March 2020

Who will feed the orphan lamb? Will he survive?

Text Austin to Cassie 23.08

30 March 2020

I'm giving him a special powder. From a baby bottle. Took a couple of hours for him to learn how to do it, but he's got a reasonable chance now. As regards the taps, you need to turn the lever in the cupboard 90 degrees and wait until you hear gurgling. Have a try now and let me know if that works.

Text Cassie to Austin 23.12

30 March 2020

Gurgling followed by water. Perfect!

Text Austin to Cassie 23.13

30 March 2020

I'm glad about that. I don't mean to be rude Ms Ross, but I have an early start in the morning and a lamb to feed in the meantime. If you have any more questions, please can they wait until tomorrow.

Text Cassie to Austin 23.19

30 March 2020

This isn't a question. Just an apology. And a thank you.

Cassie (not Ms Ross)

Text Stuart to Cassie 07.10

31 March 2020

Sorry to miss yesterday's call. Long day at emergency hub covered head-to-toe in gowns and masks, but the only other option is do-it-yourself dentistry with whisky and teeth tied to door handles. That would provoke a few letters to the papers, especially when the wrong teeth get yanked out! Missed you hugely when I got back. Caravan and Norfolk both sound grim. Why settle for one room of retro cushions when you could have whole house and feather duvet? I could move into the spare room and have no contact with Noah, or he could go to your mother, and they could isolate together. It could be fun for them both. Come home, Cassie, you're not supposed to be there. You're meant to STAY AT HOME!

Text Cassie to Stuart 07.11

31 March 2020

Noah can't possibly live with my mother! She lives in Cornwall, 200 miles away at the last count! He needs me to teach him schoolwork, to give him his meds, and we would both explode with the pain of missing each other! He absolutely needs to be with me!!!

Besides, my mother is exhausting.

Text Cassie to Stuart 07.12

31 March 2020

I can't believe you suggested such a thing.

Text Stuart to Cassie 07.15

31 March 2020

Sorry, babe, not thinking straight. Of course you and Noah must stay together. I'm just so bloody tired and you're miles away in the back of beyond and I've no idea when I'll see you again. I'm hoping next Sunday, though. Since the holiday was only booked for a week.

Text Stuart to Cassie 07.23

31 March 2020

Forgot to say two letters arrived yesterday. One addressed to you, the other to Noah. Who writes letters these days? And who would write to Noah? Forward them, or scan and email? Or keep them here until you come back...?

Text Cassie to Stuart 07.23

31 March 2020

Actual letters??? Scan and email ASAP. Super curious... xxx

Text Stuart to Cassie 07.24

31 March 2020

Going to work now. Will send tonight.

Text Stuart to Cassie 07.24

31 March 2020

X

Text Stuart to Cassie 07.24

31 March 2020

You did only book the caravan for a week, right?

Text Cassie to Austin 07.45

31 March 2020

Hi Austin, I want to say sorry again about last night. The last thing you need is texts from a tenant who doesn't know a circuit board from a stopcock. Particularly, late night ones involving 3 large glasses of wine (her, that is, not you). And particularly after a difficult lambing (you, of course, not her). Will you ever reply to a text of mine again? I hope so, because while I was scrabbling under the sink for the lever, I found an ancient-looking photo. The boy in the picture is wearing super cute shorts with a mickey mouse motif and holding an ice-cream the size of a cauliflower. Is he you?

Cassie

Text Austin to Cassie 09.52

31 March 2020

Dear Ms Cassie, the boy in the photograph must be me or one of my brothers. If he has fair hair, I fear the picture is of me.

Text Cassie to Austin 11.24

31 March 2020

Fair hair that looks like your mum has literally put a pudding bowl over your head to cut around the edge!

Text Cassie to Austin 11.25

31 March 2020

I've just reread my previous text. No offence intended :). I think the style suits you. (That's a professional opinion, by the way.)

PS How is the lamb today?

Text Cassie to Austin 15.30

31 March 2020

Oh dear. Have I offended you?

Email Austin to Cassie 15.47

31 March 2020

Dear Ms Cassie

I thought you might like to see a photograph of the lamb. He's learned to take a bottle now, and polishes off the lot, no problem, each chance he has – which is every few hours. At the moment he drinks powdered colostrum, which is what he would have got from his mother, but all being well from tomorrow I'll be able to give him milk. I've called him Ned. You're not supposed to get attached to your livestock, not in this business, but you can't spend a night persuading a helpless creature to live and not form some kind of attachment. At least, I can't. I think this one's a tough little chap and Ned seems to suit him somehow.

Anyhow I wanted to say that I hope the caravan is to your satisfaction. She's an early Avondale and back in her heyday was regarded as a classy little number. However, she's been in my family a good number of years (as you can tell from that old photograph) and although I'm used to all her little ways, I can see she might not be up to the standard you expected, coming, as you do, from London, and that I should have provided a few instructions. If you like, I could ask around to find out if there might be an alternative available. Though you'll appreciate it's not easy to find accommodation at the moment, what with the travel ban and the locals not always understanding that people might have good reasons for not abiding by it.

Sincerely

Austin

PS I wasn't in the least offended by your comments. I've never been one to mind what others think of my appearance, which most round here would say was just as well. Besides, my mum did use a pudding bowl to cut my hair and I might have to do the same myself if the barbers don't open again soon.

Email Cassie to Austin 18.13

31 March 2020

Noah and I went into town after lunch. From the moment I discovered the photograph of you with the enormous ice-cream, he kept pestering me to buy him one and to be honest, it's been so deathly quiet in the campsite I was happy to check that the locals hadn't been obliterated by the virus, or evacuated, or abducted by aliens, and that real people were living and breathing somewhere reasonably close. All the shops were shuttered up and closed though. Lockdown. I suppose the clue is in the name. We did spy a woman with a carrier bag full of loo-rolls, but she crossed the road before I could ask her where she bought them, and Noah and I could hardly chase after her when we're all supposed to be avoiding each other. We did stumble across the supermarket eventually, and Noah made do with a lolly (though I had to promise cross-your-heart style to find him an ice-cream like the one in your photograph another day). The cashier gave me a stare as chilly as the freezer cabinet and for a horrible moment I thought she might actually refuse to serve me. Luckily, an altercation broke out in a nearby aisle over the last packet of sugar and she must have decided that was enough upset for one afternoon because in the end she simply scanned our shopping looking as if her lips had been glued together. I hope this isn't a sign of things to come...

Ned is a perfect name for the lamb! He looks exactly like a

Ned to me, tough, as you say, but also with a gleam in his eyes as if he knows how lucky he is (not for losing his mother, of course, but having you to feed him all through the night). When I showed the photograph of Ned to Noah, he immediately bombarded me with all sorts of questions I couldn't answer, like if Ned knew that his mummy had died, whether they have sheep in China and how old Ned had to be before he could grow a jumper! I was tempted to ask you right away but decided I had already pestered you quite enough with demands about the caravan, so Noah and I googled them on the computer instead (though obviously not the one about Ned missing his mum). Now I know all I possibly can about lambs and even if that's not true I certainly know considerably more than I did this time yesterday. As soon as we finished Noah suddenly wrapped his arms round me and gave me a huge kiss. 'Ned can't hug his mummy anymore,' he said solemnly, 'but I can hug you.' Honestly, Austin, I didn't want him to ever let go... He's supposed to be doing a project on knights as part of his schoolwork, but I might ask his teacher if he can do one on farming instead. I can't see the point in learning about Motte and Bailey castles. Understanding the basics of the farming world would be much more practical and would probably seem just as exotic to him as Medieval England. Living in the city we never see cows and sheep, or tractors, only cats and dogs, the occasional slinky-eyed fox and nose-to-tail tractor-less traffic.

Please don't worry whether the caravan is good enough for me. Of course it is. Although the practicalities have been a challenge, that's because I am mind-bogglingly hopeless with all things electrical and mechanical. I'm really very grateful you allowed us to come here despite the restrictions and Noah and I couldn't possibly move anywhere else now, not when I've finally worked out how to operate the lights, the gas *and* the water. In fact, this is probably the time to ask if I can extend my 7-day booking? Unless you're keen to see us leave (which you very well might be) I'd like to stay here for the next few weeks. For reasons I'd rather not go into now, it's much safer for Noah to be here than in London.

By the way, getting the taps to come on was a big relief because the door to the shower block in the camp is criss-crossed with red and white tape like a crime scene. I'll have to rig up a bucket shower otherwise social distancing won't be the only reason other people want to avoid us! I'm assuming of course the tape is to keep people out rather than because there's been a murder. If so, the murderer and his victim must both have been exceptionally discreet because Noah and I haven't seen or heard anyone else on the site since we arrived.

Cassie

PS I'm sorry to say that Noah is obsessed by the photograph of Ned and has now lost interest in the one of you with the ice-cream (though he hasn't forgotten my promise).

Text Stuart to Cassie 18.38

31 March 2020

Stopping off at Trevor's for beer and takeaway. Might be home late.

Hope all good in caravan land.

Speak tomorrow. X

Text Cassie to Stuart 18.43

31 March 2020

Is that allowed? Seeing Trevor, I mean. XX

Text Stuart to Cassie 19.14

31 March 2020

We're buddying-up for survival purposes. Trevor lives alone – now I do too.

Text Cassie to Stuart 19.14

31 March 2020

Don't say that! You don't live alone. You live with me and Noah, we're just apart temporarily.

How was your day? XX

Text Stuart to Cassie 19.17

31 March 2020

Nobody else in the house. No idea when my girlfriend will return. (Something tells me not this weekend, right, Cassie?) I'm pretty confident that's enough to satisfy anyone's definition of living alone.

Day = long and tiring. Work = long and tiring. Bracing for wave of referrals.

Text Cassie to Stuart 19.20

31 March 2020

Call me when you get home. It doesn't matter how late. I'll go outside so I don't wake Noah. And don't forget to email the letters (please!)

XXX

PS Wave of referrals? That sounds awful. I'm so proud of you for being brave and seeing patients (but a little scared too).

Email Austin to Cassie 19.42

31 March 2020

Dear Cassie

I don't mind you asking me questions about farming, or anything else. I'd be happy to tell Noah whatever he wants to know. Only sometimes I may not be able to answer you straight away because I'll be doing other things and won't be looking at my phone. And you're welcome to stay in the caravan for as long as you like. Noah sounds a smashing lad and if he were mine, I'd want to do my best for him too.

Austin

PS They probably put tape over the entrance to the shower block because the door doesn't have a lock. The showers should still work better than a bucket!

Text Cassie to Stuart 23.30

31 March 2020

Stu? Are you there??? Xx

Text Cassie to Stuart 23.45

31 March 2020

???

Text Cassie to Stuart 23.52

31 March 2020

I'm sitting on the caravan step. The sky is littered with stars, like somebody has thrown handfuls of glitter into the sky. It's beautiful. And quietly terrifying. The thought that whatever happens, to me, to Noah, to any of us, the stars will keep on shining exactly the same.

Email Stuart to Cassie 07.07

1 April 2020

Cassie

Scanned letters attached below. Sorry not to call yesterday. Watched *Game of Thrones* with Trevor and didn't get back til nearly midnight. Let's speak this evening. 7.30?

Stu x

PS Hope everything OK? Your last message sounded a bit odd.

Letter Mrs Margaret Flemming MA, MoE (Leadership) to Year 6 parents

27 March 2020

Dear Parent

Dear New Best Friend...

I know exactly what you're thinking, why is Mrs Flemming writing us a letter? After all, who writes letters these days? You must all be used to getting updates from the school by email (as indeed we have become used to receiving regular emails from you!) The reason is because I want to encourage your children to participate in an initiative that will require writing letters, and to enter into the spirit of the project I thought I should start the ball rolling with a letter of my own.

You will, of course, all be aware of the pandemic, wreaking havoc across the world. The government has already announced that anyone over the age of seventy should self-isolate as a precautionary measure against the spread of coronavirus. And, of course, schools were told to close their doors from the afternoon of Friday, 20 March. These dreadful restrictions will cut off both our older generation and our young people from the myriad of normal social interactions that make up our daily life. How lonely they might become! How despairing! What can we do, I wondered, to alleviate a little of that loneliness and use this challenging time for those wonderful people at opposite ends of life's journey to learn about each other and so about the journey of life itself? Letters, I decided, was the answer. An initiative I'm calling *Dear New Best Friend*....

I'm requesting each young person in year group 6 to become the pen pal of a resident in a care home called Shirley House, a wonderful establishment with which I happen to be familiar because my own mother spent her last years there. Merely a week ago, I spoke to the manager of Shirley House about my idea and asked her to enquire of the residents, who of them would like to participate. Those who responded positively were asked to write an initial letter introducing themselves and Miss Gibbs, our Head of Literacy, has paired them with a child whom she thought would gain the most from the correspondence. I'm delighted to tell you that your child was selected as a match. Enclosed with this letter is the introductory note from the elderly lady or gentlemen in question to which I'm sure they would be excited to receive a reply. Please do encourage your child to embrace the scheme and put pen to paper as soon as possible. I am absolutely certain this will be an enormously fulfilling experience for both them and their New Best Friend!

Good luck to you all!

Yours sincerely

Margaret E. Flemming (Headmistress)

Letter Ms Ruby Summers to New Best Friend

Undated

Dear New Best Friend

My name is Ruby Summers and I'm ninety-six years old.

Ninety-six! What an extraordinary thing to write. To you such an age must be scarcely imaginable, and I can barely believe it myself. On chilly mornings, when I'm barely awake and waiting for a nice young woman called Amy to assist with my bathroom routine, I sometimes become convinced I'm a girl again, lying under the covers and waiting until the last possible moment to leap out of bed and dress at the speed of light in an unheated room. (Yes, totally unheated! Even when the frost was on the *inside* of the windows!) Nowadays I can't leap anywhere of course. However, my eyes and ears are remarkably still quite functional and when you have so few days left you appreciate every minute of them. Does your mother have an egg-timer? One where sand trickles through a little glass bowl. There can't be very much sand left in my bowl now and so I find myself noticing all sorts of everyday things I never did before. Like the nice rich velvet of the chair cushion and the robin who watches me from the windowsill. It's like somebody has turned up the volume and the colours on the television both at the same time. My only complaint is that I'm looking at the same cushion cover, and quite possibly the same robin, day after day and because of this dreadful virus I don't suppose matters will change any time soon. That is a shame because although I'm lucky enough to have ninety-six years of living to remember, I would very much enjoy thinking about somebody else for a change.

Perhaps you might be able to help?

I understand your school has suggested that children like you might be persuaded to write to an old lady like me. For my part, I can't see why any young person would be interested in what I have to say. Or want to spend so much as a minute of their precious youth writing to an elderly stranger, however frustrated they may be with the state of the world. Nevertheless, should I be wrong, should boredom, or curiosity, or simply a demanding or favourite schoolteacher entice you to put pen to paper, I can only say I would be utterly delighted to receive a reply. Please send any letter care of the Manager's Office, 103 Bucklesham Road, Ipswich, Suffolk IP3.

Your new best friend

Ruby

Text Cassie to Stuart 07.45

1 April 2020

Did you read those letters? The Head has set up a pen-pal scheme between children in year 6 with the residents of a care home in Suffolk and Noah has been sent a letter by an old woman aged ninety-six! Noah is in year 2!! What's going on?

Text Stuart to Cassie 07.51

1 April 2020

Sorry, Cass, no idea. You'd better ask the school. Just arrived at work, got to go. Will call tonight about 7.

Email Cassie to Mrs M. Flemming 09.32

1 April 2020

Dear Mrs Flemming

My apologies for bothering you at what must be a very difficult time. I'm the mother of Noah Ross (Year 2). I'm rather confused because Noah and I have been sent information about a school initiative called *Dear New Best Friend* and a letter from someone called Ruby Summers, who's a resident of Shirley House. You say in your letter the scheme applies to children in Year 6 but (as I've mentioned) Noah is in Year 2 and, because of all the school he missed when he was ill, is barely able to write more than a couple of sentences. Is there a reason why he was included? The idea sounds very interesting (if the children can be dragged from their screens –

good luck with that!) but I honestly think a whole letter, let alone a series of them, would be beyond Noah.

Kind regards

Cassandra Ross

Email Mrs M. Flemming to Cassie 13.45

1 April 2020

Dear Ms Ross

Thank you for your email. The pairing of pupils with the residents of Shirley House was done by Miss Gibbs, who unfortunately telephoned in sick this morning (from the sounds of things, I fear she has contracted the dreaded virus and won't be returning to work for a while). I can only imagine she put Noah's name on the list in error. Perhaps he has a namesake (or similar) in the relevant year group. I suggest you ignore the letter from Mrs Summers and concentrate on helping Noah keep up with his Key Stage One objectives.

Sincerely

Margaret Flemming (Headmistress)

Email Cassie to Mrs M. Flemming 14.32

1 April 2020

Dear Mrs Flemming

Thank you for your response, however I'm a bit worried about Ruby Summers. Won't she be expecting a reply? What if all the residents at Shirley House are given pen pals except her? Her own letter sounded very hopeful about the Dear New Best Friend initiative, and it must be dreadfully sad to be locked away in a care home at the moment. Perhaps you could find her a substitute for Noah from year 6?

Kind regards

Cassandra Ross

PS By the way, she signed herself Ruby, can we be certain she's *Mrs* Summers?

Email Mrs M Flemming to Cassie 20.51

1 April 2020

Dear Miss Ross

I appreciate your concern about *Ms* Summers but with a school to run, half of my staff ill or isolating, and the government's guidelines changing every five minutes, I'm afraid I simply don't have time to find another potential pen pal in year 6. Besides, her letter appears to have arrived several days after the others so all the other children considered suitable to take part will already have been allocated a resident.

If the matter continues to trouble you, could you perhaps reply to Ms Summers yourself?

Sincerely

Margaret Flemming (Headmistress)

Text Stuart to Cassie 21.19

1 April 2020

Sorry babe, just back. Is it too late to call?

Email Stuart to Cassie 22.37

1 April 2020

Cass, you're being impossible! After you hung up, I had to take a walk around the block to calm myself down – *contrary to government guidelines* (I already exercised this morning). I only phoned after we agreed because some of us have to work for a living! Even though the practice is closed to patients, tonight I had to stay late taking telephone calls under the triage system. Anyone we see in the emergency hub is in acute pain and we have to sanitise all available surfaces every few minutes to avoid spreading the virus. I tried to explain all this to you an hour ago, but you didn't seem to listen and only wanted to talk about an unfriendly cashier (who as far as I could tell didn't actually say anything rude), a lamb (why would I be interested?) and the fact that me calling late meant you had to speak to me outside the caravan in an empty campsite so that you didn't wake Noah. Well, I feel pretty lonely too. I've said it before and I'll say it again, you didn't need to go away. Come back and if you're still worried about Noah, I'll sleep in the spare room. At least, I won't arrive home to a dark house with no food in the fridge, and we could wave at each other from either end of the table or sofa while they frighten us with the next lot of graphs from Downing Street.

Stuart

PS I do love you, even if sometimes it sounds like I don't.

Text Cassie to Stuart 22.40

1 April 2020

IF, I'm worried about Noah?? Do you really think I'd be here if I wasn't?

Text Cassie to Stuart 22.41

1 April 2020

If all that matters is a dark house and a full fridge, leave a light on when you go to work. And bulk buy ready meals.

Text Cassie to Stuart 22.42

1 April 2020

Do you?

Text Stuart to Cassie 22.43

1 April 2020

Yes.

Text Stuart to Cassie 07.15

2 April 2020

Forgot to say, yesterday evening Trevor told me he'd heard a headmistress being interviewed on radio 4 about a pen-pal scheme. Must have been the one at Noah's school.

Text Cassie to Stuart 07.18

2 April 2020

I thought you were working yesterday evening? On the telephone triage system.

Email Cassie to Austin 11.22

2 April 2020

Hello Austin

Noah has been pestering me to find out how Ned is doing. He also wants to know if you live on a farm, how plants become food and what the best thing is about driving a tractor. Although I tried to explain about harvests and farm animals, I can't have done a very good job because at lunchtime Noah picked up his Dairylea sandwich, studied it closely for nearly two minutes, and then said, 'Mummy, how do you tell if this is the kind of bread that grows from plants or comes from a supermarket?!' However, if you're regretting your offer to answer his questions please don't worry. What with reading aloud practice and a new vocabulary list ('ing' words this week, a ridiculously long list of them), we have plenty to be getting on with. Though Noah did point out that farming is an 'ing' word, and I happen to think the third question is a particularly good one. I'm curious to know the best thing about driving a tractor myself.

Best wishes

Cassie

PS If, hypothetically speaking, somebody wanted to send me a letter, would the postbox that belongs to the little bronze key actually work?

Email Austin to Cassie 16.52

2 April 2020

Dear Cassie

Ned is doing well and starting to look like he might just be enjoying life. I could swear that when I bring him his bottle, he wags his tail like my bulldog, Badger – though that's probably me imagining things, which is easy to do, especially when I'm half asleep in the middle of the night.

You can tell Noah, I do live on a farm, one that probably looks quite similar to pictures he's seen in films and story books. My farm has a duckpond, chickens and a rooster that wakes me up the second the sun sidles over the horizon. Some of the barns contain machinery, but others have nothing but straw and hay and are perfect to play in without fear of anything except pants full of grass. I should know, because me and my brothers Jono and Neil grew up here. Now it's just me here with Badger (named on account of his white muzzle) who only ever leaves my side to hunt rabbits or steal chocolates. Chasing rabbits is normal but chocolates are poisonous for dogs, though Badger doesn't seem to know that. He's a sucker for them. Jono still lives nearby with his wife and children, but closer to the shops and school, while Neil has moved to Liverpool. The inside of the farmhouse is a lot messier than any picture in a book though. I'm eating my dinner at the moment and writing this has made me notice all the dirty mugs and clothes lying about the kitchen, not to mention, beds for Badger and Ned, and piles of muddy boots. A man ought to be able to clean after himself, but farming is a job with long hours and it's hard to bother with being tidy when you live on your own and nobody's allowed to visit.

As for how plants become food, you must explain to Noah that depends on the kind of plant. Wheat seeds are sold to flour mills and ground into flour, but the harvesting must be done at exactly the right time. Nowadays machines can tell you if the wheat is ready but my old dad knew just by biting on the whiskery ear and testing how much the corn crunched. Harvesting is an 'ing' word too, an excellent 'ing' word in my book, and if Noah learns what that means I reckon he'll be ahead of the rest of his class.

His last question is my favourite. Some people say the best thing about tractors is the technology and that driving them is like playing a video game. I don't agree. To me sitting in a tractor is the opposite of playing on a screen. Food is growing under your feet, the sky is changing in front of your eyes, and you can smell the rain or sun in the air as strong and as lovely as if they were dishes in a fancy restaurant.

I hope my answers aren't too long for you. Perhaps when we're not all stopped from meeting each other, Noah would like to visit the farm and meet Ned and Badger and the other animals. Though no doubt you'll have had enough of Norfolk by then and be wanting to get back to London.

Sincerely

Austin

PS The postman must still be delivering business letters to the campsite office so my box should work just fine as long as the number 17 is marked on the outside of the envelope. I hope the writer you have in mind is not hypothetical. In my opinion nothing beats a good letter for cheering someone up.

Email Cassie to Stuart 16.52

2 April 2020

OMG, the flowers are beautiful! The bouquet is enormous. And roses! How on earth did you find a florist making deliveries in a pandemic with red roses in *April*? I have to confess it was slightly weird to get a call from an unknown number, especially when the guy said he wanted to meet me outside the campsite gate with a delivery. I honestly thought he might be a posse of locals wanting to lynch me, or a policeman, or worst of all a nosy journalist. Instead, all these blooms – lilies, tulips, and agapanthus (as well as the roses) – were propped against the fence wrapped in rustic-looking paper and tied with binder twine, while the (very real) delivery driver was already retreating along the sea road. The stems were so waterlogged they dripped down my legs and I actually had to put them down twice for a rest on the way back to the caravan! I didn't even know they made bouquets this big! I've filled every size of glass and jug and still need a home for the tulips. If only I had thought to pack a vase (or five)!

Thank you, babe

Love Cassie

Email Stuart to Cassie 17.05

2 April 2020

Glad they arrived safely. I wanted to apologise for being such an idiot yesterday and flowers said it better than I would ever have managed.

Will call tonight about 7.

Xx

Text Stuart to Cassie 19.01

2 April 2020

About to call.

Email Cassie to Austin 18.32

3 April 2020

After I told Noah about the corn, he decided to test the crunchiness of all sorts of things (cornflakes, cream crackers, carrots and, less predictably, a tulip stem). He might be on the verge of developing a whole new scientific scale – a bit like the Beaufort one but measuring crispiness rather than the wind.

Cassie

PS I had been longing for the restaurants to open again. Now I'm longing to drive a tractor.

Text Stuart to Cassie 19.04

3 April 2020

About to call now. Let's make this our regular evening slot.

Text Cassie to Stuart 19.24

4 April 2020

Is now good?

Text Stuart to Cassie 19.45

4 April 2020

Popped to Trevor's for beer. 8.30?

Text Cassie to Stuart 20.57

4 April 2020

Is now good?

Text Stuart to Cassie 21.32

4 April 2020

Sorry babe, Trevor's ordered Chinese. Might be back late. Will call in the morning.

Text Stuart to Cassie 21.32

4 April 2020

XXX

Email Cassie to Mrs Rosemary Ross 21.58

4 April 2020

Hi Mum

A lot seems to have happened since we last spoke. I'd call you now, only the conversation would wake Noah and that's because – believe it or not – we're living in a caravan...

It's been an unusual week.

Do you remember I planned a week in Norfolk? The holiday park by the coast? Well, what with Stu being a dentist, and the infection rates in London, I decided not to cancel the booking and to bring Noah here instead, so we escaped last Sunday. At least that's what it felt like, driving through the night, expecting any second to be hunted down by a fast-approaching flashing siren. But we made it and have taken up residence beside pinewoods and a pale gold beach. Although the caravan is old, it's cute in a retro way that means brown and orange checked cushions, pale beige Formica and a funny graunching noise whenever the power comes on. Outside is painted the yellowy lime of an iced lolly and inside the seats convert into beds that are so close together I can rest my hand on Noah's back and feel him breathe while I'm still lying down. His nearness reminds me of all the nights we spent together in hospital, except here you can't hear any machines bleeping or squeaking nurses' shoes, just silence that's sometimes like a blanket and sometimes like standing on the edge of a cliff. Outside is mostly sky. I'd forgotten about sky. In London even if you look up (which nobody ever does), all you see are walls of brick and concrete. Here you can't not notice the sky because it seems to start right next to your feet. To be honest there's so much space it feels like I might dissolve whenever I step out of the door, and I barely dare let go of Noah's hand in case he dissolves too. Although the booking was only for six nights, the caravan owner has said we can stay as long as we like. He's called Austin, by the way – the owner, I mean – and he's a farmer with tractors, wheat fields and an orphan lamb called Ned whose photograph is now the screensaver on my phone (Noah insisted).

Anyway, enough about me. How are you coping, Mum? Although it's a worrying time for us all, I know the elderly are particularly vulnerable and that must be frightening. I'll phone you very soon I promise. I need to pick a time when Noah is awake, and I can find a spare moment from all the home schooling.

Love

Cassie

Email Mrs Rosemary Ross to Cassie 08.12

5 April 2020

Dear Cassandra

I'm coping perfectly fine, thank you. Although I might be ancient in your eyes, I regard sixty-three as merely late middle-age and I'm feeling neither vulnerable nor particularly worried. I certainly don't intend to allow an annoying little virus to slow me down when all the hullaballoo is probably a storm in a teacup. I sometimes despair of the younger generation. Your grandparents lived through a war, remember. The Blitz. Rationing. And worse. Whatever happened to good old-fashioned backbone?

Do call me later if you want but remember I'm doing my usual sea-swim at ten, then having a virtual lunch with Carol followed by a Zoom PCC meeting to discuss the August bank holiday village fete (by which time this whole wretched business will surely be behind us).

Lots of love

Your (not-so-very elderly) mother

PS What's all this nonsense about the sky being a different size and you and Noah dissolving into thin air? You need to get a grip, darling; the caravan sounds fun. Are there donkey rides on the beach? Noah would love that.

PPS What does Stuart think about you moving out?

Email Cassie to Mrs Rosemary Ross 08.25

5 April 2020

Are you taking this virus seriously, Mum? It's not like the Blitz. Having backbone or a stiff upper lip won't protect you from getting infected. Swimming and the village fete can manage without you for a while. You really should be staying inside and ordering groceries online. You do remember how to do that, don't you?

As for Stuart, I haven't moved out. The caravan is only temporary, I can't risk Stuart catching Covid in his dental practice and giving it to Noah. He misses me enormously, of course, but I know he understands. Yesterday he sent me the most beautiful bunch of flowers – they fill every single jug and glass I could find in the cupboards.

Love

Cassie

PS There aren't any donkeys here, it's not that kind of beach. And there wouldn't be rides at the moment anyway because nobody else is here.

PPS A huge bird just swooped past the window like a parachute coming into land. Its legs are far too long for a seagull. According to Google my parachute could be an Egret.

Email Mrs Rosemary Ross to Cassie 13.42

5 April 2020

Stop fussing! It seems I have no choice *but* to take this virus seriously since nobody my age is setting foot outside their gate. This morning the PCC cancelled the August fete (August!) and then Carol cancelled lunch because it clashed with her Tesco delivery slot. Backbone might not protect us from getting ill but a little bit more gumption would at least help to keep up our spirits. We've all got to die of something and at this rate I shall die from boredom or just go off from lack of use, like milk or a forgotten bottle of Chanel No. 5.

Anyway, the good news is your Aunt Dora has agreed to move in. We shall hunker down and weather the storm together, and yes, I'm perfectly able to order our groceries online, bank online, and host meetings, dinners, and book clubs online. Although I would very much prefer to take my chances with a few germs.

The flowers sound rather demanding – I hope you still have enough receptacles left for tea and gin. However I'm not surprised Stuart is missing you. He's a man who needs looking after. I told you that the first time I met him.

Do let me speak to Noah soon. I'd far rather listen to him than the riot of gloom on the BBC. There are only so many graphs and slides any sane person can stand.

Love

Mum

Email Cassie to Mrs Rosemary Ross 19.03

5 April 2020

Sorry to drag Noah away, but you'd been chatting for nearly half an hour and Stu normally phones about 7. While I'm waiting for him to call Noah has asked me to send you a message. So here it is, written by me but dictated by him!

'Hi Grannie,

Mummy made me stop talking before I had time to tell you my new animal jokes.

What do you call a cow from the North Pole? An eskimoo!

What do you get if you cross a sheep with a kangaroo? A woolly jumper!

What goes "quick, quick"? A duck with hiccups!

I've got lots more, but Mummy says that's probably enough for now and she needs to send the email so she's ready for Stuart. When can you come and see our caravan? I want to show you the beach and photos of Ned and Badger.

Love

Noah

Text Cassie to Stuart 20.03

5 April 2020

Are you home yet? Xx

Text Cassie to Stuart 21.01

5 April 2020

Stu? X

Text Cassie to Stuart 22.31

5 April 2020

???

Text Cassie to Amanda Richards 21.45

5 April 2020

If things between us were right, we would be on the phone to each other now. Or Zoom or Facetime, cracking open the Pinot and arranging a quiz or virtual cocktails, anything to make us laugh again. I know you're dealing with a lot right now, but how long can you stay mad at me? Xxx

Letter Cassie to Ms Ruby Summers

5 April 2020

Dear Ms Summers

I'm not a pupil at St Cuthbert's. My name is Cassandra Ross and your letter was sent to my son, Noah, who is in year 2 and wouldn't be able to write to you because apart from being only six, he has missed a lot of school on account of being very ill. I thought somebody should tell you because I'm aware how awful it is to be waiting for a reply from someone and not know whether you will get one.

Yours sincerely

Cassie Ross

PS The address on my letter is a caravan because that's where I'm living, temporarily.

Text Stuart to Cassie 23.22

5 April 2020

Left house keys at practice and had to go back. Only just home now as decided to catch up on paperwork. Will call in morning.

Email Cassie to Austin 10.30

6 April 2020

Hello Austin

Noah just asked me if tractors can move backwards. I assume they must do but since I've never seen one reverse and my experience of them is pretty limited to say the least, Noah asked me to ask you.

I also have a question of my own. Not a farming one and more of a request. Do you happen to have bucket and spade of the beach variety kind that Noah and I could borrow? The fact we've been here over a week and not yet built a sand-castle seems thoroughly wrong. This morning the weather was so incredible that instead of logging on to virtual school assembly, I took Noah in search of the sea. I've never been anywhere so golden. It must have been the combination of the sand stretching for miles and the sunshine. I felt like a mouse must feel in one of your cornfields! In the end we didn't see the sea. The tide was so far out we didn't go all the way down to the water as I was worried the walk might be too much for Noah.

My last question is, of course, about Ned. Does he still need feeding in the night? I hope not, as it must be exhausting when you have to get up so early. Unless, of course, you have someone to help you? In your last email it sounded as if you live alone, but it must be hard to run a farm without other people. You've been so kind and yet I've realised I know so little about you.

Cassie

PS Noah and I would love to see more photographs of Ned if you can face sending them.

Note Austin to Cassie 5pm

6 April 2020

Dear Cassie

I was sorry not to find you and Noah here. I would have liked to have met you both, even from a distance. Badger wanted some exercise and I needed some chicken wire, so I thought I would drop this bucket and spade off at the campsite on my way to the builders' merchants and walk Badger on the beach at the same time. I found them in the cupboard under the stairs. My brother Neil brought them for his boys when they visit from Liverpool but since they can't leave home at the moment, I'm sure he would be pleased for Noah to use them.

Tell Noah the trick to make proper sand-pies is to mix a bit of water with the sand and to bang the bottom of the bucket good and hard before lifting it up slowly. You can also tell him that tractors do go backwards but, because it's difficult to see behind, some have a special seat that swivels all the way round, so the driver never has to go backwards even if the tractor does.

I'll send you some pictures of Ned when I get home.

Austin

PS I'd forgotten how squiggly my writing is. I hope you can tell who the note is from.

Email Cassie to Austin 19.25

6 April 2020

Dear Austin

I was sorry to miss you too. Noah and I had gone to fetch some groceries. To be honest, a trip to the supermarket is beginning to feel like a drugs run rather than shopping, only instead of dodging the police, we have to avoid the neighbours. Most people are wearing masks so their noses and mouths are hidden, but they still look at us as though we've arrived on a spaceship. I think they would prefer it if we had.

Today, Noah was choosing sweets at the checkout when the woman behind tapped the edge of my basket. 'You're not from around here, are you?' She was staring at Noah, the downy fuzz where his hair is growing back. Although I wanted to pretend that we were locals I shook my head.

'Well, you shouldn't be here,' she hissed. And then she pointed at Noah, who thankfully was too busy choosing between a Crunchie and Maltesers to notice. 'A sick child like that could take up space in our hospital.' For a split second I didn't know whether to explain that my partner in London could give Noah Covid, or to slap her. In the end I did neither. I let Noah have a Crunchie *and* Maltesers, threw the grocery money onto the counter and hurried us both back to the caravan. I would have stayed upset for much longer if we hadn't found the bucket and spade waiting on the step.

They are perfect.

Red is Noah's favourite colour, and he was so excited we had to try them out as soon as we had finished his homework. By the time we reached the beach, the sun was splintering through the branches of the pines and their shadows were creeping onto the sand as if the trees had decided to join us. Noah crouched over the pail, concentrating so hard he looked as if he was solving maths equations, and when he lifted up the sides and none of the edges crumbled, I had to turn away. A few months ago, the odds of him leaving the hospital ward were tiny. Yet there we were together, on a beach at sunset, making perfect sand-pies.

Anyway, I've gone on for ages when all I meant to say was, thank you.

Thank you.

Cassie

PS Your handwriting is not difficult to read and the flourishes on your letters are beautiful – like dancing tadpoles!

Email Austin to Cassie 19.54

6 April 2020

Dear Cassie

I'm sure the people here don't mean to be rude. They're probably frightened and don't understand about Noah and the risk of you staying with his father.

I'm attaching some photos of Ned to cheer you up. Yesterday he got out of his pen in the kitchen and came to find me upstairs. My house is full of creaks and yesterdays, so when the bedroom door began to open in the middle of the night, I don't mind admitting I got quite a fright. It was difficult to say out of Ned and me which of us was gladder to see the other!

Austin

PS Nobody has ever called my handwriting beautiful before. Perhaps I'll try to find some other things to write.

Text Stuart to Cassie 19.42

6 April 2020

Hey Cass, I'm out tonight. Stopped off at Trevor's for a beer. X

Text Cassie to Stuart 19.54

6 April 2020

Say hi to Trevor for me. Xx

Email Cassie to Austin 22.13

6 April 2020

The photographs of Ned are adorable. Especially the one with Badger. It's lucky for you we're not allowed to drive to your farm, otherwise you'd be pestered by visits. As it is, Noah is bound to ask me for a lamb and a dog of his own and I'm almost tempted to say yes – at least I would be if there were any grass nearby, I don't imagine a lamb would be all that impressed by sand.

I forgot to say before that your note was written on the back of a letter which looked quite official. Something to do with insurance. I could email a photograph, but if you would like the actual document back, I'll need your address.

Cassie

PS Noah's father was never interested in Noah (or me, as it turned out). I live in London with my partner, Stuart, who doesn't want children of his own but just about manages to cope with me having one.

Email Austin to Cassie 07.10

7 April 2020

The letter must be a quote from the National Farmers' Union. I left it on the dashboard of my van and likely used the back of one of the pages to write my note to you. I'm sorry to ask you to go to the Post Office but I should probably have the original. My address is: Goose Farm, Blackwater Lane, Little Burnham, Norfolk. It's only a few miles from Wells.

Austin

PS It sounds to me like you're the one who does the coping.

Letter Ms Ruby Summers to Cassie

7 April 2020

Dear Ms Ross

How kind of you to write. Even though your reply was not the one I was expecting, it's been so long since I saw my own name handwritten on the front of an envelope that my heart leapt as if about to launch itself into space. For a moment I was transported back to being a girl and experiencing the same sense of anticipation I felt before I opened other envelopes, ones that changed my life in ways I'm sure you don't have the time or inclination to read about.

I should probably stop here, but your short note raised so many questions – don't we always give away more than we think? – that I can't help but pose two of them. Please put my frankness and curiosity down to old age and this paper straight into the waste-paper basket if I offend.

From whom are you waiting to receive a letter? And is it love or guilt that makes you watch for the postman each morning? I hope for your sake it's love. I've come to think that guilt is the most enduring of all the emotions. Love must be great to be timeless, but guilt never changes however lowly the cause. The years are like the mattresses in the story about the princess and the pea – however many there are, a guilty conscience never lets you sleep.

Oh dear, I've just reread the above and realised that's two questions, already. Even so I'm going to ask one more:

Why are you living in a caravan, temporarily?

Your New Best Friend

Ruby

Text Cassie to Stuart 19.42

7 April 2020

I thought we agreed 7pm is a good time to call? Where are you? The whole country is in lockdown, but you seem to be out every night.

Text Stuart to Cassie 22.42

7 April 2020

Hey Cass, sorry. Long days at the clinic and Trevor's place is on the way home. You can't blame me for wanting to stop off there rather than head to an empty house. I'll call in the morning again. XX

Letter Cassie to Ruby

10 April 2020

Dear New Best Friend

I don't know whether to say thank you for your letter or not. At first, I thought I wouldn't reply, and I still haven't decided I will. I may write this just for myself, to try to make some space in my head, because I can't stop thinking about what you said.

There *is* someone I want to get in touch. I want her to contact me very much. Though since it won't be by letter I'm not watching for a postman, instead I'm making a grab for my phone every time that hard little ping tells me another message has arrived. She's my next-door neighbour in London, and my best friend. At least, she *was* my best friend, all through the darkest days of my life. Now she may not be. To be honest, she probably no longer considers me any kind of friend at all. You see, I made a mistake, a terrible mistake. She could well say I betrayed her, but since you and I don't know each other that's all I'm going to say.

Instead, I'll tell you about the caravan, what I can see right now while I'm sitting here in the dark. It's the middle of the night, 2.45 am to be exact. The torch is my only light, creating a small white window on the paper in which the words seem to be appearing by magic. Perhaps that makes them easier to write. Outside the caravan is a campsite and next to the campsite is a beach so big it would feel empty even on a busy day. But nobody else is here. Nobody at all. When the tide is fully out the view across the sand reminds me what infinity means. The first few times I couldn't stay for very long without feelings of wild-horse panic galloping at me from over the horizon. There are woods too, all along the ridge between the beach and the campsite. The wall of silvery trunks and sharp green needles suck away the sound of the sea and create the softest, most intense silence I've ever known. So far Noah and I have only ventured into town twice – when we had to buy groceries. Our route follows the seawall alongside the harbour to the quay. The road is long and very straight and the first time we walked to the shops Noah had to rest halfway. As we sat on the bank looking at the boats, I could hear him mumbling under his breath so I asked him what he was doing. 'I'm talking to my legs,' he said. 'They need some help to keep going'!

Once you reach the quay the shop windows are full of brown speckled pottery and boats modelled from driftwood, or practical things for sailing or picnics. One of the cafes has a blackboard outside with the special for the 20th March (£9.99 for a plate of mussels and chips – which would make a nice change from baked beans, which is what I mostly seem to cook these days) while the 'Countryman's Outfitters' is still displaying winter coats. It's as if time has been frozen. At least the stores being closed means I only spend money on groceries and each time we've been to the supermarket I've been so anxious to leave I haven't even spent much on those.

We shouldn't be here, you see.

You asked me why Noah and I were living here in a caravan. The truth is because we're safer here than in London. Noah has been very ill and the medicine he has to take means his immune system doesn't work so well. In London we can't isolate properly because my partner Stuart is a dentist who has to keep working. Nobody here knows that of course. Anyone who sees us assumes we only came for a holiday and it's true that sometimes that's how it feels. After all, sea, sand – even sunshine – what more could we want? It turns out it's harder than I thought not to see anyone else apart from Noah. I speak to Stuart most days but the days still stretch as long and flat as the empty beach – which is probably why I'm awake in the middle of the night writing a letter I'll probably never send to a person I'll probably never meet.

If by chance you are reading this – and you want to reply – tell me something about you. I'll leave it to you to decide on that something.

Your New Best Friend

Cassie

PS I hope you're wrong about the guilty conscience.

Letter Austin to Cassie

11 April 2020

Dear Cassie

Thank you for returning the insurance quote. Since you said such nice things about my handwriting, I decided to send you something back, though having seen the note I wrote you, I think you must have been having a laugh – to me the letters look less like dancing tadpoles and more like a spider's crawl, a spider with hairy legs.

Anyhow, I've taken the opportunity to print out the photos of Ned and Badger. I know you have the pictures on your phone, but to my mind that's not the same. You can't hold them for one thing. And because you have to use your screen to look at them you miss out on the sideways pleasure of catching sight of a favourite one when you're doing something different.

I'm also enclosing a planner which lists the activities done on a farm each month during the year. That chart was hung on the wall of my bedroom throughout my boyhood and I suppose my mother kept hold of it for sentimental reasons. Although the print is old and faded the animals and the seasons haven't changed, so neither have the jobs. You can see how busy April is: Lambing, calving, muck-spreading, planting potatoes, drilling oil seed rape... The list goes on and makes me wonder why I'm not out in the fields now, instead of wasting time writing to you! Anyway, you mentioned Noah might want to do a project about farming, so I thought he could use my chart for his research. We can't have him deciding to learn about knights after all.

Yours sincerely

Austin

PS I don't really think writing to you is a waste of time. It was a little joke.

Letter Ruby to Cassie

11 April 2020

Dear Cassie

I'll skip the part about my surprise at your wonderful letter. Instead, I'll set the scene of my own writing environment. Far from being the middle the night, the clock in the church tower has just struck three o'clock, which means, I have exactly half an hour before the tea trolley is wheeled in by a young woman called Amy dressed in what very much resembles a beekeeping outfit. Although they say the gowns and masks are for our own protection, I would rather take my chances and see her face. Amy has a lovely smile with proper dimples you could poke a finger inside, and it's a shame not to see them at every chance we get. I would also rather have my biscuit, but because we all tend to rummage around for the chocolate ones the biscuit tin has been banned to stop germs from spreading. (I did try to tell them that viruses are not nearly as partial to Digestives and Gingernuts as humans are, but nobody wants to listen to an old woman.)

What's the room like? It's what my mother would have called 'perfectly pleasant'. I suppose it is *pleasant*, but also rather dull and drear. In the centre is an olive green, cream, and beige rug and around the circumference armchairs are interspersed with potted plants. Unfortunately, because the chairs are set too far back, we have to double over and lean forwards to talk to our neighbour, otherwise we end up peering at each other through the fronds of a rubber plant or an African fig as if we're trying to spot gorillas in the wild. When I pointed this out to Amy, she smiled her lovely smile and said if the chairs were any further forward, they wouldn't be able to vacuum the rug properly.

Not many of us sit in here anyway. Not now. Since the arrival of the virus, they prefer us to stay in our rooms, and most residents are happy to oblige. It's just the difficult ones like me who insist on a little variation to our day. Today my only companion is Beryl, a tiny woman who is barely visible under the excess of blankets tucked over her knees and shoulders. She's been settled on the other side of the room to me so we can't breathe on each other. Sadly, it also means we can't speak to each other either – although, since Beryl is nearly deaf, her conversation is random in the best of conditions. If anyone asks about her son, she's more likely to provide them with an update on the state of her bunions. Besides, Amy and the other carers like to have the radio on, which means none of us can hear each other anyway. Our routine is scheduled less by the clock on the wall than it is by the change of radio presenters. When the supervisor (Mrs Rockford) switches over from Radio 2 to Radio 4 that means it's almost dinner time and the end of another day.

The nicest feature of the room is the French windows which lead to a small patch of lawn. Although the doors are only opened on the hottest summer days, when even Beryl sheds her blankets, the view of the cherry tree is wonderful all year round. Right now, the branches are engulfed by rows of white blossom that remind me of the handkerchiefs my father and uncle used to wear in their top jacket pocket. After writing that sentence, I stopped for at least a minute to study that tree again. At my age, each spring is a miracle and every cherry tree a wonder. Perhaps that's true at any age.

Now to your letter, I truly hesitate to pose more questions, but the trouble with having a scientific background is that little things arouse my curiosity. So, at the risk of you calling me a prying old woman I'm going to ask why you said, 'she could well say I betrayed her'. Do *you* think you betrayed her? I wonder. Perhaps you think you had your reasons. Betrayal is something I've given a lot of thought to over the years. When it can be justified, I mean. Or forgiven. Still, as you say, we hardly know each other, and the wording of your letter may mean nothing at all.

Does it?

Your New Best Friend

Ruby

Text Stuart to Cassie 19.32

11 April 2020

Where are you? I called at 7pm and again at 7.30pm but you didn't pick up. It's been a long day, Cass, and I'd like to speak to you. It doesn't seem much to ask.

Text Cassie to Stuart 20.22

11 April 2020

Sorry. Me and Noah took biscuits and milk onto the beach. It's the most beautiful, peachy-orange evening and we forgot the time. Back now. X

Text Cassie to Stuart 20.48

11 April 2020

Stu, are you there?

Email Cassie to Amanda 22.31

11 April 2020

Hey Mandy

You do know I'm in Norfolk, don't you? You have been getting my messages? I had this sudden, amazing thought: maybe Mandy never received the letter I put through her letter box. Perhaps the dog ate it, or the envelope became mixed up with takeaway menus and freebie offers and got chucked out. Perhaps the Wi-Fi has been patchier than I realised and my texts are floundering around somewhere in the ether. Maybe you're wondering where I am, why you haven't seen Noah and me in the garden or out for a walk.

Then again, maybe not.

I'd really like to know you're doing OK, Mandy. Did lockdown come at the worst possible moment? Or was the timing a stroke of luck? Perhaps it solved everything, and you found a way forward. Is that too much to hope? I so badly want to hear from you, to know what happened after that dreadful evening. I've so much to tell you too, and some super cute photos to share – lambs, puppies, Noah without a tube or drip in sight, wielding a bright red bucket and spade. If they don't tempt you to contact me, then I'm guessing that nothing will.

I miss you.

Cassie xxx

Letter Cassie to Ruby

13 April 2020

Dear New Best Friend

I'm scribbling a few lines to you in the middle of the morning, sitting on the step of the caravan as Noah watches an online science lesson about the differences between wood, metal, and paper (with the help of bark, a teaspoon, and the notebook from my handbag). Sunshine is spilling over my knees while the sky is the blue of a postcard from Greece. I agree, spring is a miracle...

Who are you, Ruby? I don't know what to make of your last letter either. How can your voice seem so familiar when you've said next to nothing about yourself? I have a clearer idea of Beryl than I do of you. At least I'm aware that Beryl is very small, feels the cold and is partially deaf, whereas all you've said about yourself is that you're 96 years old and were once a scientist. Before I answer *your* questions, I want to know more about you. Tell me what you look like. Tell me what kind of scientist you were. You mentioned other envelopes, other letters, that changed your life. What were they?

Cassie

Letter Ruby to Cassie

14 April 2020

Dear Cassie

You're right, of course. How will we get to know each other if our letters don't summon an image of the writer, bent over her paper, pen in hand?

Nevertheless, describing one's appearance is a hard task at any age and at 96 almost impossible since I stopped seeing

– properly seeing – my reflection in the mirror a long time ago. That probably explains why the old woman gazing back this morning looked nothing like me! Whereas her back was stooped, her shoulders hunched, and her movements as frustratingly slow as the hour hand on a clock, I've always had wonderful posture – despite being much too tall for most men's tastes – the tendency always to run rather than walk and the inclination to dance at every opportunity. The sorry, white wisps that now pass for my hair should instead be a bob of glossy chestnut, cut considerably shorter than my mother used to like with ends that refused to turn in the same direction whatever efforts I made with the hairbrush (normally, very few). At least, thank heavens, I recognised the eyes: green or brown, depending on the light, or, more truthfully, who's asking (green always sounds so much more exotic, don't you think?) set in a face that's broader and flatter than ideal, but on the upside has enough space to house a big wide smile. I've always been complimented on my smile, though I'm sure that's mainly because most people don't smile enough.

To complete the picture, I should at least mention my clothes. I've probably worn a pair of slacks, a blouse, and a long woollen cardigan ever since I hung up my laboratory coat, and often in shades of blue. Although I'm partial to turquoise and cornflower, dull old navy suits me better. Nevertheless, I wear turquoise anyway and always have done. The main difference these days is that the trouser waistband is a little expanded; one of the few advantages of being old is that one no longer declines nice things to eat in the interests of vanity. Which makes the loss of the biscuit barrel all the more of a disappointment.

Now it's your turn.

Your New Best Friend

Ruby

Letter from Cassie to Austin

15 April 2020

Dear Austin

Thank you for the photos and the wonderful wall chart. All of them are now stuck up over the couch that's Noah's bed (I hope you don't mind Blu Tack in the caravan), apart from the picture of Ned and Badger asleep together, which Noah keeps under his pillow.

This morning – extraordinarily – there were two letters in the postbox for me, including the fabulous package from you! I'd forgotten the sense of anticipation that comes from opening an envelope that isn't a bill, or from a bank or charity. Handwriting is so much more evocative than print. I can practically hear the other person talking to me as I read, which is very odd since I've never spoken to you or my other correspondent. If you're at all interested to know, your voice sounds calm and steady, like someone who you could slip into step with, almost without noticing, whereas hers is the opposite, sharp and full of energy, like a very fast walker who memorised the route before breakfast and knows exactly where she's going. She's 96 now, I wonder if she was terribly clever when she was younger.

In my next letter to her, I'm supposed to describe myself. When I told Noah, he suggested I trim my hair first (which tells you how awful I must have looked), so I had a go this morning. It's hard to do your own hair, even for a hairdresser, which is probably why I took off far more than I intended. It's short now. *Really* short. I can feel the sun on my ears. Stuart won't like the new look (or that I didn't ask his opinion first) but this style is much more practical for living in a caravan. Besides, I like it. The hair must have been heavier than I imagined because I feel like helium balloons have been tied to my shoulders.

By the way, when I was doing the cutting, I realised that I haven't seen myself below neck level since Noah and I arrived. Is the mirror above the sink the only one in the caravan? You've no idea how much I'm hoping it is.

Cassie

Letter Cassie to Ruby

15 April 2020

Dear New Best Friend

I'm standing at the sink so I can study the woman in the mirror as I write. She appears to be about twenty-eight (I *am* twenty-eight, just trying to get into the spirit of things) with wavy dark hair, styled short like a boy's on top of a small, heart-shaped face. What she expected to see was the wrung-out pallor of a city-dweller, instead she can count four new freckles on her nose while her cheeks have acquired a slight pinkish hue that looks suspiciously like the start of a suntan. Eyes are blue (with random flecks of bronze), lashes black (naturally, not dyed), nails bitten (whenever left unpainted, i.e. nearly always) and body slight. Although she has spent as long as she can remember huddled over cots and chairs and hospital beds, to examine herself this closely she is having to stand up really straight and throw back her shoulders. Seeing the difference from now on I'm going to make her stand up properly all the time. I'm also going to tell her to buy a hat, one with a ribbon or flowers and an extremely wide brim because it would suit her hair. However, anything floral or ribbon bedecked would definitely not suit the rest of today's outfit; she's wearing cotton cargo pants in an unusual shade of orangey brown (retail name tobacco), a T-shirt in pale brown (retail name blush), while a sweatshirt (plain old grey) is tied around her waist. And the closer I look the more I realise they all need a good wash. As for the smile, she can't seem to remember whether she smiles with her mouth open or closed. When she experimented in the mirror both versions looked like she was in pain, so I'll have to rain-check that part of the description.

What's next?

Cassie

Text Cassie to Austin 16.32

15 April 2020

Where is the nearest launderette?!

Text Stuart to Cassie 20.35

15 April 2020

Photo has arrived!

Text Stuart to Cassie 20.37

15 April 2020

If you knew I wouldn't like it, why did you do it?

Text Amanda to Cassie 21.45

15 April 2020

Stop sending me texts and emails. You've ruined my life and I never want to hear from you again.

Letter Ruby to Cassie

16 April 2020

Dear Cassie

I think we've done enough scene setting. The overture at a musical serves to whet the appetite, but sooner or later the story needs to begin properly. You asked me about other envelopes, other letters, that changed my life, and I believe the time has come to tell you about them.

I could, of course, spend the next few days (possibly weeks) trying to describe the people and events I have in mind and writing you page after page. However, I doubt that way of doing things would yield a reliable account. For one thing, my memory is far from what it was. For another, I have thought about particular individuals and certain incidents so very much over the years I'm no longer certain whether I can remember the truth of what happened or only a different, rather biased, version as a result of reliving it all so often. Instead, I've decided to send you my own correspondence, mainly letters, and extracts from my diary. Not the letters I wrote myself, of course – I can't give you those since they are long gone, tucked away, and forgotten about in somebody's drawer or attic or, more probably, destroyed – rather the letters I received from other people and extracts from my diary. Unfortunately, the collection is by no means comprehensive, rather what has endured over the years through chance and sometimes choice. In any event, I believe enough has survived for you to make your mind up. About me, I mean.

I'm enclosing the first instalment. The others will follow as soon as I've had time to sort them into a chronological order. I request only one thing in return: no questions until after you've read everything. You'll know when that is, because I'll tell you. After that, you can ask me whatever you like.

Your New Best Friend

Ruby

PS Hurrah, here comes Amy with the tea trolley! She could teach anyone a thing or two about smiling, mask or no mask!

PART TWO

Diary of Miss Ruby Summers

24 September 1939

Dear Diary

We are at war. It's already three weeks since Mr Chamberlain made his announcement on the radio, but unfortunately I only thought to start my diary today. This morning old Mr Frost from the village came round with six chickens for Mother. (They have creamy white feathers and a speckled neck and are meant to be good layers.) He asked me if I still had plans to go to university. 'They're going to need people with good brains and good sense to put the country back together once the horror show is over,' he said. 'And you, young Ruby, have got both!' Mother wasn't at all pleased. She shot Mr Frost a cross look (which was not at all charitable, considering the chickens) and told him not to encourage me. 'Ruby spends too much time with her head in a book,' she said, 'and men don't care for blue-stockings.' Mr Frost seemed too busy shutting the chickens inside their run to reply, but later, he asked me to show him to the gate. Just before he left, he took hold of my hand and whispered, 'Ruby, the right man won't give a damn about the colour of your stockings. You remember that.'

After he'd gone, I thought about what he said. I decided that if I want to be an intellectual (and I do), I ought at least to keep a record of what's happening in the country because the 'horror show', as Mr Frost put it, has only just begun and it can't be very often ordinary people like us have the sense the whole world is changing in front of their eyes. A long time from now someone might want to know what that feels like.

The moment war was declared I was actually with Edmondo, wrapping up the apples from his orchard in newspaper and storing them in crates. Nobody, except perhaps Mr Chamberlain, expected Hitler to withdraw his troops from Poland and as the clock approached midday, I knew my parents would be waiting beside the wireless braced for the announcement the Nazis had not backed down. I wanted to be with Edmondo, in his father's shed, standing amongst the smell of fruit and dust, with the ink from the newsprint staining my hands and the autumn light falling in shafts through the small window. Although neither of us were wearing a watch after a while, my hands started to shake, seemingly of their own accord, as though they knew the sun must now have passed the midpoint of the sky and what that meant for the world. I looked down at the page I was holding. Staring back at me was an advert for building your own bomb shelters. What terrible stories will the newspapers contain over the next few years, I wondered? How many hours will we spend crouched in shelters listening to explosions and the crack and roar of flames?

I felt Edmondo's arms encircle my waist. We kissed. We didn't speak about what the war may mean for us. We didn't need to. All I know is that Edmondo doesn't mind that I like reading or studying any more than I care two hoots that he is Italian. He's different from all the other young men I know. We talk about important things like science and books and he never assumes that because I'm a girl I must only be interested in learning fair isle knitting or how to casserole a chicken. And he tries so hard to make me happy. Even on terrible days when wars start.

Immediately after our kiss he darted out of the shed and returned a minute later carrying a bucket of water. I stared at him in surprise. 'What are you doing?'

'Wait!' He put the bucket carefully onto an upturned crate before unwrapping four apples and placing them in the water.

'Apple bobbing?' I asked. 'When war

has just been declared!'

Edmondo touched my shoulder. 'I can't stop the world from going to war but I can at least try to stop you looking so sad.' Moving behind me, he gathered up my hair and tied it back with what must have been a bit of string or gardening twine. His fingers felt gentle, but also businesslike and strong. 'Now,' he said, turning me round and smiling, 'You must pick up an apple with your teeth before I count to twenty. Then it will be my turn!'

So, Diary, however inappropriate it may seem, that's how I spent the afternoon of 3 September 1939 – laughing and being silly with Edmondo, and getting wetter than I would ever have thought possible from one bucket of water…

Anyhow I must record what's happened during the last three weeks. The short answer is nothing. Nothing, yet everything. Although there's no sign yet of enemy planes or a German invasion, the life we knew before has completely disappeared. All of the news is taken up with the war and is all anyone talks about. Coal and electricity are rationed already, nobody is allowed to leave home without a gas mask, and everybody is obsessed with the blackout regulations. Yesterday we took it in turns with the neighbours to stand outside each other's houses and check that no light could leak around the edges of our blackout boards. Mrs Wainwright had got herself into quite a state over the threat of prison for not being thorough enough and it took Father quite a while to calm her down even though he's a solicitor and used to explaining rules. It's extraordinary to think one might be fined or locked up for having a lamp on in your own home but then the risk of giving the game away to a German bomber is simply too awful to contemplate.

NB: Mother has named the chickens Monday, Tuesday, Wednesday, Thursday, Friday, and Saturday. Maybe it's disrespectful to God or something to name a chicken Sunday. Besides, I suppose we only have six of them anyway.

Letter Mrs Clementine Isles to Miss Ruby Summers

30 September 1939

Dearest Ruby,

How's my darling sister? Still sneezing for England? It nearly broke my heart not to see you today for my birthday lunch, but Mother said your cold was such a beast she couldn't risk you giving it to the children. She didn't bother to mention that you were probably feeling much too wretched to be driven two and a half hours into the wilds of Oxfordshire only to be besieged by your adoring nephew and niece, as well as your adoring sister of course. We did our best to have a jolly time without you, though of course the war hung in the air like the smell of week-old fish. Mother kept wringing her hands and hugging the children as though she might not see them again. I'm quite aware petrol rationing means that travel will become very restricted, but I still thought she was being a touch melo-dramatic.

I must say at lunch we had a rather peculiar conversation. I said how fortunate it was for me and the children that since John is a teacher he hasn't been called up and isn't ever likely to be. That immediately prompted Mother to thank her lucky stars George is studying medicine so he isn't likely to be called up either. At this point your brother stared at his potted crab as if he'd just seen it move and wouldn't say anything at all. When I pressed him, he admitted that Merton is half-empty, as is the rest of Oxford. Apparently, many of the chaps have signed up, or been conscripted, and the ones left behind feel so bad not to be doing their bit they spend their whole time moping about, or drinking, or engaged in endless discussions of whether it will all be over by Christmas anyway. He seemed so glum I tried to change the conversation and ask if you were still as keen as ever on going to university. I should have known better of course. After exchanging a tight-lipped glance with Father, she told me very firmly that I wasn't to encourage you. 'We must all hope Ruby forgets her silly idea of becoming a scientist,' she said. 'At best it would waste three years of her life and at worst it would spoil her chances of a happy marriage.' After that, with Mother having a face like sour milk, George not eating, and Father looking like he was counting down the minutes until he was back in his study, it was quite a relief when Tabitha knocked over her glass of water and started wailing. I honestly felt like joining her!

Anyway, my darling girl. You must take no notice of Mother. Going to university wasn't my dream, but much as I adore my two gorgeous munchkins, I sometimes wish it could have been and you, Ruby, are far too clever to spend your days attending to the needs of men and toddlers!

Lots of love, darling. Please come and see us as soon as colds, petrol, and the wretched Nazis allow.

Clem

PS And, darling, do write to George. I've never known him so blue.

Diary of Miss Ruby Summers

1 October 1939

Dear Diary

I'm corralled at home, practically imprisoned in my bedroom. Mother is so determined no one else must catch my cold she's even bringing my meals to me on a tray. Not that there's any point trying to eat when everything tastes like sawdust and my throat hurts each time I swallow. Thank heavens it's Sunday so Edmondo could visit this afternoon. Since Mother wouldn't let him upstairs (or me downstairs) we played charades – he acted out book titles in the front garden while I guessed from my bedroom window. The funniest one was Swallows and Amazons. Edmondo used his coat to sail over the lawn and I nearly tipped over the sill from clapping so hard before dissolving into yet another coughing fit. Edmundo and I have been together almost thirteen months and he *still* makes me laugh every time I see him.

For the record (and for me, when I'm old and doddery and might have forgotten even the very best days of my life) this is the story of when Edmondo and I began to step out with each other.

It was September, the very first day of the academic year, and I was chatting with my friend Joan as we walked towards the school gate. Suddenly she nudged me in the ribs. 'Look who's here!'

My heart sank. A boy called Patrick with small eyes and red pimples was leaning against the wall. He'd asked me out to the cinema back in June and been quite unpleasant when I said no, pretending he'd never liked me anyway (which, apart from being rude, was very silly indeed).

'Go away, Patrick,' Joan said. 'Ruby and I are talking about our holidays.'

'That must be a laugh,' he said. 'I bet Ruby did nothing all summer but read books!' He was staring at me in a horrible way that made my clothes feel almost invisible.

'So what if I did?!' I countered. 'At least I *can* read.'

Taking his hands from his pockets, Patrick moved away from the wall. 'You're such a drip, Ruby Summers! A drip and a dullard! No boy will ever want–'

'Shut-up!' All at once Edmondo was beside me. 'Don't speak to Ruby like that!'

Patrick glared at him, clenching his fists. 'Get lost!' he said, then added with a sneer, 'Get lost, *wop*!'

'I don't know how you spent your summer,' Edmondo replied calmly, 'but I spent mine learning to box!' Taking off his blazer he handed it to me before starting to roll up his shirtsleeves. Diary, I'm ashamed to say that I couldn't stop myself from staring at him! Before the summer Edmondo had seemed no different from any of the other boys. Now he was one of the tallest, his hair blacker than ever, while his forearms had a strong, tanned gleam to them. By the time I was able to tear my gaze away, I realised Patrick was nowhere to be seen.

After school Edmondo was waiting for me beside the same gate. As we walked together down the lane we passed Patrick hanging about at the side of the road. Quick as a flash Edmondo sprang into a boxer's pose, drawing his fists up to his face and bouncing on the balls of his feet. Patrick practically ran in the opposite direction!

When we had finally stopped laughing, I asked Edmondo if he had really spent his summer learning to box. He grinned at me. 'No, mostly I played football.'

Then he added, 'But for you, Ruby, I believe I would fight anyone!'

So, Diary, even though the war and this wretched cold should by rights be making me miserable, recalling that marvellous memory has given me such a burst of energy I shall spend the rest of the evening writing letters and being productive.

Letter Professor H. Wodehouse to Miss Ruby Summers

10 October 1939

Dear Miss Summers

Thank you for your interest in Girton College. In answer to your query, young women may read any of the Tripos subjects, including Natural Sciences. However, at the present time no woman is entitled to be awarded a final degree from the University of Cambridge. That is an unfairness we are determined to rectify, once the country is no longer at war and attention can again be focused on addressing such blatant inequality.

If you happen to be in Cambridge, I would be delighted to show you our impressive facilities and give you the opportunity to glimpse the lives of our brilliant and hardworking students for yourself. If you do decide to make an application here you will need to sit a number of entrance examinations in papers that include Latin. However, I'm confident a visit to Girton would inspire your present studies to new heights. In the meantime, I wish you every success in the preparations for your Higher School Certificate.

Yours faithfully

Helen Wodehouse (College Mistress)

Letter Mr Charles Whittaker to Miss Ruby Summers

10 October 1939

Dear Ruby

How is my favourite goddaughter? I trust you are bearing up in these strange and difficult times as well as finding the odd moment to keep your parents in order.

Sadly, London looks a little bleak these days. Nearly all the shop windows on Oxford and Regent Street have been boarded up and any cars or cabs that dare to venture onto the roads in the evenings crawl around with one solitary hooded headlight or the whole of the front of the grille masked in something that resembles a bride's veil. The headlight regulations keep changing so randomly and rapidly I have to confess most of us lost track of them two or three variations ago – myself included. Please keep that last piece of information to yourself. I'm quite certain that as an employee of the War Office I'm supposed to be setting a shining example (no pun intended, of course).

In one piece of good news, the theatres reopened last week albeit with different showing times in an attempt to minimise Mr Hitler's target options. Still, I managed to see an extremely good performance of Blithe Spirit which was a blessed relief from a working day that has been rather hectic of late and mainly consumed by the arrangements for the bitter but necessary task of sending the British Army off to war. I'm bound to say I hope your brother doesn't get it into his head to sign up. Much as I admire the courage of the men who do, my own experience of war makes it hard to encourage similar bravery in those whom you know and love.

Talking of which, I hope you don't mind me enquiring whether you're still stepping out with the same young man I met in the summer? He seemed a nice enough chap, but I wonder whether you can be certain where his loyalties lie? The Italians appear to be waiting for the first opportunity to throw in their lot with Mr Hitler and when that happens the repercussions for Italians living here (and those associated with them) will be considerable.

Anyway, my dear, you've more good sense than most women your age – indeed most women of any age – so I shall leave the matter in your capable hands.

Yours affectionately

Uncle Charles

Letter, by hand, Mr Edmondo Brambilla to Ruby

13 October 1939

Mia cara

I've just read your note. Of course, you must stay with George this evening. Do you know why he's come back from Oxford so suddenly on a Friday? I wish I'd been there when you called but I was delivering groceries. Yesterday my father told the delivery boy he could no longer afford to keep him and today when I got back from school my bicycle was fitted with paniers and filled with groceries. To finish the job as quickly as possible, I pretended to be Gino Bartali, a famous Italian cyclist! I think I pretended too well because my wheel hit a tree-root as I was speeding through the village and a box flew over the handlebars. Luckily there were no eggs inside!

At least being the new delivery boy means I have an excuse to go out whenever I like. If I tell my father I'm taking a packet of tea or a tin of ham to one of our customers I'll be able to leave the house without him scolding me for wanting to be with you rather than help in the shop. I shall bring you this note tomorrow and on Sunday morning at ten o'clock I'll wait for you in the meadow.

Please come to the meadow, Ruby! Already I'm longing to see you again.

Edmondo

PS The feather is one I found when the grocery box fell out of the basket. Isn't blue your favourite colour? Turquoise like this must be the best blue of all!

Diary of Miss Ruby Summers

14 October 1939

George has joined up. He leaves for France on Tuesday. Mother was in tears all evening, trying to persuade him to change his mind. She kept threatening to go down to the recruitment office herself and tell them George had made a mistake. That the government knew what was best and they wouldn't have exempted medical students from the draft if they didn't think people like him would do more good for the country by staying at home.

We were all in the drawing room. Mother and I perched at either end of the sofa like bookends, Father standing beside the fireplace, and George by the French door looking for all the world as if at any moment he might open them and simply stride away into the garden.

Father kept saying, 'It's done, Evie, it's done. You can't undo it,' and pacing up and down while attempting to start his pipe. For some reason the tobacco refused to light and after two wasted matches Father took the bit from his mouth and hurled the whole thing into the grate where the stem snapped clean away from the bowl. Then George began to shout it was for him to decide whether to stay at Oxford or fight for his country. That he was an adult now, not a little boy, and had his own life to live. At which point Mother said, 'You have a life to lead now, but you might not have for much longer' before starting to cry again, but this time much more quietly which somehow was a hundred times worse than all the previous wailing and shouting.

I don't think I said anything at all. I felt sad and scared and frightened, and also proud of George too. Yet at the same time I was almost numb. As if my mix of emotions had neutralised each other like a very precise combination of acids and alkalis or my feelings were so overloaded they had shut down. Mother says she loves George and can't bear to lose him. I love George too, of course I do. But if nobody is prepared to fight then how will we stop Hitler? We've only been at war two months and already we're beginning to forget the way things were before. Tonight I'm wondering how we could have taken everything for granted. All that peace I mean. Waking up to different news stories, different programmes on the radio, instead of one broadcast from the BBC that means the only choice we have is listening and becoming depressed or switching the wireless off altogether. Now I can't even remember my previous worries, and I'd probably be embarrassed if I could because they would seem insignificant little niggles and not real problems at all.

To be honest I've never been all that interested in history. Compared with learning about the way things work, or how peoples' bodies are put together, it doesn't seem terribly important to know the names of battles that happened five hundred years ago, or which of Henry VIII's wives were beheaded, when it's too late to do anything to stop it. Now I've realised how everyone assumes that history, the history we read about in schoolbooks, happens to other people. And not even to real people, worrying, as they boil an egg or tie their shoelaces, about jobs or children or being in love, but to insubstantial pretend people, like characters from a fairy tale. We act as if the battles, the plagues, the natural disasters, are stories that never really took place, or happened in a fictional world that nobody actually lived in. But that's not true of course, and now history is happening to us, this very minute, and in years to come, we'll be the people on the page, the ones whom schoolchildren read about in class, and nobody will appreciate, not properly, that we really existed. That right now I'm sitting in bed wearing my duffel coat because I'm cold and can't be bothered to make a hot-water bottle. That my parents' voices are drifting from downstairs, a kind of anxious muffle punctuated by sharp little hiccups. That beyond the pool of light from the bedside lamp are only inky shadows and the faint, rather ominous outline of my wardrobe. That my hands smell of Pears soap and my finger-nails could do with a good scrub. Nobody will think about any of that. Not until history happens to them too.

It's an hour later. I've just been into George's room. It's full of all the trunks and boxes he brought back from Oxford, which he appears to have stopped unpacking halfway through the job. I don't think he's nearly so certain of what he's doing as he sounded down-stairs. When I opened the door, he was sitting cross-legged on the floor, thumbing through the pages of Gould's Pocket Medical Dictionary with a wistful expression and didn't notice me for a whole thirty seconds (I counted). He told me I could borrow any of his books while he was away and when I said it might upset Mother to see me reading them instead of him, he looked stricken and made me promise to look at them in secret because he couldn't bear for her to be any more upset than she was already. I desperately wanted to give him a hug but when I stepped forward, he sort of shrunk into himself as though he couldn't cope with any more emotion. In the end I just said good night and left the room.

Diary of Miss Ruby Summers

15 October 1939

It's the following morning now, just after a breakfast in which all anybody said was 'please pass the milk' (Father) and 'has anyone fed the chickens?' (me). I'm almost glad Tuesday is only two days away. I know that's a terrible thing to say, and I hate the thought of George leaving, but I honestly believe waiting for him to leave is even worse. We can't talk about him going to France and we can't talk about anything else either. It's like a peculiar and rather dreadful kind of party game where we have to pretend to be cheerful although we're feeling wretched and at the same time avoid saying anything about the one topic that's preoccupying us all.

And on top of everything else, the weather has turned. Before today, autumn had been glorious with the trees a riot of colour and the sun unseasonably hot. Today, there was nothing but rain. The cold, slanting kind that manages to find the narrowest gap beside a collar or sleeve. As we sat at breakfast water lashed against the window as if we were on board a ship and I got soaked simply for popping outside to put crusts on the bird-table. All at once the bleakness of the next few months (the next few years?) seems almost unbearable. Thank heavens I have Edmondo to raise my spirits. Whatever Uncle Charles might think, I don't have any doubts about his loyalties at all. Either to me, or to England.

Letter Miss E. Halifax to pupils of Northwood school

18 October 1939

Dear Pupil

I am writing to you and, under separate cover, your parents to update you on arrangements made in view of the fact the country is at war.

For the present it has been decided not to evacuate pupils in the borough of Ipswich and Northwood school will remain open. However, a number of members of staff have joined the war effort or are otherwise indisposed, consequently year groups will no longer be divided into separate forms and instead will comprise one larger teaching class.

Precautions have been made in the event of air raids. All windows are taped and covered with thick curtains while an underground shelter has been constructed between the playing field and the lavatory block where lessons can continue in the event the school day is disrupted by the air-raid siren. I take this opportunity to remind you that gas masks must not only be brought to school but carried about the person at all times. A gas drill will continue to take place every Monday morning at 9.00am.

One hundred years ago Edward Bulwer-Lytton wrote 'The pen is mightier than the sword.' Here at Northwood, we will continue to teach however inhospitable the conditions so that the might of our pupils' pens may prevail over Nazi aggression and other evils.

Yours sincerely

Edna Halifax (Headmistress)

PS Ruby Summers, you are blessed with a particularly mighty pen. Do not let the current circumstances distract you from your studies or dampen your ambition. EH

From the General Manager of the Troxy, Felixstowe

November 1939

Sunshine in November

Dear Customers

Today, I found myself ruminating on the recent unhappy period when all places of entertainment were closed and thought that cinema entertainment had perhaps been taken more for granted than any other form of diversion from the hum-drum of daily routine. Without the actual experience, it would have been very difficult to imagine the reaction of twenty-five million regular picture-goers in this country suddenly deprived of their favourite form of recreation. They were hungry for entertainment and when their demand for it echoed in the national press there appeared a gleam of hope. That gleam turned into a ray of sunshine when the authorities, realising the necessity, finally sanctioned the reopening of cinemas.

Now that we have settled down to things once again it cannot be denied that entertainment is the sunshine of life – and what a spell of it there's going to be at the Troxy in November. Just glance through the following pages and see for yourself; but before you do so, please accept my thanks for the splendid manner in which you have responded to our changed closing hour by timing your visits earlier.

Letter, by hand, Edmondo to Ruby

1 November 1939

Mia cara

We're celebrating Fragolina's birthday this Saturday, 4 November, and she's invited some of her friends from school for cake and ice-cream. Will you join us? Mother said I could ask you. It will be worth coming for the ice-cream alone since I don't know for how much longer Father will find enough sugar to make it.

How can my little sister be thirteen already!

Edmondo

Letter Edmondo to Ruby

4 November 1939

Mia cara

I've been sitting with my head in my hands for the last five minutes. Please don't mind my father. I'm sure he didn't mean to shout. He was only upset because none of Fragolina's friends came to her party. Although I've explained a little about my parents already, I've decided to tell you their whole story. If you understand the reasons why my father gets so angry these days perhaps you won't judge him too harshly…

You know the violin, the one that's kept beside the armchair in the living room? When he was fourteen my father was the most promising violin player in Lombardy. He longed to be a professional and earn his living from music. However, after the Great War there were no opportunities for musicians in Lombardy, or anywhere else in Italy, so he came to England. Here, he did find work, and he also found my mother, a pianist who accompanied singers and instrumentalists, and who, like my father had left Italy to pursue her passion. They met at a concert and only two weeks later were engaged to be married. For a short while, everything was perfect. Travelling the country together, they even became a little famous. Father has shown me programmes of their performances and told me stories of standing ovations and crowds queuing in the rain for tickets. Yet perhaps too quickly I was born, and soon afterwards Fragolina, and Father decided we needed more stability than travelling musicians could provide. So he used all of his savings to buy a house with enough room for a shop and a family, and gave up music.

His business flourished. As well as English groceries, he gave customers a taste of Italy. Ice-cream and sarsaparilla in the summer, strong dark coffee and hot pork pies when the nights became darker. The locals not only welcomed us but his ice-cream became so popular that customers came from miles around. Do you remember the first time you saw the ice-cream cart and Prince, our black-and-white horse? As soon as they heard his hooves, children like you, George, and Clementine, would come running to pay a penny for a vanilla or lemon ice. In hot weather the lines would stretch down the street – as long as they used to be for my parents' concerts – while the closest children would stand on tiptoe to stroke Prince's neck.

Now, however, when other children should be running behind the cart, the streets are quiet. Instead of calling my father's name, people turn their heads and hurry past. Yesterday someone even spat on his boot. Fewer and fewer customers come to the shop. Mother checks and rechecks the takings in the till more carefully than ever before.

I tell my parents the war is the reason why people behave like this. Who can think of ice-cream at such a time? Everyone is spending less, worried how their livelihoods will survive. But Father says it's more than that. He fears what the future holds for Italians living in England and believes that we're no longer trusted. I refuse to give up hope so easily. I'm determined to stay cheerful. However, since nobody but you came to Fragolina's party, a small part of me can't help wondering if he is right.

Ti amo

Edmondo

PS I'm enclosing a programme from 16 May 1925 when my parents performed at the Guildhall in Cambridge. On the cover is their photograph and their names: Marco and Anastasia Brambilla. See how young and carefree they look. And not so very much older than us!

Letter from Miss H. Wodehouse to Ruby

4 November 1939

Dear Miss Summers

Thank you for your very prompt response to my letter. If you are able to come to the main entrance of Girton for midday on Saturday, 25 November, one of our undergraduates will be pleased to show you around. The facilities may be a little more crowded than you expect as we are currently accommodating a number of female students who have been evacuated from Queen Mary College, London. Nevertheless, Girton's spirit remains undaunted. The onset of hostilities has only increased our conviction that the abilities of women must be recognised and permitted to flourish in times of peace as well as war.

I look forward to meeting you next Thursday.

Yours faithfully

Helen Wodehouse (College Mistress)

Letter Mrs Lillian Whittaker to Ruby

6 November 1939

Dearest Ruby,

You are of course welcome to stay with us next Friday and Saturday night. Uncle Charles and I would both be delighted to see you; despite the fact I suspect your main priority is neither Christmas shopping nor visiting your ageing godparents. In answer to your transport question, the train from London to Cambridge takes approximately an hour and a half, which means, yes, as long as the timetable remains intact, it should be perfectly possible to get there and back in a day – as indeed it would be from your own home in Suffolk. This rather makes me wonder if your parents are aware the reason for your trip to London is the opportunity to visit Cambridge? You should tell them, my dear. Although I may not have been the most dutiful of godmothers over the years, I do feel it my responsibility to impress upon you the virtue of honesty and withholding important information from your parents is nearly as dishonest as telling them an outright lie. Some might say there is no distinction between the two at all.

In any case, your proposed travel arrangements worry me for other reasons. Can it really be sensible to be heading for the capital when all the talk on the news is that the Germans might bomb us at any moment? With all the train stations full of evacuating children and their weeping mothers, it hardly seems the right time for a visit from our dearest goddaughter. Uncle Charles's work at the War Office means he and I have no option but to remain in London, but we should never forgive ourselves if something should happen to you because you were staying with us. Rather perversely, I'm certain we would feel ourselves responsible, even if the fault would lie with Mr Hitler and his dreadful bombs.

And to be frank, there's another reason for my concern. Once you've seen Cambridge, your head will be filled with all kinds of hopes – hopes, that frankly, my darling, might very possibly never come true. You know perfectly well what your mother and father think about the idea of you – of any woman – going to university, and I can't see them changing their mind. Is it then, I wonder, sensible to pursue this dream? Particularly when the world is falling about our heads and we women will have our hands full simply trying to piece it together again. I know how clever and ambitious you are, Ruby, but things truly are different for men and women. A woman has to channel her energy and abilities into homemaking. After all, if she doesn't create a home, who will? Not a man, that's for certain. And although, sadly, your godfather and I were never blessed with a baby of our own, I've known enough mothers to be able to assure you how wonderfully fulfilling – and time-consuming! – having a family will be.

Affectionately

Aunt Lillian

Letter 'anonymous' to Miss R Summers

7 November 1939

Dear Miss Summers

I hope you will forgive the forward nature of this letter. Present circumstances compel those who before the war would offer advice only when called upon to do so, to speak out more readily, particularly when troubled by matters they regard as crucial to the national interest.

Saturday evening, just gone, I happened to spot you at the entrance to the Brambillas' premises, some two hours after their shop had closed. Within moments the door opened and you greeted a young Italian gentleman in a friendly fashion (a most friendly fashion, I might say) before stepping inside.

Subsequently I made enquiries and was informed by others that you and that same young gentleman have been stepping out together for a year or more, and that the friendship has persisted these last months despite the actions of Mr Mussolini in plainly aligning himself with Mr Hitler. I cannot believe I am the only person to whom this causes consternation. The Brambilla family may have lived in the village a good number of years, but now they are aliens in a country that is at war. Moreover in my opinion an Italian alien is no different from a German alien; it is only a matter of time before Mr Mussolini lays his cards plain upon the table, and when he does, we all know which way they will face.

I wish you no ill will, Miss Summers, but my counsel, my very strong counsel, is to detach yourself from your young suitor at the earliest opportunity and before the association casts any aspersions on your own loyalties or those of your family.

Yours truly

A concerned resident

Diary of Miss Ruby Summers

7 November 1939

Today, Diary, I received two letters. Letters should be a source of joy, yet these have made me dismal beyond words.

The first was from Auntie Lilly. She had guessed the real reason for me wanting to go to London and made me feel awful for trying to keep secrets from Mother and Father. Then she practically said me visiting Cambridge was a waste of time; I should forget all about university and channel my energies into homemaking instead. I wrote straight back and told her if I put all my energy into something as dreary and undemanding as running a house the walls would probably explode and the bricks bury me alive. Besides, I don't want a home. Not like the one she has with Uncle Charles, or my parents' home, with the man doing interesting, important things and the women left with nothing to talk about other than their children, curtains, or what they might wear to somebody's garden party. However dreadful the war is, at least all the different jobs the women now have outside the home should give them better topics of conversation.

I also pleaded with Auntie Lilly to let me still come to London. While I couldn't tell my parents I planned to visit Cambridge before I left – in case they stopped me going altogether – I did promise to confess my crime the very second that I returned. I only hope the assurance will be enough to prevent Aunty Lilly from telephoning them herself. I think it will be. I have a feeling that if push came to shove Uncle Charles would stop her from spilling the beans. He has always stuck up for me wonderfully in the past.

The second letter was so horrible that if I were not this minute gazing at the sinister march of black lettering across a sheet of Basildon Bond, I would not believe a resident of our village could bring themselves to write it. The envelope was left inside the basket of my bicycle while I was at school and the writer didn't even have the nerve to put an address or sign his or her name. What a coward! He or she must have seen me arriving at Fragolina's birthday celebration. I imagine them hunched over their desk with a face made ugly by a nasty, suspicious mind. How different from little Fragolina herself, who was so brave when nobody came to her party and pretended that she didn't mind at all. (Although Edmondo says her pet-name comes from the strawberry birthmark on her neck I think it suits her sweet nature perfectly.) To begin with I put the sheet of paper from the vile mystery writer straight into the waste-paper basket. Then I had second thoughts. I won't mention the existence of the letter to anyone, least of all Edmondo, but I shall keep it. Just in case. In case of what, one might ask? Diary, I don't know. Nevertheless, I'm going to tuck the letter into these pages where nobody will find it. Then I shall go and sit under the horse chestnut trees. Three of them mark the border between our land and Mrs Wainwright's meadow and I like to say hello to them from time to time. Whenever I feel sad, I place the flat of my hand against their trunks and fancy I can feel the gnarly old bark absorb some of my unhappiness.

And at the very least I might find a conker or two.

Letter from Mr George Summers to Ruby

10 November 1939

Dear Ruby

A quick note from your bro because I know how much you enjoy getting your own letters and because, bizarrely, it seems that at least for now I've the time to write. Let me paint you a scene: Here I am sitting in the middle of a French orchard on the tailboard of my truck, surrounded by row upon row of apple and pear trees. The sky is a steady, duck-egg blue and although the temperature has dropped a little this week, I'm certain the weather is still much warmer than in Suffolk. Believe it or not, the worst of it so far, was crossing over the Channel. A fair old wind had picked up and most of us, including your dear brother, saw our breakfast reappear long before the French coast came into sight. Eventually we arrived at Cherbourg and travelled by convoy into the countryside where we spend most of our time moving around, digging out gun pits and filling sandbags to build dugouts. The nights have been warm enough to sleep in the trucks without much hardship, though I suppose even in France the winter will get cold eventually. If it wasn't for the occasional training sessions and gloomy snippets of news from Poland, I might forget why I'm here at all.

By the way, I've become pals with a chap called Frank. When I was showing the lads a family photograph, he took quite a shine to you! Of course, I told him you were far too good for the likes of him, and rather smitten with a local Italian to boot (which, I have to say, raised a few eyebrows). Still, Frank's a smashing chap and I might be persuaded to introduce you both as soon as we get some leave. Speaking of which, I've put in a request for a week around Christmas, but for heaven's sake don't mention anything to Mother because I don't hold out for my chances. Although Jerry is quiet for the moment there are plenty of men with wives and babies who will be higher up the queue than me.

Anyway, sis, have you been reading my science books? Knowing your brain, you've probably memorised the whole of the medical dictionary by now. I miss Oxford of course, the hush of the library, the mellowness of the old stone walls (when I close my eyes, I can see the rows of polished black railings like a music score), not to mention the rather too frequent nights in the bar! Even so, I know I'm in the right place doing the right thing, and in a time of war it's the only type of peace on offer. Tell Mother that when she worries. And look after everyone, Ruby. You might be only seventeen, but I have more faith in you to do the right thing than anyone else.

Your loving brother

George

Diary of Miss Ruby Summers

18 November 2020

Dear Diary,

I've just this minute got home and am bursting to talk about my day. Mother is out and, besides, would never tolerate me gushing about university, so I've run straight upstairs and pulled out my diary from under the bed. My only problem is sitting still enough to write! I've so much energy I feel like the single-handed answer to the petrol crisis. I've never cycled so fast from the railway station and could easily cover the same distance one hundred times again if I had to.

Cambridge is even more marvellous than I imagined! The spires, the bridges, the courtyards, the grass beside the river rolled out like the velvet baize of a snooker table. All of them, I rather fancied, cloaked in a mist of history and learning. I'm quite certain I could actually sense the bricks pulsing with years of striving while the moments of breakthrough hung in the air like slivers of invisible lightning. If I don't study there myself, I fear a little part of me might shrivel up and die altogether. And perhaps not even a little part, maybe the best, most exciting part…

As for Girton College, well it's the most inspiring place imaginable! I was shown around by an amazing person called

Miss Cartwright, a mathematician who is working on a frightfully important project for the Department of Scientific and Industrial Research – doesn't that sound wonderful! She couldn't say much about her work, but it's something terribly complicated to do with radars. She told me that when she was solving equations, she felt she was connecting with all that was beautiful and pure about the universe, and I replied that I thought exactly the same way when I learned about molecules. I probably made rather a fool of myself, asking her so many questions, but we were both so engrossed that when it started to rain, we became quite wet before either of us noticed the weather had turned. The only dampener as far as I was concerned was Mary mentioned a Latin entrance paper. I had been hoping rather desperately that requirement was only compulsory for history and Classics candidates. I can't see how I can possibly learn Latin when my school doesn't teach it.

By contrast, London was a sobering experience. Rather stupidly I assumed the shops would look much as they always do a few weeks before Christmas, with lights and gaiety and hundreds of enticing gifts. Of course, the blackout and evacuation has put paid to that. By five o'clock the streets resembled an inky well with only the torches of a few pedestrians flashing like lost fireflies. And even in daylight there weren't any children. Normally the pavements would be crowded with children desperate to glimpse the Toy Fair at Harrods or Hamleys but since they have all been packed off to the countryside, I saw just one little boy with his mother looking terribly on edge and not festive in the least.

Oh dear. The front door has just thumped shut, deflating my mood like a burst balloon. Now I must keep my promise to Aunt Lillian and confess to Mother where I've been.

Pause, for long sigh.

Wish me luck, Diary. Though let me formally record that those three hours in Cambridge were worth whatever happens next.

Letter Clem to Ruby

18 November 1939

Dear Ruby

Are you in terrible trouble, darling? Mother telephoned today in quite a state. Something about you slipping off for the day to look around Cambridge University under the guise of visiting

Charles and Lillian. I can barely believe you would be so bold! Apparently, Father was so cross when Mother told him what you'd done that you're not allowed to see Edmondo for three whole weeks. According to Mother, the only reasons you're allowed out of the house are either to go to school or run errands. To be perfectly honest, she sounded more worried and exasperated than actually angry. 'I just don't know what to do,' she said. 'Ruby is stubborn as a mule and so very different from other girls her age. When she's not with Edmondo, her head is stuck in some book or other as if someone has glued her face to the page. And to make matters worse the books aren't even novels! She sits in her bedroom devouring textbooks with the most ridiculous and incomprehensible names as though they were stories by Angela Brazil.' When I told Mother I thought you were quite marvellous, she said it was all very well 'fighting your corner' but I didn't understand. The world had always worked differently for men and women and always would do, because women are the ones who have the babies 'and no amount of reading would change that'.

'I want Ruby to be happy, Clementine,' she said. 'And how will she be happy if she turns into a lonely bluestocking? After the war, good men will be in short supply and they're going to want a woman who'll look after them and be a mother to their children, rather than a wife who's too busy with ambitions of her own even to cook dinner.'

Do you think she might be right, Ruby? We all hoped the war would be over by Christmas, but I'm beginning to fear we're in for a dreadful time of it. Hitler is like a nasty dog. He's busy, for now, with a bone in the corner, but he'll turn on us, I know he will, just as soon as that Polish bone is all chewed up. And after the war, you don't want to be a spinster, do you darling? Imagine a silent house without the chatter and clatter of children. Think how lonely that would be! Instead of university, why not consider something almost as demanding but less extreme? Perhaps a Cordon Bleu cookery school, or even secretarial college? That way you'd learn a wonderful skill and your stockings would acquire only the teeniest hint of blue.

I must go, dearest, your niece is howling because she's dropped Mr Paddy Paws – recently promoted to favourite teddy – over the edge of the playpen and if she doesn't stop screaming soon, we won't need Mr Hitler to bring down the walls here!

Your loving, and ever-so-slightly anxious, sister

Clem

Letter Ms M. Cartwright to Ruby

19 November 1939

Dear Miss Summers

The day after your visit I was walking through the courtyard when I spied a rather damp glove lying on the cobbles close to where we were talking. Since the colour matches that of the pair you were wearing, I assumed the item belongs to you and took the liberty of asking Ms Wodehouse for your address so that I might return it. Waste not, want not, in these uncertain times!

I will also take the opportunity to say how much I enjoyed our conversation and hope that seeing Girton in the flesh (so to speak), will encourage you to apply here when the time comes. I took the liberty of making a few enquiries and have been advised that if you are looking to widen your reading, A Physical Chemistry of the Proteins (Robertson & Brailsford) and A Textbook of Practical Chemistry (Vogel) would both be excellent additions to your personal library. On the Latin issue, from personal experience I thoroughly recommend First Steps in Latin (Ritchie) and Elementary Translation (A E Hilliard). Unfortunately, nothing substitutes for the rigorous learning of grammar and vocabulary.

Yours in friendship

Mary Cartwright

Letter Edmondo to Ruby

19 November 1939

Mia cara

Your letter astonished me! I don't mind not going to the cinema, but why should your visit to Cambridge so upset your parents? Aren't they proud of your abilities? Don't they realise how clever you are? And why do they think men don't want to marry educated women? I cannot imagine my own wife being anyone but my partner in every sense.

Ruby, I truly believe you will be that partner. Who else could ever take your place? We may be young but when I close my eyes, I see our path ahead together so clearly. Me running a business – perhaps a factory or a department store – while you conduct research in a big science laboratory. We'll talk late into the night, sharing our setbacks and our triumphs, and our home will be filled with books and energy and laughter! Despite the freezing temperature of my bedroom, the news on the wireless and our empty shop till, I cannot help but feel happy imagining such a future together.

At least you had good news about your brother. I'm glad to hear he is well and has not yet seen action. I've wondered a great deal about what it must feel like to join up. I'm not afraid of dying – though I may not feel so brave if I were standing on a battlefield – but the idea of shooting someone else, even the enemy, is terrible to imagine. Although I would fight with as much determination as the next man, I know I would remember the people I killed for the rest of my life and worry about the families they left behind and what they might have done with their lives.

Enough gloominess! I shall finish with a joke to try to cheer us both up. (I hope you find it funnier than my father seemed to do at supper!)

Hitler asks a soldier, 'Friend, when you are in the front line under fire, what do you wish for?' The soldier replies, 'That you, my Fuhrer, stand next to me!'

Are you smiling? I think you are!

Edmondo

PS I'm enclosing a page from a book of famous Italians. The woman in the picture is Senora Laura Bassi, the first ever female science professor. I'm certain, Ruby, that one day your photograph will be in a book like this too.

Letter Mr Leslie Pritchard to Miss Ruby Summers

22 November 1939

Dear Miss Summers

We have in stock First Steps in Latin and one biological work by Robertson & Brailsford, although not the specific item you requested. I have sent both books by express as you requested. We do not have a copy of Practical Chemistry or Elementary Translation so I have ordered them from the publisher. However, I'm afraid short-staffing due to conscription means there may be a longer wait for delivery than normal.

Yours sincerely

L. Pritchard

Letter Edmondo to Ruby

24 November 1939

Cara Ruby

You're crazy and I love you! When I looked through my bedroom window and saw you gazing up at me, I couldn't believe my eyes. A ghost in the moonlit shadow of the oak tree! If your parents had caught you leaving your house in the middle of the night, they might never have let you out of your room again. Instead, you've given me a silver-leafed memory to cherish for ever!

Edmondo

PS I'm sending you an oak leaf. Never forget how brave and beautiful you are. Not for a single second.

Letter Uncle Charles to Ruby

14 December 1939

Dear Ruby

I trust your period in the penitentiary has ended in time for Christmas. I must say, life in London is a curious affair at the moment. Half of the children who were evacuated in the autumn have returned. However, since most of their schools have not yet reopened, they spend most of the day roving around making far too much noise and generally causing havoc. A problem no doubt exacerbated by the absence of so many fathers. Anyhow, the reason for this correspondence is not to update you on the social ills in the capital but because your last letter mentioned a desire to learn Latin. As it happens, I recently came across a spare Latin dictionary in our library and thought the rather smart leather binding and embossed cover might brighten your learning of all that dreary vocabulary. Not, of course, that I'm encouraging you to pursue a place at Cambridge. Do assure your parents I remain strictly neutral on that score. Nevertheless, a knowledge of Latin can only be useful wherever your future leads.

By the way, I hear you're continuing to step out with that young Italian fellow. I do hope you're keeping a close eye on him. We can't risk aliens causing us any mischief, the situation is precarious and dangerous enough as it is.

Happy Christmas, my dear. Please accept the fond good wishes of your godfather.

Uncle Charles

PS I'm also enclosing an untranslated copy of Virgil's Aeneid. If that doesn't encourage you to become proficient in Latin, nothing will.

Letter Mary Cartwright to Ruby

14 December 1939

Dear Ruby

I do hope addressing you by your first name does not appear too familiar, but Christmas seems the least appropriate time to stand on ceremony. I write because a friend of mine, a Chemistry student, is selling his copies of A Physical Chemistry of the Proteins and A Textbook of Practical Chemistry to raise funds for books he wishes to purchase in the New Year. When I wondered aloud if that was rather rash, he assured me he practically knew their contents off by heart. Besides, while he would feel their absence like the loss of an old friend, they had done their job for him and needed now another mind eager for the same learning. For some reason I immediately thought of you. I don't know if you're finding it difficult to acquire the books you need, but if you want these just say the word. My friend would take four shillings for the pair (plus postage), which strikes me as eminently reasonable.

Yours in friendship

Mary

PS Happy Christmas!

Diary of Miss Ruby Summers

24 December 1939

Dear Diary

The last few days have been rather splendid, if such cheery thoughts are permissible in a time of war. Father agreed I had paid my penance for, as he put it, 'my devious behaviour' – anyone would think he'd caught me selling his whisky on the black market, rather than furthering my ambition to be educated – so yesterday, Edmondo and I celebrated by going to the cinema in Ipswich.

Without any lights inside the bus and only the dimmest of headlamps outside, the journey felt like tunnelling underground to Australia rather than a bus ride to our local town. It was so gloomy I couldn't even see Edmondo's features, just the outline of his head, and the other passengers were merely vague shapes. Everyone sat in silence, as if they daren't trust whoever might be out there listening, and when Edmondo kissed me, the darkness seemed to thicken more than ever, wrapping itself around us like the warmest of blankets. I didn't want to get there, to the cinema I mean. I was perfectly happy for the seconds to stop right then, while the night slid past unnoticed on the far side of the window. There was something timeless and magical about that bus until the moment we arrived at the city centre where all at once the clock on the town hall was staring straight at us like the face of a full moon. The driver told us the clock stays that way day after day because nobody has yet worked out how to turn off the illumination! I do hope someone does soon; they say vehicles driven only on sidelights glitter from the air like a string of beads so Ipswich Town Hall must be as conspicuous to the German bombers as a beacon.

Almost as marvellous as seeing Edmondo again, I've been showered with books!

Mary Cartwright has sent me two Chemistry books I thought I'd never be able to find. Second-hand, but incredibly good value – I got them delivered to Edmondo's house to avoid any awkwardness. And Uncle Charles has given me a very smart Latin dictionary together with the most beautiful copy of The Aeneid. They were wrapped in such innocuous brown paper Mother didn't bother to ask what was inside; she probably assumed I'd left something behind when I stayed in London. I'm very fond of Uncle Charles but I can't help wondering why he's being so helpful all of a sudden. In the past he's tended to take Father's side, rather implying a woman who can't be satisfied with a husband and children is not a proper woman at all. Still, I forgive him now. The Virgil, in particular, is divine. The only remaining obstacle is to learn Latin well enough to read it.

NB Tomorrow is Christmas Day and we're having one of Mr Frost's chickens for lunch (the one named Monday, chosen for the chop because it will actually be Monday). Since Father will do the dirty work and wring her neck tonight, I crept out and gave her a last supper of vegetable peelings. After that I helped Mother make a dozen mince pies using bottled blackberries and cooking apples as filling instead of dried fruit which is too hard to get. Although she doesn't say anything, I know she's missing George terribly. She laid the table for four without thinking so I cleared away the extra knife and fork when she went to the front door. The knock was the choir from the church, who were going from house to house with just one small torch because the government have said carol singers mustn't have lanterns. They can't ring any handbells either in case the sound gets confused with the air-raid signal! It's awful but also rather funny. Who on earth would mistake a jolly rendition of Jingle Bells for the air-raid siren? I wonder if they have the same silly rules in Germany. Or if they even have carol singers at all.

Diary of Miss Ruby Summers

3 January 1940

A New Year. A new decade. Where will we all be next January, or even when 1950 comes around and I'm the grand old age of twenty-seven? More than ever the future seems too remote to contemplate and the distance between 'here' and 'there' fraught with as much danger as Aeneas' wanderings from Troy to Italy. How I wish I knew that last part from understanding the Latin, sadly all I've managed to read so far is an English translation I found on the bookshelf beside Father's desk. What with Christmas and the recent turmoil, my studies have taken something of a back seat during the Yuletide.

Since all I can think about is the last few days I might as well get straight to the point. My brain is stuck on repeat, going over and over them, as if by doing so I might be able to change what happened…

I spent New Year's Eve with Edmondo and his family. The loveliest part was before dinner, when he and I went for a walk down to the river. The ferns crunched under our boots and the stars glittered as if a broken Christmas bauble had been tossed into the sky. By the time we returned to Edmondo's house, though my fingers and toes were totally numb I felt full of a warm and wonderful sense of well-being. We sat at their table in the kitchen. Edmondo's mother had cooked sausages with lentils, (apparently in Italy that symbolises wealth) while Fragolina was wearing red woollen stockings for luck. The heat from the stove, the laughter, Edmondo's foot against mine, made the war seem like a nightmare; frightening when you remembered to think about it, but not actually happening for real.

Everything changed so quickly.

At midnight, Edmondo's father opened the front door so we could hear the church clock chiming. We had all sung Auld Lang Syne, standing together in the hallway, when there was an ear-splitting crash. For an instant, everyone froze before running into the kitchen where the wind was gusting through a hole in the window over the sink, and a brick – an ugly, red builder's brick – was lying in the place where Fragolina had been eating stewed apples only minutes earlier. Mr Brambilla's face turned as grey and cold as yesterday's fire grate. Grabbing his coat and a lantern from the dresser he left the room without saying a word. The Brambillas' kitchen overlooks their back lawn, and he was plainly going in search of whoever had broken into the garden.

Fragolina, herself, was quite hysterical. Her face was ashen, but the little birthmark on her neck seemed to pulse crimson. 'It would have hit me!' she kept crying in English (which I suppose is the language she's grown up with). 'The brick would have hit my head!'

'It would only have caused a bruise,' Mrs Brambilla replied, before adding something in Italian I didn't understand. Her cheeks were white with shock too. 'A small bruise, that's all,' she repeated, as if to convince herself. She didn't convince me. A brick is a heavy thing, and whoever threw it must have used a lot of force. I probably should have gone home immediately, but Edmondo couldn't leave his family to escort me and I didn't dare to walk back on my own. Instead of the safe, happy place I had grown up in the village now seemed darker and quite menacing. I felt almost afraid about living here.

While Mrs B and Edmondo tried to comfort the girls, I began to clear up the mess. The window glass had fallen into the sink and all over the floor – tiny shards glinting all the way to the skirting boards – while Fragolina's pudding plate had been smashed to pieces and the tablecloth stained with stewed apple. I lifted up the brick to clear away the broken china and stopped. A piece of paper was tied to the brick covered in black handwriting. Silently, I passed the note to Edmondo. For a moment he stood staring at the words, before suddenly flinging the paper down. I couldn't help but read what was written.

Everyone is watching.

Soon you will be locked up too.

'What does it mean?'

Edmondo spoke slowly. 'The government is interning aliens who they suspect of being a threat to security. All the Germans and Austrians must appear before a tribunal to prove their innocence. The ones that cannot do so, will be imprisoned.'

'But what… how…?' The words fell over themselves in my throat and died. I glanced at Mrs B. Huddled beside Fragolina, she barely appeared older than a child herself. 'But we are not yet at war with Italy,' I managed.

'Nobody can pretend they don't know where the sympathies of Mussolini lie,' Edmondo said.

'The sympathies of Mussolini, perhaps. Not your sympathies.'

'We are Italian. That's enough in the eyes of some to make us enemies.'

'Yesterday,' Mrs B's voice was surprisingly clear, 'yesterday we made ice-cream and sarsaparilla for the village, for parties and for weddings. We laughed and danced alongside our friends. They would call to us across the street, linger in our shop to taste our pastries and tell us their news. Now they believe we will help the Germans invade their country, endanger their families, perhaps even shoot them in the night. How can they believe that of us? How can they treat us as friends one day and enemies the next when we have done nothing at all in between those times?'

Before either I or Edmondo could reply, Mr Brambilla returned, slamming the front door so loudly the echo reverberated like the wash from a boat. He came into the kitchen and unbuttoned his coat without speaking. For a second the thunder in his face made me a little relieved he didn't seem to have found the culprit. I decided to steel myself for the dark walk home and announced I must go. Edmondo offered to come with me, but I told him to stay with Fragolina. She still looked so shell-shocked and, besides, I didn't want to risk Edmondo coming across the brick-thrower himself. If too many New Year beers could make someone hurl a rock into a family kitchen, where else could it lead? The possibilities were too awful to contemplate.

As I was leaving, I glimpsed the note again and my stomach jumped into my throat. The handwriting, those black spindly letters were horribly familiar. Whoever was responsible for spoiling the Brambillas' New Year's Eve, was the same person who had told me to stay away from Edmondo.

Letter Uncle Charles to Ruby

6 January 1940

My dear goddaughter

Happy New Year! I hope you and your parents managed to enjoy the festive season despite the absence of your brother. How is the Latin progressing? Have the books I sent you proved useful? I'm quite certain a brain like yours will be able to pick up such a logical language in no time. Here, in the War Office we remind ourselves every day: *In absentia lucis, tenebrae vincunt.* (In the absence of light, darkness prevails; though I'm rather hoping you've had sufficient success with the dictionary to make my translation superfluous.)

Well, my dear, I must attend to the pile of papers on my desk. I repeat my seasonal greetings and entreat you to begin the New Year with the fortitude and resolution that the coming months may well demand of us.

Yours affectionately

Uncle Charles

PS I nearly forgot, one last question: Do you happen to know anything about the father of that chap of yours? In particular, the circumstances in which he came to leave Italy?

Letter George to Ruby

15 January 1940

Dearest Sis

Belated Merry Christmas and Happy New Year. I meant to send you at least one letter over the festive period, however events didn't quite roll out according to plan (nothing ever does here). I'll try to take things in order and not jump ahead of myself…

Shortly after my last letter the regiment got moved to a mining town in the North of France. Although the place isn't nearly as pretty as the fruit orchards, the bright spot is we're allowed to use the pithead baths on a rota that works out about one visit a fortnight. I can't tell you what a relief it is to get clean, even if the feeling only lasts a day or two. We're still spending our days digging out gun pits or training and while a gun pit might not sound big the circumference is often the size of a circus ring, so you can probably imagine how sweaty and dirty we men get. You can probably imagine the smell too – though I wouldn't try too hard on that score if I were you!

It won't surprise you to learn that most of us chaps became rather homesick as December progressed. Christmas Eve started out a dismal affair until word went round that one of the local Estaminets (that's a café to you and me) had opened up to cook the English soldiers a Christmas dinner of egg & chips! I tell you, Ruby, 'Pommes de Terre Frits avec Oeuvres' has never tasted as good, especially since the food was washed down with a fair amount of 'vin rouge' and 'vin blanc'. We sang a lot of songs and Frank (the pal I mentioned in my last letter) borrowed an old accordion from the owner of the restaurant and drove everyone mad trying to play 'South of the Border, Down Mexico Way'. Just recalling the evening now makes me smile and want to hum about stars over Mexico and falling in love!

After Christmas, matters took a bit of a downturn, however. I managed to catch some damn bug or other that caused me to run a jigger of a fever. Don't tell Mother, but I ended up being taken by field ambulance to a casualty clearing station. Not that anyone could do much for me there. All I can remember is lying on a stretcher beside a blazing stove and being given a tin basin full of 'beef' tea so vile a puddle of grease was floating on the top. I suppose the bug must have burned itself out (or died of food poisoning!) because after a few days I began to feel better and eventually the Medical Officer said I was fit to return to duties.

The second I was in post again the weather turned bitterly cold. When I think back to October, and sleeping under an apple tree, it's like remembering a holiday! Now the water freezes in our water bottles and we wash our faces in the snow. Still, the regiment is all in one piece, which is the main thing. And perhaps I'll get some leave soon, you never know your luck!

I hope you're working hard and making the most of the books in my room, Ruby. Oxford seems like a dream I once had and can barely remember.

Your loving brother

George

PS I've just this minute been promised leave in March or April! I can hardly sit still enough to write. If only I had enough paper to make a calendar and cross off the days! It's another thing you mustn't tell Mother, though – nothing is certain in this game 'til it happens, and I don't want to get her hopes up only to have them dashed.

Diary of Miss Ruby Summers

27 January 1940

Dear Diary

Am I allowed to complain about school-work when there's a war on? Well, I'm going to complain here where nobody can lecture me about how silly and trivial my worries are compared to the country being at war. Of course, I know the truth (my problems are dreadfully silly and trivial), but who can think about the war all the time, except perhaps people like Mr Churchill and Uncle Charles? It's not even as if much seems to be happening except rationing, and the growing numbers of posters at the bus-stop exhorting everyone to turn their gardens over to vegetables, and that's hardly enough to occupy the mind for long. I've rather misstated the problem anyway, which is not so much schoolwork as Latin!

When I study George's medical books, the hours simply disappear. I honestly don't understand how anyone could fail to be captivated by the incredible miracle of the human body. It seems to me the most extraordinary feat of engineering by God, or nature, or whatever combination of the two you happen to believe in. Yesterday evening as I was lying in bed, I thought about my ears hearing the rain rattling on the outhouse roof, the heat from my hot-water bottle seeping through the capillaries on the soles of my feet, and the pupils in my eyes widening to adjust to the dark. And then I remembered the thinking part too. Not only was I aware of each and every sensation I was aware of being aware of them! I could ponder them in the most objective fashion and even attempt to understand how all those processes work. In fact, the brain is probably the most extraordinary part of the whole machine!

But compared to all that wonder, Latin is so dreadfully, bone-achingly dull. And pointless too, as nobody now even speaks the language. I keep trying to learn the grammar and vocabulary but whenever I attempt to translate a passage the words never look the slightest bit familiar because their endings keep changing. Besides, if I do ever manage to make any sense of a paragraph or two, they turn out to be about slaves, or gladiators, or a complicated system of hot and cold baths. I simply don't understand how anyone could possibly believe that mastering this subject will make me a better scientist. Instead, all the stupid conjugations and declensions will take up space in my head I could use much more fruitfully for more important things. Surely there must be a way to study science at Cambridge without Latin?

Letter Mary Cartwright to Ruby

1 February 1940

Dear Ruby

Thank you for enquiring about my research. Although it's proceeding rather slowly at the moment my fascination with differential equations remains undimmed and with luck a breakthrough is just around the corner. I'm a firm believer that patience and optimism are the cornerstones of any research project worth its salt! As for Latin, I'm afraid the subject is compulsory and I don't believe the university makes any exceptions to the standard entrance papers (although I suppose there can be no harm in asking). I agree it does seem rather unfair pupils from schools that don't offer Latin should be so thoroughly disadvantaged.

By the way, you will be rather chuffed to hear that Ms Wodehouse asked after you the other day. She enquired whether I knew if you intended to apply to Girton or Newnham. Shall I tell her you would be delighted to apply to Girton if she can make the Latin requirement disappear?

Yours in friendship

Mary

Diary of Miss Ruby Summers

15 February 1940

Dear Diary

The evenings might slowly be getting lighter but the last couple of days have cast nothing but shadows. The day before yesterday somebody posted a newspaper page through the Brambillas' letterbox. The article was about a young German man whose family had been living in England since well before the war. Apparently, he was spotted taking photographs of a wrecked airplane with a film camera owned by the local rector's daughter! Goodness knows how the German got hold of the camera or whether the rector's daughter knew what he wanted to do with it, but the Home Secretary decided the actions of the German were very suspicious and he ought to be interned immediately. What's more, apparently the government might now intern all the Germans who weren't locked up at the beginning of the war. Whoever put the newspaper through the Brambillas' letter box had circled the article in thick black pen and written, 'We should do the same to you'. I asked Edmondo if he thought the handwriting was the same as that on the note with the brick and he said he thought it was. After he left, I looked at the letter from last November warning me to stay away from him, and I'm certain the writer of all three nasty notes is the same person.

As if that wasn't bad enough, yesterday Police Constable Dodds visited the Brambilla house. Mr and Mrs Brambilla have been ordered to hand in their wireless set to the police station and the whole family has been told they mustn't go more than five miles from home without informing the police! Edmondo said his father was very upset indeed. Then he told me that on the way to my house he had the queerest sensation someone was following him. We were sitting in the garden at the time, in the one patch of grass beside the swing that hasn't been dug for potatoes and carrots. Immediately – I couldn't help myself – I twisted to look over my shoulder towards the horse chestnut trees and across the boundary with Mrs Wainwright's land. The meadow was empty of course. 'I'm sure you imagined it,' I said. 'Nobody could follow you without being seen.'

Nevertheless, after Edmondo had gone

home, I took a letter to the postbox for Mother and had the most peculiar feeling of being watched myself. Although I told myself I was suffering from an over-active imagination, I definitely glimpsed a patch of colour behind the hedge that runs alongside our lane. It was probably only a pheasant or fox, but once I'd posted the letter, I found myself running faster and faster back to the house as if my legs had a mind of their own.

NB: I've just read the above again and the notion of being followed seems very silly indeed, not to say hysterical. Particularly for a scientist. I've a good mind to cross out the entry altogether.

Letter Edmondo to Ruby

6 March 1940

Mia cara

Since you're not at home I'm leaving you a note. I started to explain everything to your mother, but she said the message was too complicated to remember and told me to write it down.

Next weekend my father is taking my family to Felixstowe, to a boarding house that belongs to an Italian school in London. Before the war children from the school used to go there for seaside holidays and sometimes my parents would give them music lessons. At the moment hardly any children remain in London, and nobody is available to take them on holiday in any case, so the school has offered my family the opportunity to spend a few days there instead. On Friday afternoon we'll catch the bus to Orwell station and from there the train to Felixstowe, returning on Sunday. Although it's early in the year to visit the beach, the shop is doing less and less business and my father wants some time in the sea air to distract him from his worries. (I overheard my mother tell him that yesterday we only sold two hot pies and a jar of condensed milk.)

Ruby, if your parents allow, would you like to come to Felixstowe with us? We will of course tell the police about our trip and I know my parents will take good care of us. The mere thought of walking along the beach with you has brought the sun out from behind the clouds and cast a bright yellow beam across your kitchen floor!

Edmondo

PS I'm enclosing a cornflower from the bunch I picked on my way to your house.

(I presented the rest to your mother who told me no one had given her flowers in a very long time!)

Diary of Miss Ruby Summers

9 March 1940

Dear Diary

An odd thing happened today when Uncle Charles visited. Not that it was odd for him to visit – he normally comes to see Father every few months, mainly it seems so they can drink whisky and reminisce about the days they played rugby together at school. No, the odd thing happened when I mentioned the Brambillas' trip to Felixstowe during dinner. Mother and Father had been quite adamant there was no point in me going to the seaside in March. Especially when the government was in the process of covering all the beaches with barbed wire and mines and it would mean missing Friday afternoon school. I had a feeling though that those weren't the real reasons and that if some other friend had invited me, they would have said yes without a second thought. Ever since Christmas they've seemed increasingly uncomfortable about me spending time with Edmondo, so I decided to ask about the trip to Felixstowe when Uncle Charles was there, and they couldn't change the subject or suddenly decide they had an urgent errand to run.

Anyway, as soon as Mother had served oxtail soup (we always have two courses when someone comes to dinner, and the first is always soup), I told her Miss Beale (my form teacher) didn't mind in the slightest if I took a half day the following Friday because she knew I was such a hard worker, and I didn't mind not walking on the beach as it would be relaxing simply to hear the waves, so would she and Father please think again about allowing me to go to Felixstowe with the Brambillas. Mother exchanged a pained glance with Father then put her spoon down with a sigh. However, before either of them could actually say anything, Uncle Charles practically spit a mouthful of soup back into his bowl and Mother and Father turned to look at him instead.

'Felixstowe,' Uncle Charles spluttered. 'Why is Edmondo's family going to Felixstowe?'

I told him about the boarding house and the Italian school in London, and that Edmondo's parents were allowed to stay in the hostel as a thank you for entertaining the Italian children when they used to be brought to Felixstowe on holiday before the war. All the while I was speaking Uncle Charles didn't take his eyes from mine. He didn't even seem to blink, he simply stared at me as if I was reciting Hitler's strategy plan for the war word for word. The very second that I finished, Mother said, 'Don't worry, Charles, we've already made it clear to Ruby she's not going. It's really quite wrong of her to bring it up again.'

Uncle Charles swung around first to face her and then to face Father, swiv-elling on his chair as though in slow motion. After a moment he cleared his throat with a swallowing sound. 'Perhaps you shouldn't be too hasty, Evie,' he said. 'After all, Ruby does work terribly hard at school and a breath of sea air might put some colour in her cheeks.'

Mother's own cheeks coloured, with surprise rather than sea air. 'It's not the weather for the beach, Charles. And besides' – she peeked again at Father, before adding much more quietly – 'it's hardly the time to be seen gadding about on holiday with a lad who isn't British.'

That seemed to put an end to the matter. Uncle Charles remained quiet for the rest of the soup and the meatloaf. And I did too. Although I'd made my parents admit their true objection to me going to

Felixstowe, I didn't feel any satisfaction about the achievement at all. Instead, a rather queer air hung over the dining table like fog or damp or the unsettled feeling that lingers in some old houses.

After dinner my offer of help with the washing up was declined and I was ushered upstairs 'to finish my homework'. As soon as the door to the dining room shut behind me conversation erupted the far side but although I could hear Uncle Charles's voice rising and falling, I couldn't hear what he was saying.

About forty minutes later, footsteps sounded on the landing outside my bedroom. There was a moment of silence before the door opened halfway. Mother peered through the gap. 'Well, Ruby, you'll be pleased to know your father and I have decided you can go to Felixstowe with the Brambillas after all.'

I blinked at her for a moment before scrambling off the bed. 'Is that definite? Can I let Edmondo know?'

She nodded. A quick, uncomfortable jerk of the head. A second later Uncle Charles's face appeared over the top of her shoulder and when he spoke she seemed almost to flinch. 'Ruby,' he said, 'I would like you to do me a favour while you're in Felixstowe.'

I stared at him. 'What kind of favour?'

'A very easy one. Nothing difficult at all.' He paused. 'I want you to notice everything very closely.'

I kept staring. Uncle Charles cleared his throat again. 'What I'm trying to say is that it would be useful to know if you run into anyone of interest at the coast.'

'Do you mean if I meet someone I know?'

'Possibly, possibly… Or perhaps someone you don't know.'

'Why would I meet people I don't know? I'll be staying with Edmondo and his family.' Mother's gaze, I noticed, was fixed on the floorboards.

'Well, if you do see somebody, or notice somebody, anyone whom you're not expecting to see or who looks suspicious, make a note of it. Make a note of everything about them. Write it all down so there's no chance of forgetting it.' His voice had become quite sharp.

'What about Edmondo?' I asked. 'Should I ask him to keep an eye out for strangers too?'

Uncle Charles shook his head. 'No need for that. In fact, Ruby' – there was a small pause – 'in fact it's probably best you don't mention this to anyone at all. Although nothing useful may come of the little favour you're doing me, the less people who know about it the greater the chance that something might.'

Mother lifted her head. Under the bedroom light her fair hair seemed closer to grey than blond. 'We'd better let Ruby go to bed, Charles. It's nearly ten o'clock already.' She blew me a kiss and shut the door, but not before Uncle Charles fixed me with a hard, serious look that made it perfectly clear his favour was much more of an instruction than a request.

So, Diary. The good news is that I'm going away to Felixstowe with Edmondo. The bad news is I've been given a sleuthing task by Uncle Charles. He obviously thinks Felixstowe is the most likely place for a German attack and wants me to keep an eye out for anyone who might help Hitler invade. But he can't be expecting much – even if Felixstowe happens to be choc-a-bloc full of Nazi sympathisers, they're hardly likely to make themselves known to me. Anyway, all that matters is that I'm going away with Edmundo and if the price I have to pay is watching out for suspicious strangers, so be it!

Letter Uncle Charles to Ruby

10 March 1940

My dear Ruby

How very nice to see you yesterday. Once you return from your weekend by the sea I wonder if I might tempt you to make the trip to London again. They still do rather a good menu at the Savoy Grill and I'm hoping lunch there might be a suitable substitute for an Easter egg this year. What do you think? How about Wednesday, 20 March? I imagine school will have finished for the Easter holidays by then.

Yours affectionately

Uncle Charles

PS How is the Latin progressing? *Vincit qui patitur!* (He who endures will succeed!)

Diary of Miss Ruby Summers

20 March 1940

Dear Diary

Uncle Charles surpassed himself on the Easter egg front. Lunch at the Savoy was marvellous. I had 'Le Vol-au-Vent de Volaille à la Royale' – sliced chicken with mushrooms in a cream sauce and utterly divine. I'm jolly glad the menu was in French and not Latin, though, or else I'd never have understood a word of it (sadly, my Latin is not progressing at all). The dining room was terribly grand too: leather-backed chairs, brilliant white tablecloths grazing the carpet like swans' wings, and the most amazing silver light that bounced between the chandeliers, the crystal glasses and the mirrors making me feel quite dizzy.

I do hope the lunch was not supposed to be a reward for my spying efforts in Felixstowe. If so, Uncle Charles would have been bitterly disappointed because I told him even before we sat down that I hadn't seen anyone taking suspicious photographs – or indeed anyone acting suspiciously at all. He did appear a little crestfallen, but we still had a lovely chat over our watercress soup, and I thought that was the end of the Felixstowe business altogether. I was quite wrong, however. No sooner had my vol-au-vent arrived (Uncle Charles had chosen kidneys, which seemed a missed opportunity) than he leaned ever so slightly forward and said, 'Now Ruby, I'd like you to describe your trip to Felixstowe in as much detail as you can remember.' I reminded him I'd already explained I hadn't seen anything of interest, but he simply waived his fork and said, 'I'll be the judge of that. Tell me everything that happened, just as if you were writing it in a diary.'

So, Diary, this is what I said:

The Friday we left home was sunny with cotton clouds scudding over a clean blue sky in a purposeful and rather optimistic way. I've only ever cycled to Orwell station before but because of our weekend bags we went by bus, which was not only quicker but a lot less sweaty. The platform seemed deserted until a police constable appeared from inside a little office and asked us where we were going. 'Felixstowe,' Mr Brambilla replied. 'For the weekend.'

The policeman gave Mr Brambilla a quizzical glance. 'And where have you come from?'

'We live here,' Mr Brambilla said, growing a little straighter. 'In Bucklesham.' As the policeman continued to gaze at him, he reached inside his jacket and produced a bundle of identity cards.

The policeman studied them for ages, throwing glances from time to time around our little group. Mrs Brambilla took hold of Fragolina's hand and Edmondo put down his bag, as though about to do or say something, but at that moment the policeman returned the papers to Mr Brambilla and with a single nod of his head walked away.

Mr Brambilla tucked the identity cards back into his jacket. 'I suppose they have to be careful,' I said to break the silence. 'Particularly around here.' Mother had warned me to expect to see policemen or soldiers on the trains, guarding the exclusion zone. A strip of England along the east coast has been made a no-go area for anyone coming from outside the area. If we lived more than twenty-five miles away from Felixstowe, we wouldn't be allowed to go there at all! It's quite extraordinary to think nobody can travel here except on official business. (Perhaps those restrictions don't apply to Uncle Charles because of his War Office work? Or else he had official business reasons for coming to see us I don't know about. I didn't say that last bit to Uncle Charles during lunch because I've only just thought of it.)

Anyway, at Orwell station Mr Brambilla was still watching the retreating back of the constable. 'Nobody wanted to see your identity card,' he said to me. 'The policeman only asked my family because he heard our Italian accents. Like everyone else, he thinks we are the enemy.' There was a fixed, dark look to his face that made it seem as if the sun had dipped behind a cloud.

I felt my hand being squeezed and realised Edmondo had come to stand beside me. 'We should climb on board,' he said. 'Before we miss the train.'

Mrs B tried to revive everyone's spirits by chattering gaily and pointing out of the window, but the incident put rather a dampener on things and when the guard came to check our tickets Mr Brambilla glared at him so hard the poor man practically scampered into the next carriage.

By the time we arrived at Felixstowe it was nearly three o'clock. The station was barely busier than the one at Orwell and though a piece of cardboard propped against the glass of the information booth said 'Back in ten minutes' I had the strong impression that ten minutes had been and gone a long time ago.

There seemed little point waiting for a taxi, or even a horse and cart, so we walked into town. A lot of the shops were boarded up and most of the ones that weren't were still closed. However, a sign outside a hotel, the Felixstowe Grand, was advertising afternoon tea. The menu promised scones and sandwiches and buttered teacakes, and my stomach began to rumble so loudly from lack of lunch I was certain the others would hear. We waited expectantly in the lobby before a harassed-looking woman appeared at last and told us (quite crossly) they had stopped serving tea weeks ago. At least, near the promenade we came across a man selling ice creams from a hand waggon. I wondered if Mr Brambilla might complain they weren't as good as his gelato, but in fact he bought us each a vanilla tub which cheered us all up and made it seem like we were on holiday after all.

Unfortunately, the feeling didn't last long. Whereas the station and streets had been practically empty, the seafront was full of soldiers and trucks. Two young men, barely any older than Edmondo and me, were rolling out coils of razor-topped barbed wire along the boundary between the coast and the road while the beach resembled a building site. Two wedge-shaped concrete battlements had already been constructed on the edge of the shingle and a huddle of men was gathered around a cement mixer, some shovelling sand into the barrel as others loaded wheelbarrows from a pile of wet-looking slop. Strolling along the sand was plainly out of the question. You could hardly hear the waves above the grind of machines and the shouts of the soldiers.

The boarding house was tucked down a side street just off the promenade. All the rooms, with the exception of the kitchen, seemed to be square and brown and with only the minimum of furniture absolutely essential for sitting or sleeping. There was a heavy sort of dampness too, as if the air hadn't been disturbed in an age. After the trek from the station and the disappointment of the beach, nobody much fancied venturing out and we played cards all afternoon. It was rather dreary to be honest, but I tried to enjoy myself for Edmondo's sake. He kept giving me anxious little looks and, unlike him, snapping rather impatiently at Fragolina. By six o'clock it was beginning to get dark, and it was then we realised that hardly any of the lightbulbs worked! Luckily Edmondo's mother found a drawer full of candles in the hallway and cooked us big plates of pasta under the sputtering gaze of a row of tea-lights. Just as we finished eating there was a knock at the door. Mr Brambilla exchanged a glance with Mrs B before pushing back his chair. Two minutes later, a man like a human pipe-cleaner wearing a pork pie hat was standing in the entrance to the kitchen and speaking rapid Italian with Mr Brambilla.

Diary, I must record that at this point Uncle Charles, who had been starting to seem faintly bored, leaned right across the table, his fork dripping gravy and his tie practically dangling into his plate.

'You said you didn't meet anyone in Felixstowe, Ruby!'

'I meant that I didn't meet anyone suspicious. The pipe-cleaner man turned out to be a musician friend of the Brambillas. He brought his violin with him and later in the evening he and Mr Brambilla played to us in the sitting room.' Nestling close to Edmondo, the music melting into the candlelight and our hands still and entwined in the dark, had been the first romantic part of the weekend and made me glad I had come after all (I didn't tell Uncle Charles about the other romantic parts of the weekend, those incredible moments belong only to Edmundo and me...)

At bedtime I shared a room with Fragolina. I could have had my own room because there were plenty of them – the building seemed to go up and up forever, staircase after staircase winding towards the attics – but the lack of lightbulbs and echoey emptiness made the place quite unnerving and I was glad to have company. However, that first night, sometime around midnight, I needed to go to the bathroom, and when I crept downstairs, I heard voices coming from a room we hadn't been using. The pipe-cleaner man and Mr Brambilla were sitting on upturned crates talking intensely, the violins at their feet like sleeping dogs. On the wall behind them the shadows of their head and shoulders were enormous, as if I had climbed to the top of a beanstalk and entered a land of giants. Then as I watched the pipe-cleaner man picked up his violin and started playing something so incredibly sad it seemed to latch on to all the unhappy things deep inside you and bring them spilling out.

Uncle Charles made a throaty, impatient noise. 'And what were they talking about? Before the music started again.'

'I don't know. They were speaking Italian.'

'Did they see you, Ruby?'

'No. I went to the lavatory and then tiptoed back to my bedroom.'

I dropped my gaze and busied myself with my Volaille. Mainly because I was hungry and the Volaille was delicious, but also because I couldn't tell Uncle Charles what really happened next in case he got the wrong idea and became suspicious of the Brambillas. I'm not sure I can even bring myself to write it here. Diaries are funny things. Mostly you regard them like a confidant to whom you can say anything, but part of you wonders, perhaps even hopes, if one day all the little dramas of your life might be of interest to somebody else and while what happened at the boarding house probably would be of interest to someone else the interest would be for all the wrong reasons and simply because the Brambillas are Italian. Anyway, luckily, Uncle Charles didn't appear to notice my discomfort. Or perhaps, I'm a better liar than I give myself credit for (if credit is the right word).

'What about the next day?'

'We went for a walk. All the way to Felixstowe Ferry and back, although with so many places off-limits there wasn't a great deal to see.'

'I meant about the other man, the pipe-cleaner man. Did you see him again? Or anyone else?'

I shook my head. I was on firmer ground now that I was remembering the walk along the front. The trouble with all the wire and concrete wasn't the ugliness, or even that we couldn't go on the beach, but rather the sight of them kept reminding you in a constant, jabbing way, like a stitch you get running, that we were at war. And when I looked across the sea, I realised that George was far away on the other side. Fighting somewhere, or getting ready to fight, or possibly even injured (or, I hardly dare write it, worse), and the second I had had those thoughts watching the foamy swell of waves and hearing them heave their way up the sand immediately lost their appeal.

Uncle Charles speared a kidney and muttered, 'Well, that's better than nothing, I suppose.' After that final-sounding assessment, to my great relief the conversation moved onto other topics. It was only as we got up to leave that he asked casually but quite suddenly, 'Why did you call him a pipe-cleaner man, Ruby? It's rather an odd description to use.'

I found I had to think about the question. 'Because he was so thin and pale,' I said eventually. 'And he seemed all the time to be hunching up his shoulders as if he was trying to fit through a narrow gap. Except when he was playing music,' I added. 'As soon as he picked up the violin, his whole way of being became bigger.'

Although Uncle Charles nodded, he appeared lost in thought. Several times before we left the restaurant, he looked to be on the verge of making an announcement but in the end he merely said something innocuous about the food or the waiters or my schoolwork and thankfully left me in peace to enjoy the novelty of being out on the town.

Letter, by hand, Edmondo to Ruby

21 March 1940

Mia cara

Our last night in Felixstowe is all I can think about. I don't have the words to describe how wonderful you are. When I opened my bedroom door and saw you standing before me in that ivory dressing gown, I believed I must be dreaming or had been taken straight to heaven. Ruby, you should probably burn this letter! We must never tell a soul! If our parents were to find out what happened they might never let us see each other again… I would marry you tomorrow if I could, though I fear what it would mean for you to choose an Italian as your husband. A leader who I hate makes your country consider me a danger, when every particle of my being so detests Mussolini I would sooner die than support him or Hitler.

Please come to me tonight! Meet me in the Wainwright's meadow at ten o'clock. Now term has ended we have so little time together, yet without you I barely feel alive.

I love you

Edmondo

PS I'm enclosing a postcard of Felixstowe. The building on the left is the Felixstowe Grand. One day after the war, we will go back together and I will buy you cake and champagne!

PPS My father found me as I was about to seal the envelope. He insisted I tell you not to mention the presence of his friend, the musician, to anyone because this friend was not supposed to enter the exclusion zone. I'm sorry to ask such a thing but my father is waiting for me to write this before he leaves the room.

Letter George to Ruby

12 April 1940

Dearest Sis

All leave has been cancelled. Hitler invading Norway and Denmark has put paid to any chance of me seeing the horse chestnuts in bloom this year (obviously I'm more upset not to be seeing you and Mother and Father but if I carp on about that I'll make us both sad). At least for now our location isn't too shabby – we're camped in the grounds of some chateau or other, tall grey turrets rising high above a canopy of elms. In another time you, me and Clem would unpack a picnic, lie on our backs under the trees and argue about who was on the throne when the castle was built. Clem would swear she could hear the sound of hooves thudding the turf, the ghosts of huntsmen and noblemen who used to ride the woods, and though you and I would say she was daft we'd listen for them, nonetheless. No time for picnics now. The elms are used for camouflage and we're tired, dirty (and probably stink) from having to dig a 6ft slit trench by every vehicle. There's a sense that things are hotting up at last, and morale amongst the lads is good. Frank thinks now Hitler has come out in the open so to speak the Brits will have the chance to give him the kicking he deserves and the war will be over much more quickly. I hope he's right. How wonderful it would be to return to Oxford, an essay or two to write at my desk and a pint or two to sink in the bar. In the meantime, you'll have to do the writing for me, though not the beer drinking!

Your ever-loving brother

George

Diary of Miss Ruby Summers

18 April 1940

This page from the Daily Mirror arrived in the post today, in an envelope addressed to me.

There are more than twenty thousand Italians in Great Britain. London alone shelters more than eleven thousand of them. The London Italian is an indigestible unit of population. He settles here more or less temporarily, working until he has enough money to buy himself a little land in Calabria or Campania or Tuscany. He often avoids employing British labour. It is much cheaper to bring a few relations into England from the old hometown. And so the boats unloaded all kinds of brown-eyed Francescas and Marias, beetle-browed Ginos, Titos and Marios and now every Italian colony in Great Britain and America is a seething cauldron of smoking Italian politics. Black Fascism. Hot as Hell. Even the peaceful, law-abiding proprietor of the back-street coffee shop bounces into a fine patriotic frenzy at the sound of Mussolini's name and we are nicely honeycombed with little cells of potential betrayal. A storm is brewing in the Mediterranean. And we, in our droning, silly tolerance are helping it to gather force.

The phrase 'nicely honeycombed with little cells of potential betrayal' would be rather impressive if only the article wasn't so revolting. The Daily Mirror sells thousands, maybe millions of copies. How awful to think of so many ordinary people reading that families like the Brambillas are their brown-eyed, beetle-browed enemy and believing that to be true simply because they see those words in newspaper print. Merely copying that description here makes me feel slightly sick. How can a newspaper be allowed to write such dreadful, inciteful things about a community who can't say anything back to defend themselves?

NB: I'm still troubled by having mentioned the pipe-cleaner man to Uncle Charles before I received Edmondo's letter. I've wondered and wondered whether to say to Uncle Charles I shouldn't have told him or instead confess to Edmondo he made his request too late. The first course of action would raise Uncle Charles's suspicions and the second worry Edmondo, so I've done nothing. I can't decide whether that implies good sense or cowardice.

Letter Mr Leslie Pritchard to Miss R. Summers

18 April 1940

Dear Miss Summers

Thank you for your recent communication. Unfortunately, I'm not aware of any books published under the name 'An Easy Guide to Mastering Latin' or any similar such title. On the basis of my own experience, I am highly dubious such a work exists and if it does, I fear the contents would in all probability fail to deliver the promised learning experience.

Yours faithfully

L. Pritchard

Letter, by hand, Edmondo to Ruby

20 April 1940

Mia cara

Tonight? Our usual time and place?

Edmondo

PS I enclose a lilac from the meadow. In anticipation.

Letter, by hand, 'anonymous' to Miss R Summers

21 April 1940

Dear Miss Summers

You may recognise my handwriting. I wrote to you some months ago, but you don't appear to have heeded either the gravity of my warning or the consequences of your actions. You are cavorting with the enemy, my dear! As the future of Europe becomes more perilous the sympathies of Mussolini become ever more apparent. Why then, do you persist in stepping out with that Italian young man, that foe in our midst, who should by now be securely behind bars along with the rest of his family? The fact that you timed your last meeting after dark suggests you are well aware of your wrongdoing and wish to hide your liaison not only from fellow Englishmen like myself, but from your family too. The time has come to put an end to such irresponsible behaviour. If your parents cannot lay down the law, I hope you will heed the warnings of a stranger, one who will not hesitate to inform the police of your behaviour should he come to believe it is driven by my more sinister motivations than the reckless ardour of youth.

Yours truly

A Concerned Resident

Diary of Miss Ruby Summers

21 April 1940

Dear Diary

I'm grounded again. No meeting Edmondo for a whole week!

Mother discovered I slipped out to see Edmondo last night. She came to find me about five o'clock this afternoon, carrying a familiar-looking piece of writing paper. 'Ruby, is this true?' she said, waiving the page at me. 'Somebody has sent me a note saying you were with Edmondo yesterday evening. At quarter past ten!'

From the handwriting I could see the author was the same ghastly person who has sent me another letter warning of the dire risks of cavorting with Italians. Whoever he (or she?) is, they must spend all of their time creeping about in the hope of finding someone doing something they can tell tales about. I said to Mother I thought she and Father didn't mind me seeing Edmondo. After all, they let me go to Felixstowe.

'That was quite different,' Mother said sternly. 'Edmondo's parents were there. You can't possibly leave the house after dark to meet a young man on your own! Whatever will people think? And him being Italian too!'

I could have told her Edmondo's parents were not always with Edmondo and me in Felixstowe. They weren't with us when we found a gap in the barbed wire and lay on the beach under a dazzle of stars. (Is dazzle a noun? If it's not, then it jolly well ought to be.) And they certainly weren't in Edmondo's bedroom that unforgettable night when I decided life was there to be lived and our bodies became a wonder of dazzle. I could also have said I didn't much mind what people think. People in general that is. Of course, I mind what people I care about think, but since I find I only like people who don't bother about the outward show of things that isn't much of a restraint. However, Mother was staring at the anonymous note with such a shocked, worried expression, though by then she must have read it twenty times, I thought better of answering her back and went up to my bedroom without a fuss.

A little while later there was a tap at my door. 'Can I come in?' Mother paced twice around the room before perching on the edge of my counterpane. 'You love him, don't you Ruby? I know you love Edmondo very much.' When I nodded, she swallowed so hard the skin rippled across her throat. 'Mussolini will join the war soon. Everyone is talking about it. And when he does, Italy will take Hitler's side.'

I kept very still. 'Perhaps Mussolini will change—'

'—Out there' – interrupting me she

waved her hand towards the window – 'out there, your brother and many thousands of other young men are risking their lives to fight Hitler. Every day there is more loss, more terrible suffering. If the government come to believe that Italians living in England are a danger, Edmondo and his family could be locked up.'

'But Edmondo is against Hitler! And against Mussolini. He wouldn't ever want to help them invade England. He believes in freedom, in the cause of the Allies and defeating fascism. They wouldn't lock him up, surely?'

'There might be a tribunal first. To hear the evidence.' She spoke quietly.

'Well, that's all right then, isn't it?' By contrast I was shouting. 'Because there won't be any evidence against Edmondo or his family. They've lived in the village for, for… years! They're one of us! Edmondo's father gives away ice-creams free to children who can't afford one. On the King's birthday he hangs a Union Jack over the counter in his shop!'

'Supposing there were some evidence?'

I stared at her. 'There can't be!'

Mother's head was bent. She was picking at a loose blue thread on her skirt, though if she had seen me doing the same thing she would have slapped away my hand and told me I was making the problem worse. When she looked up, her face seemed loaded with pain. 'No,' she said, 'I suppose you're right.'

After a moment she folded up the letter and got to her feet. 'I managed to buy sausages for supper. I'll call you when they're ready.'

I had a sudden awful premonition. 'I will be able to see Edmondo again, won't I? Once seven days is up. You won't stop me from doing that?' Either she didn't hear me or she wanted to avoid the question because the bedroom door closed quickly behind her, like a heavily inked full stop.

PART THREE

Letter Austin to Cassie

16 April 2020

Dear Cassie

How useful to be a hairdresser. I wish you could cut my hair. These days I'm shaggier than either Ned or Badger and have to wear a bandana to stop the ends from falling into my eyes.

Your other letter writer sounds as if she wants to know a lot about you. I wonder why. Hearing about her questions made me realise I don't know what you look like either. However, I'll wait until I meet you in person to find out. In my experience descriptions of the kind they write in books and letters don't help very much. Finding out a person is tall or short or has blue or green eyes doesn't help me picture them. I need to see how they react to other people. If their face and hands move when they talk and what makes them laugh. Or maybe I'm just more interested in those things than whether they have big ears or a button nose. For the record, I'm a tall man with brown eyes and my nose is normal size but the way you'd recognise me now is by the big red handkerchief tied around my forehead and the fact I'm followed everywhere by dog and a lamb like Mary from the nursery rhyme. At this rate I shan't be able to send Ned to the slaughterhouse because Badger will miss him too much. It's just as well there's a lockdown in force and nobody can visit, otherwise my credibility as a farmer would be long gone.

You're right about hearing someone's voice when you read their letters. To me, yours sounds bright and spring-like, like a crocus or a daffodil.

Austin

PS The small mirror over the sink is the only one in the caravan. I hope you still consider that to be good news.

PPS You could always grow your hair again if Stuart doesn't like the new style. (For what it's worth, I've always imagined you with short hair.)

Letter to Cassie to Ruby

17 April 2020

Dear New Best Friend

Did you marry Edmondo? Did you go to university? What happened to George?

I can't wait for the next instalment.

Cassie

Text Cassie to Austin 08.43

17 April 2020

You can't possibly send Ned to the slaughterhouse! What are you thinking of? Never mind Badger, that would break my heart and Noah's!

Text Cassie to Austin 08.45

17 April 2020

If you promise to keep Ned, I'll give you a free haircut – just as soon as we're allowed to meet each other.

Text Cassie to Austin 08.46

17 April 2020

Make that free haircuts for life!

Text Austin to Cassie 08.55

17 April 2020

That's a big promise. My hair might be dreadful to cut and I'm planning to live a very long time.

Text Cassie to Austin 09.10

17 April 2020

I don't mind what your hair is like, but as my home is in London a lifetime of free hairdressing is not much of an offer.

Please don't send Ned to the slaughterhouse.

Text Austin to Cassie 09.15

17 April 2020

So long as you promise not to tell anyone. I can't have other farmers calling me soft.

Text Cassie to Austin 09.15

17 April 2020

Deal.

Letter Ruby to Cassie

18 April 2020

Dear Cassie

Remember what we agreed. No questions until the end. However, I don't mind telling you now, I have never been married. My work was my life partner, and our relationship was very fulfilling. What about your life partner, Cassie? Have you met The One yet? Perhaps you might indulge me with some reciprocal storytelling of your own.

Your New Best Friend

Ruby

PS For what it's worth, I believe you have a smile that lights your face like stained glass with the sun behind. You might be out of practice now, but once the freckles on your nose are too numerous to count, I predict that smile will be back.

Letter Cassie to Ruby

20 April 2020

Dear Ruby

A life partner. Such a romantic expression. I wonder what Stuart, my boyfriend, would think of the idea. I'm not sure he'd be terribly keen. I've not been a very good homemaker. Or earner. And I've not much future income potential either. I'm a hairdresser, you see, and though I never set out to be one, now I can't ever imagine doing anything different. Most of all, I like my clients. Some never stop talking while others say nothing but 'hello', 'goodbye' and a 'bit more off the fringe, please' so the only sound for the entire hour is the snip of my scissors. A few are desperate to get something in particular off their chest. All they need is the right question to open up a space into which they can drop the receipt for underwear on the floor of their husband's car, or the blister pack of pills under their son's bed, or the daughter's diary that just happened to fall open as they were hoovering. I honestly believe a trip to the salon can be better than therapy: think of the endless free coffee and the enormous boost of looking a whole lot better going out than when you come in! Police detectives should interview a victim's hairdresser because that's the person who'll know about the secret lover or the gambling habit.

Cutting hair is how I met Noah's father, seven and a half years ago, in an Australian youth hostel about a thousand miles from the sea. All I did was walk into the kitchen. Sitting on a table playing a guitar was the person who was going to change my life. The first thing I noticed were his hands, broad and confident, running over the strings. The second that his matted hair resembled a fox's brush. The third was the tan line underneath the sleeves of his T-shirt that ran all the way round the muscled brown skin. He didn't look up, but he must have known I was staring at him.

'What do you want me to play?' Not an Australian accent, but close. A Kiwi, I guessed, about five years older than me.

I blinked at him.

'Dylan or Mayer. You get to choose since they don't care.' He jerked his head at the other occupants of the kitchen who were either heating up beans or peeling back beer cans.

'Dylan.' My tongue seemed to have doubled in size.

While he strummed, I cooked some kind of vegetarian chilli thing, pretending I'd forgotten about him as I chopped and fried as slowly as possible. Once all the others had left the room, I finally sat down at the table and found I couldn't take even a single bite.

The guitar guy stopped playing and watched me push the food around my plate. The sudden silence felt as loud as jungle drums.

'Are you going to eat that?'

I pushed the dish towards him and tried to look away as he worked his way through the chilli. A second later, I heard myself say, 'Would you like me to cut your hair?'

It was his turn to stare.

'I cut hair back home in England. I know what I'm doing.' It was true. I've always had a knack for hair and earned money through uni that way. Five pounds for a trim. A tenner for a restyle. No one ever complained and before the biggest parties there were queues outside my door.

We carried a kitchen chair out to the back porch of the hostel and under the glow of a single bulb with the night air rattling to the tune of a million crickets, I cut his hair short like stubble. So short I could see the two tiny moles on the back of his neck and feel the shape of his skull reveal itself under my fingers as the locks fell away. Just as I was finishing a dingo howled. The wild, eerie wail of it made me drop the scissors in fright and when I bent down to pick them up his hand closed over mine.

He never knew about Noah. Although we planned to travel together to the Northern Territories, at the last minute he said he wanted to hang on a couple of days to hook up with a friend. 'Wait for me in Darwin,' he said.

I did.

Three days became a week became two weeks as his texts became shorter and less frequent. The last one attached a photograph from Western Australia, Wave Rock – a huge granite cliff, curved like a wave about to break. There was a girl in the picture, gazing at the camera with his guitar case at her feet.

I honestly don't mind, Ruby, not for my sake. Noah is enough for me. While I was pregnant and back in England with my mother, I used to think back to that night in Alice Springs. The oasis of the porch in the ink-black wilderness, like an island in the middle of a sea. Every time the doorbell rang, I imagined a tall New Zealander standing on the step with a guitar slung across his back. But Noah shoved everyone else off the stage. Once he arrived nobody else mattered. It was as if my Australian romance had been a dream and I had woken up to find that real life was even better. Now the only time I think about Noah's father is when Noah asks about him, which isn't often at all.

Well, this is probably the longest letter I've ever written and I have to stop because Noah is pestering me for milk and the most extraordinary sunset is happening behind the pinewoods – the sky is on fire with oranges and pinks.

Cassie

PS Was that reciprocal enough for you?

Text Stuart to Cassie 15.21

22 April 2020

Sorry, I can't speak properly right now. My next patient is due at 3.30 and I need to change my gown and mask. I know you're upset, Cassie, but the answer is obvious. Come home! You've been gone over four weeks. How many more do you plan to be there? Eight? Ten? Indefinitely? You can't hide away with Noah for ever. These people plainly don't want you and will only make your life more unpleasant the longer you stay.

Besides, we need to talk. X

Text Cassie to Stuart 15.22

22 April 2020

What do you mean, we need to talk? We talk most evenings.

Letter Cassie to Austin

22 April 2020

Dear Austin

A horrible thing has happened. I almost called you but decided writing would be less intrusive. You could even throw this letter away without reading it, or skim read while you're watching TV or feeding Ned. And putting down on paper what happened is already oddly cathartic. As if the act of picking up a pen and searching for the right words has put a fence around my feelings and stopped them from running out of control.

Anyway, the thing that happened, happened while Noah and I were at the supermarket. When we got back, we found a heap of dog poo on the caravan step. Right in the middle. I would have trodden in it – the step is brown, so the poo didn't show up – only I dropped the key and when I bent down the stench was inches from my face. Of course, I pretended to Noah the poo was an accident. I said a dog must have been sniffing about the park and happened to do its business there. It wasn't an accident, though. An envelope had been jammed into the door hinge of the caravan. Inside was the back of a take-out menu from a pizza place on which in huge letters someone had scrawled:

'Go home! People are dying because of morons like you.'

Is that what you think too, Austin? That people might die because I brought Noah here? At first the note made me want to leave straight away. I even started to gather up some of our stuff, pretending to Noah I was just having a tidy-up. Then Noah asked if we could go to the beach and look for shells.

We walked all the way to the water's edge and while Noah filled his bucket (*your* bucket, I should say), I watched the shadows creeping longer over the sand. The tide was so far out the beach-huts looked tiny in front of the pinewoods, like a single string of fairy lights in an enormous Christmas tree. Nobody but us was there and every direction seemed to roll on for ever. It's funny to remember how, when we arrived, all that space used to make me panic. Now the feeling is more like one of somebody dabbing antiseptic cream on a cut finger – a kind of cooling calm. Anyway, I thought about how careful Noah and I have been since we arrived. Apart from the checkout lady in the supermarket, we haven't seen anyone. Not to talk to anyway, only occasionally to pass on the pavement. We haven't even met you. We spray our hands with antiseptic before we enter a shop until they're wet and wear our masks the moment we go inside. And I'm certain that Noah is stronger for being here. When we first came here he wouldn't have had the energy to walk all the way to the sea at low tide. Today, the moment we reached the beach he let go of my hand and ran!

Give me some advice, Austin? I want to do the right thing, but what's right for Noah isn't the same as what the people here want me to do. Or what Stuart wants me to do. Am I allowed to make Noah my priority?

Your demanding tenant

Cassie

PS Don't worry, I scrubbed the step with Fairy Liquid until my wrist ached. It's probably less smelly now than it's been since the caravan left the factory – the step that is, not my wrist!

PPS I can't believe I nearly forgot to ask about Ned. (That's the trouble with letters, there's no way to delete and copy and paste. Or maybe the stream-of-consciousness thing is more honest? At least you can tell what's really on someone's mind.)

Text Stuart to Cassie 18.42

22 April 2020

I only meant we need to talk properly; when you're not worried about waking Noah or the connection doesn't disappear halfway through the call. Ideally, when we're actually in the same room.

Text Cassie to Stuart 18.44

22 April 2020

The connection is never an issue with anyone else. Perhaps it's Trevor's Wi-Fi that's the problem. Or that you never have much to say to me.

Text Stuart to Cassie 18.45

22 April 2020

Being 150 miles away from each other is the problem. The pandemic is the problem. Me not doing anything except dealing with dental emergencies and people complaining about their teeth over the telephone is the problem. Going home to an empty house and eating ready meals is the problem. And I've just noticed the whisky is finished, so now that's a problem too.

Text Stuart to Cassie 18.47

22 April 2020

Sorry. I just miss you, that's all. I'll call tomorrow. Going to Trevor's for a whisky.

PS Aren't you tired of living in a rickety old caravan the colour of a grape?

Text Cassie to Stuart 18.50

22 April 2020

I'm thinking of coming home at the weekend.

Text Stuart to Cassie 18.50

22 April 2020

Fantastic! XX

Text Cassie to Stuart 18.51

22 April 2020

Actually, the caravan is a wonderful example of an early Avondale and she's in extremely good condition for her age.

Text Stuart to Cassie 18.51

22 April 2020

I won't have time to shop before Friday so pick up whatever you want to cook for dinner on the way back! X

Letter Mrs Rosemary Ross to Cassie

22 April 2020

Dear Cassandra

Your talk of letters must have inspired me because we only finished our chat five minutes ago and already all sorts of things have popped into my head that I want to tell you on paper. All at once writing you a letter feels important. I might even send them to lots of people, starting with those I've only exchanged Christmas cards with for ever and a day. For once in my life, I've got the time to do more than scribble a few lines about where I've been on holiday and how we really must meet up *this* New Year, and since I haven't been anywhere since March and goodness knows when we might meet anyone at all, I shall have to dig a little deeper for something to say. I'm rather curious about that particular exercise. Now I come to think about it, I've realised I'm not terribly interested in Esme's latest theatre trip, where Jocelyn went in Turkey or whether the Browns have another grandchild. Trying to ask after all those places and baby names is as testing as an episode of Countdown and a lot less entertaining. I'd much sooner hear about the highs and lows of their last twenty years (which is probably the last time we had a proper conversation), how they're coping with later middle age (not old age) and what their plans are for the future once this wretched pandemic is over. (Yes, Cassandra, we still have a future in our sixties – decades of it, I hope, if your grandmother is anything to go by.) Even your new penfriend (Ruby, did you say?) has a future, a very precious one if she's 96. Don't forget to ask about that, as well as her past. You could be in for a surprise.

What have I been doing to fill the time, apart from planting a herb garden and a daily walk to the duckpond and back? I forgot to mention my new sewing venture. I'm making facemasks out of your old T-shirts (washed of course, otherwise the poor recipient might catch something a good deal worse than Covid). Once I've made a big enough batch, I leave them in a shoebox on the counter at the Post Office for anyone to help themselves. I initially intended them for essential workers but then decided they should be for anyone who wants one. Anyway, Cassandra, my new resolve means I'm not going to pad this letter out with a description of your Aunt Dora's latest bread-baking or today's Netflix time-filler. Instead, I'm going to give you some advice: You mentioned you were thinking of leaving Norfolk and going back to Stuart.

Don't.

Stay where you are.

The author of the dreadful note, the dog-poo depositor, is *one* person. Probably a lonely and frightened individual who knows nothing about you or Noah or why you came to Norfolk. But I do. It was exactly a year ago today you did that marvellous marathon haircutting session to raise money for the hospital. You were exhausted and pale, yet so determined to do something positive, and you did. Fifty haircuts in eighteen hours and over ten thousand pounds raised for the children's ward (no wonder you made the papers!) How different your voice is now from those dark days. For more than a year every word you uttered was like a cartoon character squashed flat by a steamroller. Today your tone was entirely different and you're back to sounding twenty-eight rather than eighty-eight. In short, you're starting to seem like my daughter again and I'm thrilled to have her back. Please don't spoil it now.

By the way you'll probably get a postcard from your father soon (who plainly believes a worldwide pandemic is no reason to curtail his adventures). He telephoned the other day from a village in Central America to check we were all still alive. I'm well aware he's travelling with his latest girlfriend because she and I belong to the same gardening club (not that she seems to know much about gardening). I managed to get the full story last November at a tulip planting morning – despite him being far too coy to tell me anything himself. Perhaps he thinks I might actually mind, when all I feel is relief that I'll never have to spend another second in that wretched camper van. The man keeps forgetting we separated ten years ago!

Give Noah a hug from me.

Mum

PS If any of my Christmas card friends should ask about my highs and lows over the last twenty years, you becoming pregnant, and having Noah, would be a high. (While your grandmother used to tell you that, I probably haven't – at least not enough. That's why the sentence is underlined.)

PPS Has anything happened to your friend Mandy? You used to talk about her all the time but recently you haven't mentioned her at all.

Letter Ruby to Cassie

23 April 2020

Dear Cassie

A short one today because the nurse is here. She comes to the home every Thursday and Monday to check who of us are still breathing before shoving a swab down our throats to test for the wretched virus. At the moment, she's with Beryl, who made a valiant effort to hide under her blankets the second she spotted the approaching march of the light blue trouser suit. For good reason, in my opinion – once that nurse gets a cotton bud in her hand she goes for the tonsils as if trying to hook a plastic duck at a funfair. It can take me the rest of the day to recover from a jab down the gullet too.

I wanted to say, Cassie, you might be very good at being a life partner if you have the luck and good judgement to find the right person. I'm not convinced you have yet. It sounds to me as though the role of being Stuart's girlfriend comes with a job description, and from the skills and attributes he appears to value, I can't help wondering why you applied. Noah's father, on the other hand, seems like a different type entirely, and not in a good way. Perhaps the guitar was an early clue.

Your new best friend

Ruby

PS Ignore my comment about the guitar. I'm rather prejudiced against musicians, particularly string players.

Letter Austin to Cassie

23 April 2020

Dear Cassie

I'm glad you wrote to me. Although we haven't met, you and Noah seem better friends than many people I've known for years. I wish in a way you'd telephoned instead, so I could have tried to cheer you up straight away, however I understand why it helped to write down what happened. Words are like tent pegs, which is both a good and bad thing. Pinning down a worry is good but trying to pin down some other kinds of feelings can make them sound different to what they are and less special. Perhaps that's just my experience. Or maybe it's because I don't know the right words or the best order to put them in.

You asked for my advice: If you want to go back to London because you're missing Stuart or you feel worried for your safety, I think you should go. If you're only leaving because of what someone else wants you to do, or because a local had nothing better to do than frighten a young mother and her child, I think you should stay here.

I'm not sending you any more photographs of Ned for now. He and Badger look such a sight together you would want to stay just to have the chance to meet them, but that wouldn't be a good enough reason. I'm enclosing a book instead. My local supermarket has a table where people donate books that cost whatever you want to pay and all the money goes to charity. Since the lockdown I've been buying books and reading about things I would never normally have time for. Last week I bought one called A History of Pineapples and a Guide to Making Kites. With this letter I'm enclosing the Cloud Collector's Handbook, one of my earlier purchases I thought Noah might enjoy. Every page has a photograph of a different kind of cloud with space to record where you saw it, so if he's getting bored of learning about farms he can become a cloud-spotter instead. Besides, when you're living in a caravan it's useful to understand about the weather and even if you go back to London, it will still be nice to look at the clouds. My favourite is the Cumulonimbus because I like the name. However, since it's a storm cloud and I'm a farmer I don't like to see them too often.

Austin

PS I hope you decide to stay here.

Postcard Mr Stanley Ross to Cassie

Postmarked 14 April 2020 arrived 24 April 2020

My beautiful daughter!

Voila! A picture of San Felipe Fort, Guatemala! Penelope Anne and I managed to cross from Mexico just before the borders closed! The old camper van is still holding up, so we've decided to keep travelling rather than try to get home! Next stop, Mayan ruins at Quirigá! Trust Noah is staying well, give him a high five from me!

Love to both

Dad & PA

PS I spoke to your mother the other day. She told me you're in Norfolk and gave me your address. Spreading those wings again at last, Cassie? It's about time! As the French proverb says, *There's no flying without wings*!

Text Cassie to Stuart

24 April 2020

You'll have to get your own shopping. I've decided to stay here another few weeks. X

Letter Cassie to Ruby

24 April 2020

Dear Ruby

You're right about Noah's father. Though the longer I waited at the Darwin youth hostel the more I convinced myself I loved him. It took a teenage receptionist with an ivory blond micro-braid to sort me out. On my ninth morning, as I was moping about with my phone in my hand, she leaned so far over the desk six copper bangles slithered the length of her forearm. 'He's not coming, sweetheart. Today or any other.' The bangles gleamed with hard Australian sunlight. 'Shoot on through and forget him!'

I didn't realise I was pregnant until I got back to England. As soon as I knew I fired off a couple of texts to say we needed to talk. He never replied, not even when I said it was urgent, that we *really* needed to talk. I tried again – literally saying I'd had a baby and it was his – after Noah was born, but the message pinged straight back – undeliverable. When Noah got sick, I thought once more about how I might contact him, yet even if I had found a way, what could I say to someone on the other side of the world? 'By the way, you have a gorgeous little boy who might be about to die?'

So, it was Noah and me on our own – until Stuart came along. I met him at a party held by my best friend Mandy. He was her next-door neighbour. Soon afterwards Noah and I moved in with Stuart and for a brilliant while life was perfect. Then Noah got sick. A little over a year ago now. He started to say his legs hurt. I wanted to believe the problem was just growing pains, but I knew in my gut it wasn't and – eventually – after they'd done some tests the doctors told me Noah had Leukaemia, Acute Lymphoblastic Leukaemia to be precise. That same night Noah had a blood transfusion and injections of chemotherapy into his spinal fluid and went from being my happy, boisterous five-year-old to a tiny little boy in a huge hospital bed with tubes coming out of his hands and feet. We left the hospital after thirteen days armed with more medicines and leaflets than I had ever seen before in my life.

Six days later we were back.

Noah was ill again. Horribly, terrifyingly ill. He had sepsis. For a week it was touch and go and every bit of him was monitored on a bleeping screen I didn't dare tear my eyes from in case the signals changed and nobody but me noticed. Mandy was brilliant. While I was in the hospital with Noah, she brought me in goody bags. She'd fill a plastic carrier with magazines, and chocolate and tubes of lavender hand cream. Once there was a packet of pink stripy M & S pants and a new white T-shirt. She was great to Stuart too. She used to take over a portion of whatever she was cooking in the evening so that I didn't have to worry about him as well. That's why I feel so awful about what happened. She did all that for me and now I've ruined her life.

I haven't responded to what you said about Stuart, have I? Whatever I wrote before must have given you an unfair impression of him because I'm sure he's much nicer than you made him sound in your last letter. It's true he's the polar opposite from Noah's dad. Stuart wouldn't be caught dead with a guitar (as they remind him of camping) and he's *driven*. He works incredibly long hours and is always taking extra qualifications so he can do ever more complicated things with people's teeth. On top of that, he's actually very good looking in a groomed sort of way that involves ironing, expensive shoes and a perfect smile (naturally). When Noah got sick, I worried how he would manage but he totally understood I needed to stay at the hospital and never once moaned about me being away. Although he's found it difficult to cope with me coming to Norfolk, I think the strain is a temporary blip. Lockdown must be causing all sorts of blips in lots of relationships. My mother says the problem is that Stuart is 'a man who needs looking after'. I'm hoping the real problem is that Stuart is missing me.

Cassie

Letter Cassie to Mrs Rosemary Ross

25 April 2020

Dear Mum

A letter? I can't remember the last time you sent me one of those! Come to think of it, *have* you ever sent me one? I've had birthday cards, and boring stuff like bank statements and credit card bills forwarded to Stuart's address, but I can't remember an actual letter. Even so, I recognised your handwriting as soon as I picked the envelope out of the letterbox, and when I began to read it was like you were walking into the room. Why are letters so much more special than emails and texts? I've been pondering this a lot since I've begun to write so many of them and decided it's because they take much more effort – after all a letter only a few sentences long is hardly worth the bother. Still, now I have a ritual for writing them that turns the effort into pleasure. Once Noah is in bed, I sit with my paper and pen and a glass of wine on the caravan step, which is where I am now. If I'm not distracted there's long enough to finish a letter before the sky deepens to indigo and the pine trees solidify into a single black shadow. Sometimes, I am distracted though, particularly by the geese. They start to gather at dusk and hang around for a while as if waiting to see who's going to show up before heading towards the sea in an enormous scraggy V shape. If even the prospect of a limp British summer is too much for them, they must be geese that really, really like the cold!

Talking of weather, Noah and I have definitely hardened up since we came to Norfolk. When we first arrived both of us waddled about wearing all our jumpers at once. At teatime today I realised Noah had been cloud-spotting for over an hour in only his shorts and a T-shirt. I hardly dare commit the words to paper but he's starting to look like a country kid. One of those ruddy, grass-stained children who any minute you expect to turn a cartwheel or produce a caterpillar in a matchbox. Cloud-spotting, by the way, is his new hobby (second only to tractors and the wonders of crop rotation). Austin gave him a book called the Cloud Collector's Handbook and already Noah claims to have seen more than twenty different kinds. I think he might be confusing his Cirrus with his Altocumulus (yes, I did have to borrow the book to look those up – cloud-spotting is strangely addictive) but he says I'm not looking closely enough.

Anyway, the moon is out now, as well as the most impatient stars, and I want to ask you something before it gets dark. I thought you regarded Stuart as a catch, particularly for a single mum and unqualified hairdresser. And I'm certain you said he was a man who needed looking after. So why haven't you advised me to go back and look after him?

Love

Cassie

Letter Ruby to Cassie

27 April 2020

Dear Cassie

I'm determined to write and send this letter immediately after receiving yours (despite the fact that the nurse with the tonsil-probing cotton bud departed a mere thirty minutes ago) because a single, pressing question has stamped itself onto my brain.

What happened between you and Mandy?

You've tantalised and teased an old woman about your guilty conscience far longer than is fair. I shall struggle to continue our correspondence if I'm left in the dark for much longer.

Your New Best Friend

Ruby

Letter Cassie to Stuart

27 April 2020

Dear Stuart

You were right to be a little fed up on the phone yesterday. I didn't mean my message to sound as abrupt as it must have done, and I know you didn't just want me to come home in order to pick up a Tesco shop (though in my defence groceries was the one thing you mentioned in your text... I'd draw a smiley face here if you didn't find them so annoying).

I realise how difficult you find me being away, but I have to do this for Noah. Even if the scientists are becoming more confident young people are not at risk from Covid, Noah is *flourishing* here. You honestly wouldn't believe the difference. Our daily walks on the beach are definitely making him stronger so even if he does catch the virus, I'm optimistic he'll be able to fight it off like most children. One day hopefully I'll be able to explain all that to the locals. For now, I'll have to take the rough with the smooth and cross my fingers the dog-poo person is in the minority.

Anyway, Stu, I really wanted to say thank you for understanding. It was sweet of you to hide how upset you must be and not make me feel worse about me changing my mind than I do already. I'll make it up to you when I get back – that's a promise!

Lots of love

Cassie XXX

Letter Mrs Rosemary Ross to Cassie

28 April 2020

My dear daughter

I may well have said Stuart is a man who needs looking after. I didn't say you should be the one to do it.

Love

Mum

PS Who is Austin?

PPS Any one of the above three sentences would justify putting pen to paper. Content, Cassandra, not length, that's what I'm learning about letters.

Letter Austin to Cassie

28 April 2020

Dear Cassie

I was very glad to get your call to say you had decided to stay. Not because of the rent from the caravan (I assume that suggestion was a joke) but because getting to know you and Noah has been the part of lockdown I've enjoyed the most. Now I'm looking forward to the day the government allows us to meet properly and, like everyone else, I hope that day comes soon. Although I'm a farmer and used to spending time on my own, I'm surprised to find how much I miss not having small interactions with strangers and acquaintances. Before the pandemic I never appreciated the chance to exchange a few words with the newsagent or lady next to me waiting to buy a coffee. Now we're too far away from each other to speak normally and because of the masks and scarves you can't tell whether the person wants to chat or not. I think the truth is mostly not. I'm sorry to say a part of me is glad my parents are no longer here and don't have to cope with all the rules. My mother died a long time ago (I was five at the time and can only remember the smell of Pears soap and hair like bedsprings) so it's hard to guess how she would have managed. My dad was a tough countryman who wouldn't have taken kindly to being told what to do by a scientist with a graph and, not being one for the internet, he would have missed having a pint with his friends a great deal. He passed away last autumn. I couldn't bring myself to sit in his armchair until I first tried to hand-feed Ned and found that his old seat was the only one big enough for us both. I dread to think what he would have made of a lamb in the sitting room but it's too late to worry about that now.

I'm glad Noah is enjoying the Cloud Collector's Handbook. When you told me that when he grows up, he wants to be a part-time farmer and a part-time cloud collector I couldn't help but laugh and the memory has made me chuckle all day. In my opinion being a cloud collector should be a job, so perhaps Noah will be the first. But if he sticks with farming, you can tell him April is as busy a month on the farm as March. We still have lambs arriving and we've started drilling the oil seed rape and spraying the barley with fertiliser. One good thing about lockdown is how nature has been allowed to bloom. Without the noise of planes overhead, and all the traffic and visitors, the birds seem to be singing louder and even the wildflowers look brighter, as if they've been given a touch-up with some poster paints.

Well, I warned you I didn't have much news, but you still wanted another letter, so here it is. Perhaps next time I should write one that's shorter, unless I have something more interesting to say.

Austin

PS Tell Noah to keep a special eye out for a cloud that appears to be wearing a white beret. It's called *pileus* and if he spots one of those, I'll send him a pound for an ice-cream because I've only ever seen two of them in my life.

PPS Since you've decided to stay, here's a photo of Ned and Badger in my garden. Look how much Ned has grown. It won't be long before he's fully sheep-sized with a smelly fleece and horns, and then I'll wonder why I promised you not to send him to the slaughterhouse.

Email Cassie to Austin 12.42

29 April 2020

Hi Austin, just to say I was sorry to hear about your parents though I understand why you think they might not have coped with lockdown. My own mother seems to be doing fine (actually she appears to be *thriving*) but my lovely grand-mother may well have struggled. She died last year and I still miss her.

Cassie

PS I never knew my grandfather because he died before I was born, while my father's parents live in the wilds of the Yukon and probably aren't even aware of the pandemic.

Email Cassie to Austin 12.44

29 April 2020

You won't ever wonder why you didn't send Ned to the slaughterhouse because even when he's a smelly old sheep he'll still be Ned.

Letter Cassie to Ruby

30 April 2020

Dear Ruby

Alright, the time has come. I'm in my usual spot on the caravan step with a particularly large glass of wine and the tops of the trees are whipping about in a breeze that's shooting clouds over the sky like racing sheep. In case you're interested the clouds are called cumulus (soon, one glance at the sky and I'll be able to provide an hour-by-hour forecast for the next seven days). I'm bundled up in my thickest hoodie, woolly socks and Noah's Disney scarf, and I'm also digressing because this won't be easy to write.

It began about the time Noah came out of hospital after the sepsis emergency. Normally Mandy is the most laidback person I know. Someone who approaches any crisis with a bottle of Chardonnay, a brief reacquaintance with Marlboro Lights and a blousy confidence that whatever the problem all will be fine. When Ben, her husband, was made redundant and had to take a job in Yorkshire, she shrugged it off and said a few nights apart each week wasn't a big deal, and while Noah was sick, she never appeared to worry, telling me every day without fail he would be fine and that all we had to do was keep going. Then last October, even with my head crammed to bursting with Noah, I noticed how different she seemed. One minute she was tense and bubbly as a shaken bottle of soda. The next she was so distracted I had to wave a hand in front of her face to get her attention. As soon as I did, her eyes would take on a sad, closed-off expression for the rest of the day before the whole wretched cycle would start over again the very next time we saw each other.

Eventually, I asked her what was wrong. Or rather I

asked if she was having an affair. It was Saturday, 3 November 2019. I remember the date because Noah was desperate to see fireworks, so we had all gone to a bonfire celebration at the local park. Stuart and Ben had taken Noah to fetch mulled wines and hot chocolate, and Mandy and I were standing side by side, staring at the towering blaze that was chomping its way through crates and logs and a massive stuffed guy.

The question was out my mouth before I knew what I was saying. Before the words *Mandy* and *affair* consciously entered my head in the same sentence. I knew immediately I'd hit the nail on the head. In the spotlight of the flames her guilt had nowhere to hide. I saw the shock widen her eyes and travel like an electric current down to her throat.

She swallowed twice. 'I don't want to talk about it.' When I opened my mouth, she cut across me. 'I know it's wrong.' She leaned further over the rope barrier that was supposed to stop us getting too close to the flames, 'I'm going to finish it, OK?'

I didn't say anything. In the distance, the others were slowly coming across the grass. Noah kept pausing to sip from a paper cup. The men were each holding two plastic glasses, the steam curling into the air. Mandy straightened up and swung around in front of me. 'Promise me you won't tell Ben!' she hissed. Although her face was now in shadow, the emotion burned through the dark.

The boys were getting closer, I could hear Noah asking about the fireworks; how long we had to wait before they started and whether there would be rockets. 'Cassie?' Mandy tugged the sleeve of my jacket. 'Or Stuart. You can't tell him either.' I must have nodded or shook my head or did whatever I had to do to reassure her because her fingers gripped for one more second before letting go.

I hardly saw her for the next few weeks. There was

always an excuse: work, parties, Christmas shopping, but I knew she was avoiding me and if she didn't want to see me that meant the affair must still be happening.

On the Friday before Christmas, there was a thump at the front door, like someone had fallen against the panelling. It was nine o'clock in the evening, Stuart had a late surgery, and I was chilling on the sofa listening to Taylor Swift. Although I didn't want to see who was there, I didn't want Noah to be woken either. Reluctantly I opened up. The visitor was Ben and he had clearly been drinking. I'd had a couple of glasses myself, but I was sober enough to notice how much weight he'd lost since Bonfire Night and that his hands kept jumping from his trouser pockets to his hair. He was wearing a new jumper and aftershave and initially the thought crossed my mind that he was having an affair as well. The next instant I realised he knew about Mandy and that he was trying to improve himself, to hang onto her, and just at the moment I understood those things he said, 'She's having an affair, isn't she?'

'Who?' I said.

It was the most stupid, idiotic reply and as Ben stared at me, I felt my face heat up like a gas hob.

'Mandy, who else?'

I wanted to lie, to say, 'Of course not, don't be ridiculous.' Or 'You're being paranoid, she's probably just stressed about Christmas,' but the way he stood there, so hurt and helpless, made saying anything like that impossible. Then the music stopped, and the sudden silence felt like someone was digging nails into my skin and I realised my fists were so clenched my fingernails really were digging into my palms. Ben said nothing. A second later he stormed towards the door, before stopping on the threshold.

'Who is he?'

'I don't know.' I shook my head as hard as I could. 'I honestly don't know. She said she was going to finish it.'

He gazed at me with glazed, shiny eyes. 'Well, she hasn't.'

After he left, I sat on the stairs and tried to compose a message to Mandy, but I didn't know what to say and ended up deleting them all. At about 2am I got a text from her. 'Ben gone. Hope u r satisfied.' And that was the end of our friendship, and as far as I know of Mandy's marriage. Recently, Stuart told me Ben had moved in with his brother and has stayed there for lockdown.

So, you see, Ruby, if only I'd been a better friend, Mandy would have finished her affair, Ben would never have known, and they would still be together. And Mandy and I would be the same inseparable pair we've always been. Doesn't life sometimes suck?

Cassie

Letter Ruby to Cassie

1 May 2020

Dear Cassie

Being a good friend is not the same as being a good liar.

Yes, sometimes life sucks. It's still rather wonderful.

Love from Your New Best Friend

Ruby

PS I'm enclosing the next tranche of my letters.

PART FOUR

Letter Clem to Ruby

13 May 1940

Dearest Ruby

I'm sitting on a blanket in the garden because the news is so bleak the only way I can think to cheer myself up is by writing to you. I've just finished listening to Mr Churchill. I imagine you heard his address to the House of Commons, along with Mother and Father. As he was speaking, I could picture all the families up and down the land crouched around their wireless sets, spellbound, and frightened. Separated from loved ones living in other parts of England by wretched petrol rationing and blackouts, while fearing for the lives of their sons, husbands and brothers fighting overseas. Just like we're all terrified for George. 'I have nothing to offer you but blood, toil, tears and sweat.' That's what Mr Churchill said. I know because I wrote down his words. I can't imagine Mr Chamberlain saying anything quite so stirring – or so awful either. How can it have come to this so quickly, Ruby? A week ago, the war seemed distant, almost manageable, but the invasion of *France*, then Belgium and Holland, has brought Hitler to our front door and I can't seem to stop asking myself how we will keep him from getting inside? Do you remember when we were children, and Mother used to read us the story of the three little pigs and the Big Bad Wolf? I feel like we're in one of those houses now, the horrible wolf is rearing over us, huffing and puffing, determined to blow it down. We shall just have to hope and pray we're in the house made of bricks, the one that didn't crumple, and however much Hitler huffs and puffs those bricks will stand firm.

Precious Ruby, forgive the wild outpouring of your sister. If we were together, I know a hug from you, tucked up together on the sofa with a mug of cocoa, would calm this sick sense of panic and help me be strong. Instead, I shall go upstairs, cuddle my two angels, and vow to keep them safe whatever the Big Bad Wolf does next. Then I shall brush my hair and put on some lipstick so I shall seem quite the epitome of calm by the time John gets home from work. Only you, my darling, know the truth.

Write to me soon

Your loving sister

Clem

Diary of Miss Ruby Summers

15 May 1940

Dear Diary

How can I possibly have been fretting about Latin? How absolutely idiotic and selfish. This morning I received Clem's unhappy letter in the post, later the news came on the wireless that Holland has surrendered, and to cap it all on Saturday when I ran into Mr Frost (of the chickens) he told me the Germans will drive us out of France within days. 'Stay strong, young Ruby,' he said patting my shoulder. 'Stay strong. We're in it now. For the long haul.'

These are the darkest days so far. Mother and Father are desperately worried about George. Whenever I go in search of Mother, I find her either cleaning or gardening with a demonic kind of energy or else sitting in the drawing room doing absolutely nothing except staring out the window with milky eyes. When I got back from school I asked if I could go and meet Edmondo. She thought about the question a surprisingly long while, before saying, 'Yes, Ruby, do go and see him, it will cheer you up,' in a way that sounded positively encouraging. It's all very confusing. One moment my parents appear desperate to keep Edmondo and I apart, imparting dire warnings about me being seen with an Italian, while other times they seem to remember the Brambillas are not really foreigners at all.

I was so excited to visit Edmondo that I cycled to the shop straight away, hair flapping loose, and my coat undone like a parachute. I arrived to find him scrubbing the window with a bucket of soapy water lodged between his feet. When he turned around his face was mottled.

'What happened?' I asked instinctively, though no sooner were the words out of my mouth than I saw for myself what had happened. Someone had daubed red paint all over the glass. Edmondo had cleaned off most of the mess, but an 'a' an 'r' a 'd' and an 's' were still visible. He followed my gaze. '*Italian bastards*, that's what it said, *Italian bastards*, in great, big letters.'

I shook my head in disbelief. 'Who was it?'

'We didn't see. The shop was closed for lunch.'

'It was broad daylight! *Somebody* must have seen.'

Edmondo shrugged. 'Even if they did, nobody who will tell. I think everyone in the village agrees with the painter.'

I dismounted from my bicycle and propped the frame against the wall. Bending down, I took my handkerchief from my coat pocket, dipped the corner into the water, and side by side with Edmondo began to rub out the 's'. It took us a long while to clean the window, all I seemed to do at first was smear red paint over the glass like blood. Although I had my back to the road, I could feel the stares of passers-by gouging into my back as if they were drills that builders use to break up cement.

After we finished, I felt exhausted. We sat for a while in the meadow, but the only thing in our heads was the window which was too upsetting to talk about, so in the end I simply went home. On the way back I wondered how Edmondo could stand it. How anyone could stand to become hated by people you had thought of as friends, when it was the world that had changed and not you at all.

Letter Uncle Charles to Ruby

20 May 1940

My dear Ruby

I will be paying you all a flying visit this Friday afternoon, bombs, blackouts, and Mr Hitler permitting. While I shall of course be delighted to see your parents, it is you to whom I particularly want to talk. Please humour your devoted godfather by being so good as to ensure you stay at home after school. Who knows, I may even be able to sweeten my visit with a little help from a rather splendid bakery in Mayfair that, despite the current limitations, still manages to bake a very respectable Victoria sponge.

Fondest

Uncle Charles

PS I do hope the Latin is progressing. World events are no excuse for not studying. In years to come the country will need women like you to help rebuild it. I can only pray your endeavours will be to the benefit of a British rather than a Nazi government.

Diary of Miss Ruby Summers

24 May 1940

Dear Diary

I'm so terribly angry I can barely write. My heart is thumping like a train and my wrist is jumping all over the paper. Even if I manage to gather my thoughts into some kind of order the words will never line up properly on the page.

It was a trap! The whole afternoon was a trap! Uncle Charles arrived on the dot of five o'clock with a cake in a parcel as big as a hatbox. After Mother had fetched the best china plates and made tea in the silver teapot the four of us sat in the drawing room as though it was someone's birthday or the King was about to arrive. For nearly thirty minutes Mother and Father made small talk almost gaily but as soon as their last crumbs were gone, they melted away with barely a murmur leaving me with Uncle Charles who immediately deposited his teacup on its saucer and fixed me with a look of steel-hard grey.

'I understand you're still stepping out with that young Italian chap?' Although I was nibbling my cake, determined to make the treat last as long as possible, his tone turned the sponge to sawdust.

'Mother and Father don't seem to mind,' I mumbled, which was half true. Or rather, appeared to be true for half of the time, which is not quite the same thing. I didn't want to add that Mother especially couldn't seem to make up her mind whether she objected to me seeing Edmondo or not.

Uncle Charles inhaled through his nose and then blew out so hard that his chest heaved like an accordion. 'Perhaps,' he said slowly, 'they understand your friendship might be of some use.'

I blinked at him. 'What do you mean, *of some use*?'

His gaze didn't leave my face. 'Of some use to the government.'

'How can me knowing Edmondo help the government?'

There was a pause. Then Uncle Charles said, 'It's more a question of knowing the Brambilla family, Edmondo's father in particular.'

I didn't reply. From the hallway, the grandfather clock rang the three-quarter hour. It seemed odd, the same regular peals chiming throughout the day and night regardless of the dreadful news from Europe, and I could never decide whether the oddness was disconcerting or reassuring. Hearing them now made me more on edge than ever and I dropped my plate onto the tea-tray with a clatter.

Uncle Charles took another of his great big breaths. 'Listen Ruby,' he said leaning forward, 'the man you saw in Felixstowe, the one who played the violin–'

'–the pipe-cleaner man?'

'Yes.' There was another pause. Then, 'We have… the government has reason to think he's a fascist. A supporter of Mussolini. The description you gave me when we had lunch together, well apparently it fits the picture of somebody who is of interest to the War Office.'

'Why?'

'Why?' Uncle Charles repeated. He looked a little perplexed.

'Why is the pipe-cleaner man of interest to the War Office?'

Uncle Charles frowned. 'I couldn't possibly tell you that, even if I knew myself.'

'Well, the War Office must be wrong!' My voice came out louder than I meant it to sound. 'The man who came to see Mr Brambilla was just a friend, another musician. I heard him playing his violin and it was beautiful. He wasn't talking to Mr Brambilla about Mussolini, or which side Italy would take in the war…' I stopped, as it occurred to me that since I didn't speak Italian, I didn't actually have the first idea of what the men *were* talking about.

Uncle Charles didn't reply. The longer the silence lasted the more it seemed that he was weighing up his options. He must have decided the benefits outweighed the risks because eventually he said, 'The place where you stayed in Felixstowe wasn't an ordinary guesthouse, Ruby. The building belongs to a group of fascists in London. The biggest association of fascists in England.'

I opened my mouth to protest, but Uncle Charles raised the palm of his hand. 'The London school that makes use of the house, and the boys and girls taken there on holiday, are either fascists or the children of fascists, and anyone associated with the place and who knows the people who own it is very likely to support Hitler and Mussolini.'

My head was spinning. 'Not Mr Brambilla!' I said hotly. 'Even if you're right about the boarding house and the fascist school, Mr Brambilla couldn't have known about it. He and his family have lived in our village for years. In the summer he hands out free ice-cream to children whose parents can't afford to buy them one. I'm sure he just gave some of the boys from London music lessons and was invited to go to Felixstowe as a thank you.'

There was another silence and as we sat there staring at each other a piece of the jigsaw puzzle fell into place. 'That's why I was allowed to go with Edmondo to Felixstowe, isn't it?' I said at last. 'You persuaded Mother and Father to let me, and it's the reason why you invited me out for such a nice lunch afterwards. You knew everything you've just told me *before* I went to

Felixstowe. It wasn't random strangers you wanted me to keep an eye out for, you used me to spy on Mr Brambilla and find out what he knew!' All at once the soft velvet of the sofa seemed as spiky as the back of a hedgehog and I jumped to my feet.

Uncle Charles patted the sofa cushion. 'Sit down, Ruby.'

'Why?'

'I've not finished…' He patted the sofa again, only this time it was more of a thump. Although his cheeks were the same purply-red as when he and Father tucked into the after-dinner whisky, his eyes gleamed with an intensity I didn't ever remember seeing before. Reluctantly I lowered myself down, perching on the very edge of the seat to make it clear I might stand up again any minute.

'The situation in Europe is bad, Ruby.' He paused. 'Worse than most ordinary people have yet to realise. And soon Italy will join the war too and Mussolini will throw whatever weight he can muster behind Hitler. It's imperative for the government to uncover any fascist networks in England, any fascist sympathisers, who might help Hitler to invade our country. And the government has reason to believe – good reason, so I'm told – that the violin player who visited Mr Brambilla at the guesthouse is such a man.'

'Then why don't the police arrest him? If the government is certain he's so dangerous?'

'Because he's disappeared.' Uncle Charles's mouth became small as a knot. 'The security forces were keeping an eye on him, hoping he might lead them to others in his network, but shortly before the Easter weekend, just after you saw him in Felixstowe, he vanished into thin air.'

'Then how can I help? I don't know where he is.'

Uncle Charles paused again. 'We believe he may surface at the Brambillas' house.'

I blinked. 'Because you think that Mr Brambilla is part of his network?'

Uncle Charles didn't reply.

'Or, perhaps,' I said, remembering the strange, sad music, 'because he knows he's being persecuted, and trusts Mr Brambilla to help him.'

From the hallway, the clock began to chime six o'clock and in a peculiar way I felt suddenly older, as if far longer than fifteen minutes had passed. I could practically see the lovely sponge cake crumbling into mould and the colour leaching from Uncle Charles's face as if we were turning into a dog-eared, monochrome photograph.

'Either way, Ruby' – there was the weight of years in my godfather's voice

– 'either way, you must let me know at once if you see anything suspicious.'

The sitting room door opened a crack and then shut again. 'It's alright, Evie. Ruby and I have finished our little chat.'

The door opened properly this time, and Mother stood on the threshold looking nervously from me to Uncle Charles. Springing from the sofa, I pushed past her without saying a word, and on my way up the staircase, I heard her say in a hushed tone, 'No wonder she's upset. We shouldn't have asked her to do it. She's still practically a child!'

Uncle Charles's reply followed my heels, and *his* voice was not hushed at all. 'In a time of war, a lot of people are asked to do difficult things. And that, Evie, is because the consequence of not asking them is even worse.'

So, there you have it, Diary. My family has turned me into a spy. I'm supposed to betray Edmondo, the person who loves me most in all the world. Who trusts me to love him back, to support him always and never let him down. The only bearable solution is to believe that I'm right and there is nothing to find out about Mr Brambilla which would be of any interest whatsoever to Uncle Charles or the War Office.

Letter George to Ruby

12 May 1940 (received 1 June 1940)

Darling Sis

God knows when, or if, I shall ever be able to post this letter. If you're reading these words, I must have found a willing pair of hands England bound...

I'm writing from the edge of a field in northern France with my back against an upturned cart that's lost two of its wheels. Frank is asleep on the grass beside me, his jacket pulled over his face. We stopped walking when neither of us could see straight any longer. The elms lining the road had turned into looming monsters and Frank was talking nonsense, as if he were strolling the streets of Manchester with his arm around a girl. At least it's still quite dark. The sky is the colour of an old bruise, with only the faintest gleam along the eastern edge, while the moon is nowhere to be seen. Perhaps she's found another orbit, a different world to gaze upon. I wouldn't blame her if she had. Forgive my maudlin tone but the last week has been hellish in the most literal sense imaginable, and I fear the worst is yet to come.

Five, or is it six, days ago – I've rather lost track of time – our regiment was sent to defend a route out of Brussels. We motored north along an empty road, passing a stream of trucks and staggering French soldiers coming in the opposite direction. After them came the refugees. Elderly men, exhausted women leading petrified children, and horses pulling carts laden with toddlers who were clinging to bundles for dear life as they swayed back and forth. And they were the lucky ones. Some were using prams or even dogcarts to ease the load, while others had nothing and were struggling to make any progress at all under the weight of crying babies and bags of bedding.

Abruptly our orders changed. The fast approach of German columns meant our only option was retreat. To leave the tarmac and head south over the fields of ruined crops, avoiding the congestion of the blocked roads. It was nearing dusk, the light thinning and the air starting to prick with damp, when we heard the drone of an aircraft over the noise of our engines. The trucks were halted and we scrambled to take up positions with rifles and Bren guns.

However, we soon realised the Messerschmitt wasn't aiming for us at all. Instead his target was the pitiful, helpless ribbon of humanity toiling along the roads behind. We fired, and fired, all of us sharing the same revulsion at the screams of terror coming from the other side of the hedges. Eventually, the nose of the aircraft dipped. Black smoke began to billow from the tail, and the plane plunged to earth as if gravity had finally begun to work. I don't know whether the German was hit by our guns or those of another convoy, but I never thought I should feel such elation at witnessing the death of a human being. My old Oxford self gazes from a distance, shocked and not fully understanding. Your brother has changed, Ruby. I'm sorry to say the sights I've seen these past few days have made me believe in the existence of evil in a way I never did before. What else can it be but evil, to deliberately kill innocent women and children as they attempt to flee their homes? I look now at my hands, holding this pen, and know, given half a chance, I would happily have placed them around the throat of that German pilot and choked the life out of him. Are you horrified at who – at what – your brother has become, or is the war changing you too? Would you also be unrecognisable to the Ruby of a year ago?

I'm in danger of digressing. I want to explain how Frank and I came to be here, alone in a field with the whole of

Europe aflame around us. I wish I could spare you, but there is more, and I must tell someone.

Hours after the attack, our regiment came across a farm. The house seemed deserted, a few bedraggled chickens pecked about a yard and a pig was roaming free, left to fend for itself when the owners had fled. Night was falling, a welcome blanket of dark after the ghastliness of the day, and foolishly we thought the outbuildings would give us the chance to sleep somewhere other than the cramped confines of our trucks. I woke before five, stirred by the dawn leaking between the roof beams. Even then, I didn't grasp the danger, our vulnerability. Instead, I went in search of a horse. For some reason I believed I heard neighing and worried the animal might have been left to starve to death I decided to investigate.

There was no horse, Ruby.

The barn door was wide open, the stall bare, yet that imaginary neighing, that inexplicable, utterly convincing figment of my imagination saved not only my life, but Frank's as well. No sooner had I discovered the empty stable than I spied the deadly green of aircraft wings more dazzling and conspicuous in the morning sun than the roar of the engine. All at once Frank was there too – he must have followed me from the haybarn. Shoving me on the shoulder, he pushed me into the stable, and as we fell the world around us collapsed. Explosions like hammer blows pounded the air into fragments while bricks rained down relentlessly. I honestly feared we would be buried alive and that you, Clem and Mother and Father would never know what had become of me.

Eventually a peculiar kind of quiet descended, barely detectable beyond the ringing in my ears. When I shifted position the stones on my back clattered to the ground.

'Frank?' My mouth was dry with fear and the stink of ammonia. 'Frank, are you there?'

There was no reply.

I hoisted myself onto my hands and knees. The stable wall was a pile of rubble, exuding dust thick as London fog. As I tried to gather my wits the ground spun in circles and made me retch onto my fingers.

Eventually I managed to lift my head.

A black boot protruded from beneath the slab of wood that a few minutes earlier had been the stable door. Stumbling to my feet, I hauled the timber to one side. 'Frank?' To my inexpressible relief, he stirred and a few seconds later sat up. Blood was oozing from cuts on his forehead, but he seemed oblivious to the injuries. For a moment or two he blinked at me in disbelief before his focus settled on a point somewhere over my left shoulder and his face froze. I twisted around to follow his gaze. The haybarn where we had slept, where we had left the rest of the men, was rent with flames and burning with a terrifying intensity. Although we rushed towards the inferno, the wall of heat was utterly impassable and we could only gape in horror as the roof beams collapsed with a groan and frenzied fire consumed our sweet, peaceful dormitory.

I stop here, Ruby, to rub away tears. I am sorry for you too. I know reading of such things will upset you dreadfully, but this letter has a greater chance than I do of returning to England, and somebody must know what happened for the sake of those men's families and anyone in England who needs reminding that this foul and wicked enemy has to be defeated whatever the cost might be.

Frank and I left the farm with the barn still burning. We climbed into the only surviving truck and drove across a dewy pasture dotted with apple trees and awash with early morning sun. Neither one of us so much as glanced over our shoulder or uttered a single word. We both knew our friends were lost and the beacon of their funeral pyre could bring more planes, more bombers, and we simply followed that most basic, most terrible, most marvellous instinct of all – to survive.

We drove and drove, with little sense of where we were going or what to do, until we reached a crossroads. As we lingered – hoping for what, I don't know, a sign from God, perhaps – a column of traffic appeared from the left and I flagged down the lead vehicle.

'Where are you going?' I asked.

'To Dunkirk, and then England,' came the reply.

Without waiting for an invitation, we joined the back of the convoy. However, before we had travelled more than twenty miles smoke began to trickle from our bonnet, a few seconds later the trickle resembled a puffing steam train, and a few minutes after that the engine stopped altogether. There was nothing else to do but abandon the truck and continue the journey on foot. And that is what we are doing now, as soon as we have strength to put one foot in front of the other again. At least we now know where we must head, the northern tip of the Pas-de-Calais. The point where the coasts of France and England appear so neighbourly on a map it looks as if a man could simply lean across and pull a friend stranded on the other side directly over the Channel. This is what Frank and I are praying for at any rate.

I will stop writing now, dear Ruby. My eyelids are too heavy to hold open, and the patch of damp grass beside this cart has the appeal of a feather mattress. Perhaps when I wake the last few months will turn out to have been a terrible nightmare and I will be lying in my bed at Oxford. Or better still at home, bread and marmalade for breakfast and nothing more compelling on the wireless than our usual British fare of bickering politicians and rain forecast for the afternoon.

Tell Mother and Father I love them. And, of course, my dearest, love to you and Clem. When I think of my sisters, I am reminded of all that is kind and good in the world and for a short time at least can believe all is not lost.

Your devoted brother

George

Diary of Miss Ruby Summers

1 June 1940

Dear Diary

I'm sitting at my desk overlooking the garden. My window is open, and the smell of the wisteria is as sweet and heady as the wine my father likes to serve with cheese. When I bend over the sill, I can see the big purple flower heads dazzling against the crumbling brick in a way that makes me think of an amethyst necklace thrown over an ageing ballgown.

I should be working – *New Practical Chemistry* is open at page forty-seven – instead I have put schoolbooks to one side and picked up my diary. Much as the combination of the glorious wisteria and May sunshine makes me want to lie my head on the table and close my eyes, neither the weather nor the garden is the problem.

Today, I received the most awful news from George. Luckily Mother was at the butcher's when the postman arrived (these days the queues mean the errand takes the best part of the morning) because I can't decide whether to tell her about the letter or not. The relief of knowing George was alive would soon give way to the horror of what is happening in France and the dreadful fear he may not make it home. Although the envelope is burrowed inside my bed (in case Mother comes into the room) every time I attempt to focus on the columns of the periodic table or the covalent bonding properties of carbon,

George's voice pierces through the sheets. Instead of the pages of Practical Chemistry, I see a burning hayloft, women and children diving into ditches, dead bodies, and injured animals, and I know the effect would be even worse on Mother, who would probably pack a bag, set off for Dover and go in search of George herself.

To depress matters further (if that's possible), a few days ago the Home Office announced the police had been ordered to intern all Germans and Austrians living in the United Kingdom. The only ones to be spared were Jewish refugees who had managed to escape from the Nazis (since nobody could think that they pose a threat to the Allies). As I wasn't completely sure what happens to people who are interned, I asked Father what it meant.

'Locked up,' he said from behind The Times. 'Where they can't do any harm.' We were reading in the sitting room, while Mother cooked dinner. The government's broadcast had only just finished.

I could hardly believe him. 'You mean locked up in prison? With actual criminals?'

'Not prisons, exactly. Special camps. A lot of them are being taken to the Isle of Man.'

It took me a moment to think where that was. In the Irish Sea, I remembered, somewhere between England and the coast of Ireland. 'For how long?'

Father shrugged. 'Until the war is over, I suppose. Or the risk of invasion has passed. Or' – his mouth twisted – 'the country has been overrun by the bloody Hun.' After a second, he half-lowered his newspaper and said in more normal voice. 'England is at war, Ruby. If the Germans were to invade, we can't possibly have a ready-made army here waiting to help Hitler.'

'But what if the people we intern don't support Hitler?'

The pages of The Times dropped to Father's knees. His eyes glittered. 'But what if they do, Ruby? Think about that. What if they do?'

In the silence that followed the sound of the wireless flared from the kitchen. The news must have finished because through the wall I could hear Jimmie Davis singing 'You Are My Sunshine'.

I took a breath. 'What about the Italians? Will they be interned too?'

'There's a very good chance of that, yes.' My father's gaze didn't waver. Immediately, I saw Edmondo's face. The way his eyes gleamed like dark molasses and his hair fell over his cheeks in black curls. How serious, how earnest he was, yet how he always managed to raise my spirits, and find the hope, the humour in the worst situations. He was my sunshine. 'Isn't there the right to a hearing first?' I said, remembering something Mother had said. 'Before a tribunal. Like in court when someone has been accused of a crime.'

'It's too late for hearings now. The purpose of internment is to stop possible traitors *before* they betray England. Waiting until after a trial would give them time to do their dirty business first.' My father must have seen something in my face that made him soften because he added more gently, 'Sometimes a person can appeal to a tribunal, to prove he isn't a threat.'

My grip on the sofa cushion relaxed slightly. Surely, I thought, Mr Brambilla would have no trouble convincing a tribunal of his innocence.

Abruptly the music in the kitchen stopped and a moment later Mother appeared in the doorway. With a start, I noticed how pale she looked, her face etched with lines. She wiped her hands on her apron. 'Dinner's ready. Cauliflower cheese and bacon. Without, I'm afraid, a great deal of either cheese *or* bacon.'

That was three days ago and I've hardly done any schoolwork since. On top of worrying that Edmondo and his family will be locked up, since this morning I can't stop thinking about George trapped in France and whether we'll ever see him again. When I stood in his bedroom with my eyes closed, to try to sense if he's still alive, all I felt was an achy kind of silence.

The wisteria may be beautiful, but everything else is twisted and ugly with war.

Letter Clem to Ruby

5 June 1940

Dearest Ruby

Showing George's letter to Mother and Father was definitely the *right* thing to do! Of course, they're worried sick but at least they know he was still alive when he wrote. And to be honest I don't believe the dreadful business with the barn upset Mother much at all. When she spoke to me, all she cared about was George, his chances of getting to Dunkirk and being rescued. I think she even wanted to believe that George avoiding the fire was somehow a sign he would survive.

To be honest – and I feel terrible saying the truth – the news is so full of ghastly stories I don't think many of us can take them in anymore, and if we did, I'm not sure anyone would manage to get out of bed. We'd all be pinned to the mattress under the weight of our own misery. At any rate, all I seem able to do is concentrate on my nearest and dearest – protecting Greg and Tabby as best I ever can, keeping John fed and his spirits up, and sending my best love to you and Mother and Father. And, of course, I pray hard for George every morning and night. I imagine everyone is like me, emitting rays of love like tiny spotlights, and you have to hope in the end those thousands and millions of little beams will be enough to keep the darkness at bay.

Darling, Ruby, I hope you can feel my beam of love.

Clem

PS No normal news worth recounting except the hens have stopped laying (perhaps they're depressed by the war too). I hope you're having better luck with your days-of-the-week chickens. Unless ours are having a temporary blip, John will soon insist that we eat them, so I'm jolly glad we never got round to giving them names.

Letter Edmondo to Ruby

5 June 1940

Mia cara

You must be wondering why I posted this letter instead of bringing it myself. The truth is I was halfway across the meadow when I encountered the owner of the tobacconist's shop, that white-haired man who never seems to smile. He tapped his cane in front of my feet as our paths crossed. 'You're that Italian lad from the grocery store, aren't you? The one who goes about with the lass who's the daughter of the solicitor.' He looked over the grass towards your house with a hard gaze. 'I suppose that's where you're going now.'

I nodded. 'I have an invitation to give Miss Summers.' I went to step past but he raised his cane and blocked my way as if he were herding a cow or sheep!

'You listen here, sonny Jim! A girl like that can't be associating with the likes of you. Not if she knows what's good for her. You turn around and go back home!'

I couldn't believe my ears. 'Ruby wants to see me!'

He pushed his face so close to mine I could feel the hatred pulsing from his skin. 'Does she indeed? I doubt that very much. The freedom of this great country is on a knife-edge because of that bastard Hitler and every day your Mr Mussolini gets closer to throwing in his lot with him. You bloody Italians should be rounded up with the Germans right this minute, and Ruby Summers ought to know a whole lot better than to gad about cavorting with the enemy!'

I stood up as straight and tall as I could and looked him directly in the eye. 'I'm *not* the enemy! I don't support the Nazis. I support the Allies. I'm almost English myself, I was born in England and I've lived here all my life.'

His expression didn't flicker. 'You're an Italian. Your blood is Italian. Your parents are Italian. That's enemy enough for me.'

For a while we simply stared at each other.

My heart was racing and I knew I could easily push past. I'm ashamed to say that for a moment I imagined him lying on the ground, too winded to speak. Instead, I made myself turn around and walk away.

'Hey, sonny!'

I stopped.

'There's no such thing as *almost* English. There are only two sides now. Us and them. And if you don't support the Nazis, then bloody well pick up a gun and fight against them! And until you do' – he waved the cane wildly – 'mind my words and stay away from that girl!'

And so Ruby I'm sending you this invitation by post. Out of the kitchen window I can see Prince eating his tea in the yard. To him today is like yesterday and tomorrow will be the same. All he feels is the sun on his back, munching steadily with his head in a bucket. Whereas I can be certain of nothing. I hate to think like this, but I have to ask myself if the old tobacconist could be right? Perhaps you don't want to see me. Perhaps you're being kind and loyal and don't know how to tell me the truth. And even if you do still want to be with me, perhaps I shouldn't let you? Would I be a stronger or a weaker man to have brought you this letter in person? To love you best, should I let you go or hold you tightly? I can't disentangle the right from the wrong, the honourable from the selfish. I can neither bear to lose you nor to put you in danger. It's like an impossible maths problem, only a thousand times worse because the problem is the whole of our lives.

I will send you the invitation, Ruby. You're so much better than me at maths, maybe you'll find a solution. I only know the seconds are like the pieces of chaff in Prince's bucket, to be tossed out of the way for the only moments that matter – my next chance to be with you.

I love you.

Edmondo

PS I'm enclosing a notecard from my mother, asking you here to celebrate my father's birthday this Sunday at three o'clock.

Diary of Miss Ruby Summers

9 June 1940

Dear Diary

How does one indicate a pause, other than by way of a tedious and time-consuming explanation? The truth is, I wrote, 'Dear Diary,' before stopping and putting down my pen for a complete ten minutes. That might not seem so very long, but it was time enough for the shadows of the horse chestnut trees to pull another yard of lawn towards them and the evening light to dip from gold to a pale grim grey. I've decided, though, that I have no choice other than to set down the happenings of the afternoon in full. Already I didn't record the whole truth of my visit to Felixstowe and if I continue to keep secrets from my diary then what is the purpose of keeping one at all? The main point of a diary is to find solace in confessing within its pages the things you can't tell an actual human being – even your closest friend or parents – and commit important events to paper so that one faraway day, when the memory of even the most startling incidents has faded, you can read about them and marvel at the extraordinariness of life – the good and the bad – astonished at how you can possibly be the same person who once sat hunched over the page wondering where to begin…

This afternoon I went to Edmondo's house. The festivities were no more ambitious than afternoon tea, but the weather was fine and the Brambillas had slung bunting between the apple trees in their orchard and dressed a trestle table with a blue and white cloth and enamels jugs of long-stemmed poppies. Although I seemed to be the only guest, the number of chairs together with the plates stacked beside a pile of forks made me think other people from the village might also have been invited but decided to stay away. Mrs Brambilla said nothing about that however, and simply cut the apple cake into slices the size of door-stoppers. She and Fragolina seemed determined to be gay, maintaining a buoyant chatter despite the fact Mr Brambilla himself didn't seem to share in their gaiety at all. He failed even to finish his cake before laying his plate on table, muttering something in Italian and striding towards the house. Seeing the look that passed between Mrs B and Edmondo, I guessed his departure was not unexpected and wondered if I should simply go home. To be honest, I had some sympathy with Mr Brambilla. Pretending to be happy when you're not is difficult and brave, and living in a country which regards you as an enemy is hardly conducive to a jolly birthday tea. Nevertheless, Mrs B would not give up easily. After a few minutes of rather prickly silence, she hovered close to my shoulder.

'Ruby,' she murmured. 'Would you please go into the house and ask my husband to come back outside. His behaviour is spoiling the party.'

'Me?' I blinked at her in astonishment.

'I think perhaps he would find it more difficult to refuse you, than one of his own family.'

What choice did I have? After a moment's hesitation I pushed back my chair and made my way through the poppies and grass towards the back door.

As soon as I stepped into the kitchen my body tensed, reacting to something unexpected even before my brain had quite processed what that something was. The room looked the same as it always did if slightly untidier than usual, the dresser piled with newspapers, crockery, and a number of cooking items – flour, oatmeal, and powdered eggs – that nobody had managed to put away. As I scanned the scene, the front page of the Daily Star caught my eye, the headline blazing with fervour and relief. *Tens of Thousands Safely Home Already*. I was thinking we still hadn't heard from George, had still had no word *he* was safely home from Dunkirk, when I realised I could hear voices, a low patter of Italian so quiet the sound was barely louder than distant rain.

I crept towards the hallway. Crept because all at once I felt the need to be quiet too. On the other side of the passage, I could see Mr Brambilla standing just within the sitting room and facing the opposite wall. Though the door was barely open, I could glimpse the cotton of his shirt and flashes of movement from his arms. Perhaps because I was closer, or my imagination was getting the better of me, the voices seemed to be gathering intensity like clouds amassing on the horizon. All at once Mr Brambilla turned around and strode into the hallway. Flinging wide the front door, he took up position sentry-like beside it. I watched, open mouthed, as after a moment the other occupant of the sitting room emerged and without another word scuttled through the open gap and into the street beyond.

By the time Mr Brambilla came into the kitchen, I was standing beside the dresser holding the Daily Star. Mr Brambilla stopped when he saw me, and I lowered the newspaper slowly, as though I had been engrossed and he was disturbing my concentration.

'Ruby! What are you doing inside our house?'

'Mrs Brambilla wanted me to find you and ask you to come back to the party.' My voice sounded shaky, and my hands were shaking too, making the newspaper rustle. I couldn't stop thinking about what I had seen, *who* I had seen.

'Have you been here long?'

'I only arrived a minute ago. I thought I should wait for you to come back to the kitchen, and then I spotted the newspaper and began to read the front page.'

'You don't have a newspaper at your own home?'

'We only get The Times, which disappears into Father's study the moment it falls through the letterbox.' This much was true and the relief of arriving on firmer ground gave me confidence. 'Will you come back out to the party, now? Mrs

Brambilla seems to have gone to a lot of trouble and she was terribly upset when you left.'

Mr Brambilla stared at me. His eyes were sharp and bright, as if searching for a tiny object he had dropped on the ground. Then he inclined his head. 'Very well,' and he gestured towards the back door, indicating I should go first. I wondered if he might not follow me, if the moment I departed he would double back inside the house. Walking across the meadow, I strained to hear his footsteps, but the ground was too soft, the swish of grass against my skirt too loud, and it was not until I arrived at the table, and he said in English, loudly and suddenly, right behind my ear, 'Here I am. No need for a search party,' that I knew my mission had been successful.

Mrs B clapped her hands and cut me another slice of the cake. Although I smiled, I could look neither at her nor at Edmondo, and when I tried to eat, the cake seemed to have turned to cardboard and I had to gulp mouthfuls of cold tea even to swallow. I stayed for as long as I could bear, but I fear it wasn't very long because the whole family seemed surprised when I said I had to go.

Edmondo asked if he should walk me home. I declined and told him not to break up the party. He looked dreadfully crestfallen and probably assumed I didn't want to be seen with him in the village when I simply needed some time on my own. Time to think about what to do, if I should tell Father or Uncle Charles that I had seen the pipe-cleaner man actually inside the Brambillas' house. As I said my goodbyes and thank-yous, I could feel Mr Brambilla's eyes upon me again, that same magpie stare, and it was all I could do to meet his gaze with what I hoped was an inscrutable look of my own.

What should I do, Diary? I don't for a moment believe Mr Brambilla to be sympathetic to the Nazis, but if I tell Uncle Charles I saw the pipe-cleaner man in the Brambillas' house, then Mr Brambilla will be arrested, and perhaps Edmondo too. Yet if the pipe-cleaner man is working for Mussolini, giving Uncle Charles the chance to catch him might be the biggest single thing I could do to help my country win the war.

I stare at these pages, then I stare out of the window. I wish I could stare inside myself and find the answer but all I see is darkness and the lonely responsibility of an impossible decision.

News Chronicle (*The Times*)

11 June 1940

Mussolini Declares War On The Allies

At 4.30pm yesterday afternoon, Ciano, the Italian Foreign Minister, summoned the French Ambassador to the Palazzo Chigi and handed him this statement:

'His Majesty, the King-Emperor, declares that Italy considers herself as at war with France as from tomorrow, June 11.'

Fifteen minutes later the British Ambassador (Sir Percy Lorraine) was given a similar declaration.

At 6pm Mussolini appeared on the balcony of the Palazzo Venezia, where 250,000 fascists, following their orders to do so, had gathered. To them Mussolini declared, 'We are now in the field with Germany'.

Letter, by hand, Edmondo to Ruby

11 June 1940

Mia cara

You must have heard the news by now. The very worst has happened. Our countries are at war! At six thirty this morning a policeman we had never met before came to our door. He told us that because we live near the coast, we must abandon our shop and find somewhere else to stay. I've copied out the letter he gave my father so you can read the exact words for yourself and understand we have no choice but to leave.

'No foreigner can enter into, or reside in, any area declared to be a Protected Area without the written permission of the Chief Constable. Notice is hereby given to you that you, being an alien and being resident in an area declared to be a Protected Area, are required to take immediate steps to remove from this area, and that if you are found in this area after the expiry of three days from the date of this notice, steps will be taken to enforce the Order against you.'

It's now the afternoon and already there are people outside, yelling insults in angry voices. At the moment they are few in number, but the crowd is growing, the mood darkening. They truly hate us now, although we are the same people who sold them bread and ice-cream and they are the same people who used to stand at our counter chatting like old friends. What can I do? How can I stop this nightmare from happening? It feels as if my family and I are being drowned. Swept out to sea, away from the shore of our home and the people we love.

Ruby, I don't know when we will next see each other. My parents have a friend who will let us use his house in Essex until we find somewhere else to live – if we can ever find a landlord willing to rent a house to an Italian family or a way of paying for it without the income from our shop. *Non importa*. Never mind. Don't worry about me. Worry only for the safety of yourself and your own family. One day soon we'll be together again. I swear.

Ti amo

Edmondo

PS I enclose a small photograph of myself with Fragolina. Please keep it hidden – I've written our new address in Essex on the back.

PPS It's an hour later… I ran all the way to bring you this note, wearing an old hat and raincoat as a disguise. I hoped to see you and say goodbye in person but somebody else is here, calling for you at the back of the house…

Note (by hand) Mr Wilfred Frost to Miss Ruby Summers

11 June 1940

Young Ruby, I shouted and shouted but you must be out. A mob is gathering outside the tobacconist and from what I could hear they intend to raid the Italian grocers. There are too many men to stop but it may not be too late to alert your Italian friends.

Sincerely

Wilfred Frost (of the chickens)

Diary of Miss Ruby Summers

12 June 1940

Diary

I'm almost too exhausted to pick up a pen. It's two o'clock in the morning. The grandfather clock is beginning to chime the hour and the familiar peal of the bell is like a steadying hand on my shoulder.

I hardly know where to start. After school there were two notes waiting for me, one from Edmondo and one from Mr Frost. (Mother said she must have been out when Edmondo came, taking eggs to Mrs Wainwright, but I don't know if I believe her.) 'The Brambillas are being attacked!' I cried, thrusting Mr Frost's note into my father's hands. 'We have to call the police!'

Father's eyes remained fixed on the

page, though he can hardly have needed more time to read so few sentences. He'd just got back from work and was wearing a dark grey suit as if in mourning. 'The village isn't very big, Ruby. I imagine Constable Dodds is already aware of the situation.'

His voice was so calm, for a moment I thought I might be worrying about nothing and felt my pulse steady. 'Is the danger over, do you think? Will the looters have been arrested? Mr Frost seemed to believe there were a lot of them, but perhaps Constable Dodds asked the police from another village to help.'

Father didn't reply. I saw him exchange a glance with my mother, who had paused her knitting and was gazing at me across the sitting room, the pockets under her eyes even deeper and darker than normal.

'Father?'

'Ruby…' he began and stopped.

The penny dropped. 'Constable Dodds won't try to stop the hooligans, will he? If anyone asks questions later, *which they won't because the Brambillas are Italians and therefore the enemy*, the police will simply pretend they didn't find out what was happening until it was too late.'

Father was holding my gaze the way you might hold the hand of an eight-year-old reluctant to cross the road. Eventually, he said. 'Something like that could happen. Yes.'

I could barely contain myself. 'But… but that's *awful*. Until this beastly war started, the Brambillas were our friends. And not just our friends, they were friendly with everyone in the village. You never heard a bad word said against them. Edmondo has sat around our kitchen table, played cards with us on a Saturday night and he helped George mend the fence at the bottom of the orchard. Yet because of a man in Italy who is as much stranger to the Brambillas as he is to us, it's now perfectly alright to destroy their property, threaten to hurt them and hound them from their homes like foxes being gassed out of their burrows! Well, it's not alright with me! I'm going to the shop this minute and if the villagers want to attack the Brambillas they'll have to push me out of the way first!'

'No, Ruby!' Flinging her knitting down, Mother jumped to her feet. 'You mustn't do that. That mob could be dangerous, anything could happen!' But before she reached the end of the sentence I was already in the hallway. As I rummaged for a coat, Father appeared in the sitting room doorway.

'Don't try to stop me. I'm going whatever you say!' By way of proof, I hauled myself into an ancient mackintosh and began to do up the buttons.

He didn't move. 'I can see that.' Then, 'Ruby…'

'What?'

'I know you want to help Edmondo, however you might not understand the situation as well as you think you do.' I opened my mouth to protest but Father raised his palm. 'Be careful, that's all. It's bad enough for your mother' – he gave a peculiar little gulp – 'bad enough for both of us not knowing if George will come back, without watching you plunge headlong into a mob of angry people.'

I hesitated, then nodded, and opened the front door.

Father needn't have worried. As I approached the village centre the streets were quiet. Eerily quiet. Even the bench on the green, normally a hub for gossip, was bare. A stray newspaper blew over the grass in a wind that had the damp, heavy quality of stewed fruit. Pulling my coat tighter, I braced myself as I rounded the corner. Even so, the moment the Brambillas' shop came into view, an ache engulfed my chest and my feet came instinctively to a standstill.

All the windows on the ground floor were smashed and the shop door swung loose and lopsided by a single hinge like the last moments of a dangling tooth. On the pavement a wooden pallet – the kind used in deliveries – lay on its side. For a moment I stared, perplexed, before understanding that it must have been used as a battering ram to force a way into the Brambillas' home. I moved towards the broken building and glass crunched under my shoes, the fragments coated with dust that had the texture of flour or custard powder.

At the doorway, I hesitated, before walking around to the house entrance. I knocked, then slowly eased the door handle. 'Edmondo? Are you there? Mrs Brambilla?'

The passage was gloomy and deserted. As I edged down the hall, the only sound was the echoey slap of my sandals on the tiles. I reached the curtain of beads that led into the back of the shop and pulled them aside slowly, the cords rustling like a rain shower. All at once a small blond-haired figure shot out from behind the counter. Before I could say a word, a boy of no more than eight or nine darted to the broken front window and began to climb over the sill, his arms bulging with two bags of Tate & Lyle sugar. For a split second his eyes met mine in a defiant sort of apology, then he was gone. Stunned, I gazed around the silent shop. The drawer of the till hung open, its compartments hollow. The shelves had been emptied from floor to ceiling with only a couple of dented tins lying beside the skirting board which someone must have dropped in their rush. Even the lampshade had been removed. The sight of the bare bulb, dangling naked and forlorn over the ravaged room filled me with a hot rage that felt more like a fever than anger.

I turned on my heel and made my way back along the corridor. There was nobody in the kitchen or the sitting room, but at the foot of the staircase I thought I could hear voices upstairs.

'Hello!' I called and started to climb.

Immediately, the voices fell quiet.

A door opened. 'Who's that?' Mr Brambilla was standing above me on the landing, leaning over the balustrade.

'It's me, Ruby.'

His face didn't soften. 'What are you doing? Why are you here?'

'I came to see you. I came to help.'

He stared at me for a moment, gave the briefest of nods, then turned away. Almost immediately, Edmondo took his place. 'Ruby!'

I raced up the stairs and into his arms.

Inside the nearest bedroom, two suitcases were lying open on a bed surrounded by piles of clothes and books. Fragolina was folding garments into the bottom of the cases in a hushed and business-like fashion. Although her head was bent, even from the distance of the doorway I could see the streaks on her pale cheeks.

Edmondo squeezed my hand. 'A crowd of people was here. Shouting all sorts of horrible words!'

Fragolina lifted her chin, so that the birthmark on her neck was quite visible. 'Bloody Italians,' she whispered. 'Italian bastards! Take what you can! Do the Tally shop in!'

'The *Tally* shop?'

'It's the slang used for Italians. Like Hun or Jerry is used for Germans.' Mr Brambilla spoke from the landing, as though he were informing me of a football result or the weather forecast for tomorrow. In his hand was a third suitcase. Behind him, Mrs Brambilla was barely visible beneath a mountain of skirts and dresses.

Her gaze swung from Edmondo to me and back to Edmondo. 'Have you told her?'

I looked at Edmondo too. 'Told me what?'

He pressed my fingers again. 'We're leaving tonight. My mother and sister are too scared to stay here one more night, and since we are only allowed to stay three more days at the most, we may as well go now.' His grip on my hand tightened. A single tear ran down his cheek and fell onto the collar of his shirt.

I was too full of sadness to dare to open my mouth. A stone seemed to have lodged in my throat that threatened any moment to explode. Through a blurry veil I watched Mrs B lower her armful of clothes onto the bed. Amongst the jumble of colour, I recognised the green frock she had worn for Mr Brambilla's birthday. I would have given anything to have been sitting next to Edmondo in that sunny orchard again, when being with each other was something we still had the power to choose.

Mrs B pulled me back to the dismal bedroom. 'Ruby, pass me my coat *per favore*. The grey woollen one that is hanging in the wardrobe.'

Mr Brambilla interjected, 'You do not need your winter coat, mia cara. It is June.'

'Yes, *now* it is June but in six months' time it will be winter.'

'There is no space to pack a thick coat.' His tone made my hand freeze on the cupboard handle.

'Then I will wear it and sweat like a pig!' Two bright spots had appeared in the centre of Mrs B's cheeks. 'Pass me my coat please, Ruby. It is perhaps at the very back of the wardrobe.'

Peering into the gloom, I reached

behind the empty hooks and last remaining folds of fabric. To my surprise, my hand brushed against something hard and as I pulled the grey wool free of its hanger, I caught a glimpse of polished wood and black knobs, gleaming at me from the darkness. I was standing upright again, passing Mrs B her coat, before I was able to register what I had seen. It was only when I noticed that Mr Brambilla was staring at me, scrutinising my face with his searchlight gaze, that the discovery struck me, and I realised both the shock of what I had seen and the need to hide my feelings in the same instantaneous moment.

Before anyone could speak, the high, hard crack of breaking glass filled the room. Although I flinched, the Brambillas barely seemed to notice.

'Another downstairs window has been broken,' Fragolina said. 'That is why we must leave tonight. Soon the only way to inflict more damage will be to attack the bedroom windows – or us.'

'I should go home and let you concentrate on your packing…'

I saw Edmondo gulp, the sudden spasm of his Adam's apple, before he turned to lead me downstairs.

Dear Diary, I can't even begin to convey how impossibly awful it was, saying goodbye to Edmondo. Worse even, than when George left for France.

Perhaps I shouldn't admit that, but I have, and surely it can't be too terrible of me to think that way? Although I was worried something awful might happen to George, I believed deep in my bones – still believe – he will come home to us. Yet when I try to conjure up that same feeling of hope for Edmondo, it's like hearing a telephone ring and ring in an empty house. I am more than worried about Edmondo, I am frightened. Frightened for him, for his future, frightened for the whole of his family. And frightened for me, that I will never love anyone else as much as I love him for the whole of my life… I am putting down my pen.

It's now twenty minutes later because tired as I am, I cannot sleep: What about the radio, Diary? (I am whispering, rather than writing, these words.) Why was a radio set hidden in the back of the Brambillas' wardrobe? I've checked back through my diary and found the entry for 15 February where I recorded Mr Brambilla being very upset because PC Dodds had ordered him to hand in his wireless set at the police station. And what I didn't say at the time, didn't dare to write about my visit to Felixstowe, was I'm almost certain that when I saw Mr Brambilla and the pipe-cleaner man playing music in the middle of the night, I caught a glimpse of a wooden box, a box that might, just might, have been a radio, in the corner of their secret room...

Diary of Miss Ruby Summers

13 June 1940

Dear Diary

Today we received a letter from a soldier in George's regiment, a Lieutenant Doyle. George is alive – thank heavens – but took a bit of a knock and is expecting to be returned home for a period of convalescence once he is well enough to be discharged from hospital. The letter is so dreadfully vague Mother is tearing out her hair – quite literally. I saw a clump of locks in her hand as she paced about the kitchen, bemoaning the inadequacies of the letter writer. 'He doesn't even say what has happened to George, let alone where he is or when he'll be coming home. How can Lieutenant Doyle possibly have missed out such essential information!'

'At least, George is alive,' I ventured. 'And on the mend, by the sounds of things. A lot of people would envy us for that. And thank Lieutenant

Doyle for making the effort to contact us.'

Mother came to a halt and the hand holding the letter dropped to her side. 'I know that, Ruby. Of course, I know that! But George has been hurt. Quite badly hurt by the sound of things and to be kept in the dark like this about my son, when it would have been so easy, so natural to tell us more… How could Lieutenant Doyle have been so… so careless?' For a moment she held up the letter again, as if she could stare the missing details into existence, before taking a little gasp of breath and hurrying from the room.

Between you and me, Diary, I wonder if Lieutenant Doyle really has been careless, or whether he missed out the details of George's injuries quite deliberately. I expect he would have shown the letter to George before he sent it, which means it was probably George who wanted to spare Mother the grief of reading about whatever has befallen him before she could see him for herself.

Perhaps I'm being pessimistic. I've had rather a miserable day thinking either of George or the Brambillas while the news seems to grow more terrible with every passing day. From this Sunday, the church bells are to be silenced. Instead, they will ring only to inform us of an invasion. Although it's sad not to hear the bells, it's far worse to realise England could soon be invaded – and that German troops might land only a few miles away. I try to tell myself history is full of darker more unhappier times than these but that's of little comfort when everyone you love is either in deepest peril or worn to a shadow of themselves by worry.

I shall study to take my mind off all the gloom. I may even tackle some Latin grammar (which is so fiendishly difficult, thinking about anything other than cases and declensions becomes quite impossible). After that I shall write to Edmondo, and then I shall write to Clem, and count myself fortunate that my letters will bring a smile to the faces of two such marvellous people.

And I won't mention the radio in the wardrobe to either of them.

Letter Clem to Ruby

14 June 1940

Dearest Ruby

Tabby raced to the door the moment she heard the clunk of post falling through the flap. Imagine my delight when I saw the envelope she had fetched bore your handwriting. It's so dreadfully perverse that being close to the ones we love feels more important than ever yet the terrible shortage of petrol means I can't possibly say when I'll next be able to visit you all.

Once I had read your letter though, I realised I have nothing to complain about at all. The poor Brambillas! If I had heard about the attack on their shop from anyone but you, I don't think I would have believed them. Do you remember the first village fete after they arrived, when we were all so thrilled to buy their ice-cream? You were so excited you dropped your cone on the grass! Edmondo kept insisting you should have his one instead but then Mr Brambilla gave you another ice-cream that was even bigger than the first! It seems extraordinary the government has forced him and his family to move out of their home and leave their own shop simply because they happen to live near to the coast.

Oh Ruby, how dire can things get? Is there no limit to the madness human beings inflict on one another? Literally the very next moment after I read your letter, it was announced on the wireless the Prime Minister has ordered that all Italian men must be sent to an internment camp. I can only imagine how awful you must feel. And how helpless. Do you know if the new rules apply to all Italian men or only to those in a certain age-group? Where are all these internment camps anyway? And what are they like? We surely can't send people to prison indefinitely simply for being the wrong nationality. I've no doubt most of the Italians living here, including the dear Brambillas, despise bloody Hitler and Mussolini just as much as the British do.

Let me know the moment you hear from Edmondo. I'm worrying about him too, and my worry is made all the worse by knowing how much more worried than me you must be. What did we worry about before the war, Ruby? Looking back, those days seem so rosy and carefree, but at the time we didn't think so. What a waste! If we'd had the slightest inkling of what was around the corner we would have cherished every moment of being safe with food in the larder and our loved ones within arms' reach.

I'm reaching out my arms to you, darling, in a hug to stretch across the miles.

Clem

PS The letter from Lieutenant Doyle does sound rather frustrating (and frankly rather inept), but I doubt its shortcomings are sinister or deliberate. I suspect the poor Lieutenant simply dashed off a note without thinking. Writing to the family of an injured friend is hardly likely to be his top priority. Let's be jolly thankful for the news that George is safely out of France and will be home again soon.

PPS Kippers for supper here. I read in the paper we need to eat more herring to stop them being wasted. At least there's something we won't be short of!

Diary of Miss Ruby Summers

14 June 1940

Dear Diary

Nothing from Edmondo. I've written twice to the address he gave me. Why hasn't he written back? It's been three days now. Has he been arrested? I swear last night I heard the clock chime every single hour, yet the instant Mother came to wake me I couldn't keep my eyes open.

I could barely see a reason to get out of bed anyway.

Letter Professor Helen Wodehouse to Ruby

14 June 1940

Dear Miss Summers

I trust this letter finds you as well as can be expected in such difficult times. At the suggestion of Miss Mary Cartwright (with whom I believe you are acquainted) I am writing to inform you that one of our research alumni, Miss Dorothy Hodgkin, will be making a presentation in our Great Hall, this Tuesday, 18 June at 3pm. The subject is the X-ray diffraction of crystalline proteins. Should your school be willing to release you at the relevant time and date, you would be most welcome to attend. Light refreshments will be served after the event.

I appreciate the war has changed lives across the globe and presented us all with personal tragedies and unwelcome challenges. Nevertheless, the current circumstances have only strengthened my conviction that educated women are needed to take up the reins in all aspects of life with the utmost urgency.

With this concern in mind, permit me to enquire if it is still your intention to apply to Girton College? Your friend Miss Cartwright mentioned the Latin requirement might present a difficulty.

I'm afraid Latin is unavoidable, but with application I'm confident you will overcome that particular hurdle.

Yours truly

Helen Wodehouse (College Mistress)

Diary of Miss Ruby Summers

15 June 1940

Dear Diary

I have nothing to say. There is still no word from Edmondo, and I can think of no explanation for his silence that does not involve something awful. I cannot express my feelings in words. If I had paint, I would simply colour the entire page black. As it is, I will study, force myself to eat supper with Mother and Father and pretend I am acting in a play that, miraculously and unexpectedly, turns out to have a happy ending.

NB: The situation is, dire, Diary. It's now nine thirty at night and my attempts to concentrate on Latin are both futile and pathetic. The truth is I understand no more of the language now than I did three months ago. I'm as likely to grow a second head as pass the entrance exams to Cambridge. And why should I mind about that? When the whole world is suffering so badly, what kind of person cares about their own future? A selfish, egotistical one, that's who.

Letter Uncle Charles to Ruby

16 June 1940

My dear goddaughter,

Forgive me, the pressures of work require me to disregard normal pleasantries and get straight to the point. Have you heard from that Italian lad you're so fond of? As soon as you do, you must telephone me on the number below. Without fail, Ruby. Without fail. No harm will come to him, however it is imperative you pass me whatever information you have at the earliest opportunity. I trust you will not let me – or your country – down.

Affectionately, and in haste

Uncle Charles

Letter Edmondo to Ruby

16 June 1940

Mia cara

I'm writing against the express instructions of my father who demands I break all contact with you. For almost a week, I've tried to do as he asks, but I don't understand his reasons and find I can't obey him. It seems that when forced to choose between loyalty to my parents or to you, I choose you.

I will always choose you.

The day we said goodbye will probably be the most terrible day of my life. Yet my clearest image is not the crowds pressing against the shop, the noise of shattering glass, or seeing ordinary men and women clear our shelves like locusts and steal the money out of the till. My lasting impression is not even the moment we said goodbye when I felt you reach into my chest and pull away my heart. No, my strongest memory is the instant I saw you in the hallway. Resolute and beautiful, an angel in the moonshine.

We are safe, my family and I, at least, for now, but the stories we hear from our Italian friends are worse than I could have imagined. The security forces come at night. At 2 or 3 a.m.

there is a knock at the door. If nobody answers, the officers force their way inside. Outside a police van is waiting, painted black with a grille at the back like the bars of a cage. The men are told to pack a suitcase before being arrested and driven to a police station, their wrists handcuffed. After that, I'm not certain what happens. We hear rumours they are searched naked and washed with disinfectant before being locked away, but I try not to believe such things. I understand England is at war, Ruby. That Italians could be traitors. All I want is the right to prove *our* innocence… I'm afraid, not for myself, but for my father. I worry about his health, whether it could endure such hardship. And what about my mother and Fragolina? If my father and I are taken away, how will they manage without us and the shop?

Still, I'm determined to stay positive. Our family is together for now. The place we are living is small, but the rooms are comfortable and we have enough to eat. Mainly I spend the days reading, drawing, playing cards with Fragolina – and thinking about you. Although my father doesn't like us to go out, I'm allowed to take one short walk each day. I watch from the upstairs window and wait until I spy the postman at the end of the lane before I leave the house. Then I can intercept your letters before my father sees what I'm doing. Please don't ever stop sending them, Ruby. When I read your handwriting I feel you next to me again.

I love you

Edmondo

PS I enclose a sketch of our new home. The upstairs window on the left is the bedroom I share with Fragolina and where I am sitting now, writing to you.

Diary of Miss Ruby Summers

17 June 1940

Dear Diary

Uncle Charles has written to ask if I have news of Edmondo. Edmondo has written to me because he trusts me not to inform anyone of his whereabouts. Professor Wodehouse has written to invite me to a presentation in Cambridge. I cannot reply to Uncle Charles because I can neither lie to him nor give away Edmondo's location. If I reply to Edmondo, I shall feel I am betraying Uncle Charles. And answering

Professor Wodehouse would be both pointless and misleading because I have no hope of becoming one of the women that she wants to lead the country. The only reins I'm capable of holding are those of a docile and very ancient pony. I have never felt more alone.

NB It's an hour later. I have written to Edmondo again. We must stay true to each other.

Diary of Miss Ruby Summers

18 June 1940

Dear Diary

The only way to grasp today's events is to record them here. Perhaps in a few days' time, when I read the entry back, I'll know what to do. In the meantime, as soon as I've finished writing, I'm going to hide this book behind the headboard of my bed. It seems ridiculous and melodramatic to think I can't risk my own parents finding my diary, but the world has gone so crazy perhaps nothing is that ridiculous any longer.

It all began shortly after supper. Mother was in George's room, brushing the carpet again, (although the floor, windows and cupboards are already so spotless you would think we were welcoming royalty rather than a member of our own family) while I was in my own room struggling to memorise a list of Latin vocabulary and desperately wishing I was in Cambridge listening to Miss Dorothy Hodgkin.

Anyway, the crunch of rubber on gravel was followed by the chime of the front door. A few moments later the unmistakable voice of Uncle Charles expanded up the stairs, slipped under my door and clutched hold of my stomach like a gymnast grabbing at rope. I sat very still. I was aware of Father calling Mother, followed by the steady descent of my mother to the drawing room.

And then, hush.

Of course, I could no longer study. I imagined Uncle Charles telling Mother and Father about his letter to me – and my lack of reply. I pictured Father pacing in front of the fireplace, his torso bent forwards and his hands clasped behind his back. All the while he would be throwing glances at Mother as they wondered what to do for the best. I had just about reached the part where Father would come to a halt, square his shoulders, and open his mouth to call me down, when a voice really did shout up the stairs, only it was Mother, sounding angrier than I could ever remember hearing before.

'Ruby. Come here at once.'

In the drawing room, the three adults were standing in a semi-circle facing the door. I stopped on the threshold; the simple act of breathing was making me dizzy. For a moment, none of them spoke, as if they were all hoping someone else would start.

Eventually, Father cleared his throat. 'Your godfather says he sent you a letter.' He paused. 'Asking if you know the whereabouts of Edmondo and his family.'

There was a long silence. I seemed to have forgotten how to talk even if I wanted to.

Mother stepped forward. 'For heaven's sake, Ruby! What are you thinking of! Lives are at stake. Young British lives like those of your brother and his friends...'

Father held up his hand. 'Ruby,' – his tone was gentle, even placatory – 'There's a problem, I'm afraid. Mr Brambilla was supposed to inform the authorities of the address to which the family were moving and then register at the police station when they arrived. He did provide an address in Westbourne, Ipswich before they left, but it seems the Brambillas are not there and have not registered at any police station in that vicinity. In short, nobody knows where they are' – his pupils narrowed and his gaze became heavy with sadness – 'except perhaps you.'

Three pairs of eyes encased me. I felt like a fish, trapped, and gasping for air and at that moment two cyclists went past the window, calling gaily to each other. The scene seemed so removed from inside of the drawing room it might have been in a different country. At last, I whispered, 'I can't help. I don't know where the Brambillas are living.'

Mother came forward again. This time she caught my arm. 'That's not true, Ruby! Don't tell fibs! I know you've been corresponding with Edmondo! I've seen you heading to the postbox carrying an envelope! He must have given you an address.'

I swallowed. 'I expect the address I have is the same one Mr Brambilla gave the police. After all,' – oh Diary, it was so dreadfully, shamefully easy to lie – 'I don't know whether he has received any of my letters or not.'

'What address have you been writing to?' Uncle Charles was curt.

'I don't recall the details off the top of my head. Except' – remembering the earlier part of conversation – 'that it's somewhere in Westbourne, Ipswich.'

Father let out a sigh of relief. Uncle Charles made a harrumphing sound. Mother didn't say anything at all but after a moment she let go of my arm.

'Can I go back to my homework now?'

Father nodded.

At the doorway I turned back again. 'What will happen now, Uncle Charles? How will you find the Brambillas?'

'We'll bring some trained men up from London to conduct a thorough search of the shop and house, and hope something turns up from that. Otherwise' – he regarded me steadily – 'we'll need a lucky break.'

I can't write any more, Diary, my hand is shaking too much.

What have I done?

Or perhaps the better question is, what *haven't* I done?

PART FIVE

Letter Cassie to Austin

3 May 2020

Dear Austin

I think we might both be in trouble. Last night the police were here.

I had the feeling *something* was going to happen as soon as it began to get dark. The sky was crowded with dollops of clouds that looked like a jar of cottonwool balls had been knocked over and the setting sun was turning the horizon fiery pink. It only needed the silhouette of a witch on broomstick (or ET, I love that film!) to complete the scene. I woke Noah in case he was missing something special in the Cloud Collector's Handbook and together we watched until the flame colours were gone and the dusk had taken on a still, luminous quality that was more like the echo of light than light itself.

Anyway, I was steering Noah by the shoulders up the caravan step when all at once a torch beam appeared, bobbing steadily closer along the ridge of the sea road. Nobody comes to the caravan park at night. Nobody normally comes in the daytime either – except the bin man (on Tuesdays) and a very occasional dog walker looking so hot and puffed they must already have walked several miles – but at night Noah and I might as well be on the moon. Bundling us into the caravan, I whispered, 'stay quiet' and raised my finger to my lips to show I meant business.

Staying quiet made no difference. Footsteps smacked against the path and the torch shone briefly through the window, flashing over Noah's face. There was a brief hush as the walker crossed the grass followed by a sudden rap of knuckles. For one mad moment, I imagined not answering and hiding for ever in the dark while Noah and I grew hungrier and hungrier and our hair grew longer, before sanity finally prevailed and I turned the handle just as the door opened from the outside and a stranger tumbled through the entrance like coal being delivered.

It took about a minute for us all to recover but when we had finally switched the lamp on and the torch off, the stranger turned out to be a gangly lad of about twenty wearing a policeman's uniform. He had a long nose in a very long face that was probably made to seem longer because of the helmet he had to retrieve from underneath the table before he could put it back on. 'Good evening,' he said – and I almost expected a knee bend – 'My name is PC Lane.' I knew he was trying to sound assertive, but the way he held his torch close to his chest reminded me of how Noah clutched Elephant when he was nervous.

PC Lane ran his finger under the strap of his helmet. 'There's been some complaints at the station,' he said. 'From local people. The caravan park is closed, you see. Nobody is supposed to be here at the moment.'

I didn't reply. Several seconds passed and my head began to fill with all sorts of thoughts I couldn't tell PC Lane about because he would have thought I was mad. He looked alarmed enough as it was, as if of all the reactions he had anticipated silence wasn't one of them. At least not one that kept going for such a long time. 'As I was saying,' he said eventually. 'The caravan site is closed because of government rules. It means you have to go home tomorrow morning.'

'But we are home.'

At the same instant PC Lane and I turned to look at Noah.

'This is our home,' Noah repeated. 'Isn't it, Mummy? That's what you said. This is our home for now.'

It felt like a football had lodged in my throat. 'For now,' I managed at last.

PC Lane stared. 'Don't you have somewhere else to go?'

The same crazy notion I couldn't possibly tell a stranger – or even you yet, Austin – made me say very firmly, 'No, we don't,' and I tried hard not to blink.

PC Lane looked at Noah, then at me, and then at Noah's tractor parked in the squares of the cushion cover, but I think it was the medication that swung it, Noah's box of tablets sitting next to Elephant on top of the fridge. I saw the policeman's gaze snag on the box and his long, thin face seemed to get longer and thinner. 'My little sister had those,' he said, and we all ran straight into another silence.

I wanted to know if his sister had suffered from the same illness as Noah. If she had got better, and if so, how many years it was before their mother stopped worrying every time his sister so much as yawned. However, I didn't dare mention any of those questions. Not in front of Noah. So, instead, I asked, 'Please can we stay a little while longer? Until we find somewhere else to go.'

'The park is closed,' he repeated. But more doubtfully this time.

'The park doesn't own this caravan. This one has been rented to us privately.'

PC Lane fiddled with his helmet strap again, nudging the plastic forwards and backwards and revealing an imprint under his chin like a tiny tyre-track. Finally, he said, 'I suppose the position might be different. With a private caravan. I'll have to ask back at the station.'

At the door he switched his torch back on. Just before he plunged into the night, he glanced over his shoulder. 'Should I tell them in the campsite office you're staying here because you know the owner of the caravan?'

'Maybe,' I said quickly, 'you don't need to tell them

anything yet. The office is locked up and no one is there at the moment anyway.'

After PC Lane had gone, I made Noah and I hot chocolate and didn't mind at all that it took me three attempts to light the gas. I tucked Noah into bed and opened the caravan door. The clouds had disappeared, and the sky looked as if an enormous silver saltshaker had been tipped over an expanse of black velvet. I'm drinking my own hot chocolate wrapped in a duvet, sitting on the step, writing to you, and trying not to think about the virus, the police – or anyone else. I've realised that I love living here, Austin. I can't imagine not being able to reach out and touch Noah when I'm lying in bed. Or smell the sea as soon as I wake up. Or hurry to the postbox every morning and pick out the envelopes. (My *mother* is even sending me letters. That never would have happened if we'd stayed in London!)

I do hope PC Lane doesn't cause trouble for you. I didn't tell him your name, but I don't suppose it would be difficult to find out who owns the bright green caravan. Imagine if he makes me go home before we've even met?

Cassie

PS I have two more letters to write tonight. One of them is to a penfriend. The reason for the second has come about because of what I realised while I was talking to PC Lane. Though I might just cut out the photograph of the cloud in the Cloud Collector's Handbook called *Duplicitus* and send that instead. Or maybe I won't write at all. Maybe I'll save myself the bother and let him work it out for himself.

Letter Cassie to Ruby

3 May 2020

Dear Ruby

The sky is littered with stars. The more I look, the more of them appear, which as well as being immensely beautiful is a useful reminder that sometimes you need to look for a long while simply to see what's right in front of your eyes...

I was going to write somebody a bitter and sad letter tonight. Instead, I'm going to make myself another hot chocolate and ask you a question.

I know you told me not to ask about your letters until I'd read them all, but surely you can say what you did after the war without telling me whatever it is you don't want me to know. So Ruby, this is my question: What was the very best thing you did once the war was over?

Love

Cassie

Text Stuart to Cassie 19.20

4 May 2020

Hey Cass, I'm home. Good time to call?

Text Stuart to Cassie 19.45

4 May 2020

Cass, are you there?

Text Stuart to Cassie 22.30

4 May 2020

If you're not there, where are you?

Text Austin to Cassie 09.10

5 May 2020

I got your letter this morning and it's made me worried. Not because of the policeman. Alfie Lane is a good sort and he won't turn you out of the caravan if you've nowhere else to go. But why did you tell him you have nowhere else to go, Cassie? What's happened to your home in London? Why can't you go there? I don't want you and Noah to leave but some of what you wrote sounded a bit odd. Who has got to work out what? I do hope everything is alright.

Austin

PS I don't think there's a cloud called Duplicitus. Do you mean Duplicatus? It's when a cloud forms at two altitudes at the same time, though I don't understand how the picture in the book would take the place of a letter.

Text Cassie to Austin 09.21

5 May 2020

Duplicatus then. Though being in two places at the same time was exactly what I meant, even if it's not worth cutting up the Cloud Collector's Handbook to make the point. Perhaps I should say, it's not worth cutting up the handbook for him. Anyway, don't worry, Austin, I'm fine. Stronger than ever. And no more visits yet from PC Alfie Lane, so I think you're right about that too. Please go back to writing me letters. The moment I see an envelope waiting in the postbox I feel like someone has switched on a light. And if the envelope has your handwriting on the front, two lights come on.

Text Stuart to Cassie 19.10

5 May 2020

I'm home. Ready to chat?

Text Stuart to Cassie 19.45

5 May 2020

Cass?

Text Stuart to Cassie 22.38

5 May 2020

Cassie, what the hell is going on? You won't answer my texts. You won't answer my calls. For God's sake let me know you're OK. I'm beginning to think you've been struck down by the virus. Or carbon monoxide poisoning. Or a mad farmer with a shotgun. Or you've drowned or got lost. Christ, the list is endless. If I don't hear anything by tomorrow, I'm going to call the police.

Text Cassie to Stuart 22.39

5 May 2020

I'm fine.

Text Stuart to Cassie 22.39

5 May 2020

WTF???!!!

Letter Ruby to Cassie

6 May 2020

Dear Cassie

The very best thing I did once the war was over? That's a difficult and thought-provoking question. A proper answer goes back so many years the memories might not come in the right order. At my age the past feels like an overcrowded drawer – while everything might be in there, finding anything in particular requires a lot of delving around and once located is liable to be buried beneath a host of other unexpected and forgotten items. Still, today, I'm happy to spend some time doing a bit of rummaging because I'm sorry to say the morning is tinged with sadness.

Beryl's chair is empty.

At first, I thought the problem might be my eyes, or that Beryl had shrunk even more, because all I could see on her usual seat were the maroon flecks of her favourite blanket. After several minutes of squinting and staring, I realised the fleece was folded on top of the cushion and nobody at all was sitting there. My worst suspicions were confirmed when Amy came round with the tea-trolley at eleven. When I asked her where Beryl was, the lovely smile faltered. 'I'm afraid Beryl left us in the night.' Although I knew exactly what she meant, for a wonderful moment I had a vision of Beryl shinning down the drainpipe with a suitcase strapped on her back. Amy patted my arm, slipped a chocolate digestive onto my saucer, and turned up the radio as if the extra noise might compensate for the empty chair.

No matter.

I shall focus on you, and when I think of Beryl imagine her somewhere warm and sunny where blankets – particularly maroon-flecked ones – are entirely superfluous.

So, my dear friend, let's go back to the past...

The short answer to your question is that the best thing I did after the war was find a job. Not just any job, but one that ultimately led to a very special telephone call on a particular Tuesday morning. For some reason the days of the week had always seemed to me to have their own colour. Mondays were red, Fridays reliably blue, Wednesdays black and Thursdays yellow. Tuesdays, on the other hand, were colourless. Tuesdays were drab, a bland, innocuous day when nobody expected anything to happen. Yet that turned out to be terribly unfair because one of the most wonderful, show-stopping moments of my life happened on a Tuesday. However, before I explain I must tell you about some other items in my memory drawer.

I left Cambridge in 1943 with a first-class degree and first-class Masters in Biochemistry. I thought I was quite the bees' knees, that research institutions all the way from Land's End to Aberdeen would fall over themselves to employ me! It didn't occur to me I was a woman. Of course, I should rather say it didn't occur to me being a woman would matter. It did. Apparently one glimpse of me holding a test-tube would be enough to distract all those defenceless men from their noble ponderings and propel them down a different trail of thought entirely. I must say the idea of being able to distract anyone from anything might have been quite flattering, if only the door into a laboratory – any laboratory – hadn't stayed so firmly closed. During the Christmas after my graduation my father called me into his study. One hand cradled a whisky, the other the ledge of the mantelpiece. He had the expression of a man who had summoned himself to conduct a task which he was dutybound to see through. As tactfully as he could manage – which was not at all – he asked if I was stepping out with anyone suitable. Naturally he meant was I about to get married. I wasn't. Most eligible young men were either dead or fighting – or scarred in ways visible and invisible to the human eye – and the ones that weren't didn't come as close as the length of a football pitch to Edmondo. My father nodded slowly at the news. He wasn't surprised. 'In that case,' he said, 'after all that education you need to get a job. Any respectable job. And stop chasing after dreams.' At the time I was furious. Now I suspect he was trying to be kind; he wanted to protect me from yet more rejection.

So, in the new year I took a position in a girls' school as a replacement for a science teacher called away to nurse her brother. I felt like a plant that has been left inside a dusty shed and watered once a month. None of the pupils showed the slightest interest in cell replication or photosynthesis or any other wonders of biology and when I made them dissect a grasshopper one of the girls was sick over her shoes and twelve sets of parents wrote in to complain. A combination of misery, boredom, and an article in The Times despairing over the lack of available men to take up professional roles made me have one last try. One evening (I'd very much like to believe it was a Tuesday) I applied for a position as an assistant at a medical research laboratory investigating the use and development of something called purine derivatives. For the first time ever, I simply identified myself as *R. Summers* without inserting any title at all.

R. Summers was invited to interview by return of post.

The following Saturday I dressed in my dullest skirt and jacket, wore my flattest shoes and thickest stockings, flattened my hair and didn't so much as powder my nose to be certain to be as non-distracting as possible. My efforts were entirely wasted. I don't believe I would have distracted my interviewer from his focus on the anti-metabolites of purines if I had arrived wearing nothing but my swimsuit.

It was wonderful.

Professor Theodore Roberts was wonderful.

Within moments we had plunged headlong into a discussion that sailed us straight through lunch and into the afternoon before we came up for air, and he asked without so much as taking a breath, 'Can you start on Monday?' Of course, I couldn't start the following Monday but the moment the school term finished, I raced out of that garden shed and locked the door behind me.

Although a science laboratory isn't for everyone, making different kinds of chemicals with life-changing potential was my kind of heaven. I could work ten hours a day for seven days a week and nobody thought of asking if I had to leave in time to cook my husband's dinner, or if I preferred Cary Grant over James Stewart or how to get grass stains out of cricket whites. Ruby the scientist might as easily have been Richard or Roderick and, as far as I know, the only times I distracted anyone were when we were waiting for a batch of results and I used to pace up and down the corridor. You see, I believed the answers to our questions were there, waiting for us in the ether. We just had to keep the faith and find them. One particular Tuesday – *that* particular Tuesday – we were waiting for a telephone call. Five sick children had been treated with a trial drug and at eleven o'clock we would be told the results. At ten fifty-five I began my pacing and a few laps later the office telephone rang. Stuffing my hands deep into the pockets of my labcoat I kept walking until I heard Theo say, 'Ruby?' His voice sounded different, his pitch strangled and slightly higher than normal. I stopped and straightened a picture on the wall. I can see the painting now, flowers in a vase, half of them brilliant with sunlight and half cast in shadow. 'How many?' I said. I meant how many children had the new drug helped, how many were out of hospital or at the very least still alive. The pause seemed to last minutes. I wiped my sleeve across the picture frame to clean away a film of dust.

'None of them,' he said at last.

'None of them?' I felt as if a wave was breaking over my head. I had been so optimistic, so confident we had found something of real potential. As my eyesight blurred, the colours of the flowers began to bleed into one another, rather like a messy box of paints.

All at once Theo was closer, his voice right in my ear. 'No, Ruby, you don't understand. None of them have died. None have relapsed. All the children – *all* of them – are growing fitter and stronger. It's still early days, but things are looking good. Better than good' – his voice burst like a firework – 'they're looking bloody brilliant!'

That was the best thing, Cassie. The best week, the best day, the best hour, the best minute. It was the same as winning a raffle, coming top in an examination and peace being declared all at the very same moment. I realised then, we would soon discover a medicine that could save lives, countless lives. Even if the drug we were testing needed to be tweaked, those results were proof our research, our hypotheses, were sound, and more than that I knew in that instant I was going to spend the rest of my life searching for more medicines, more answers and that I would find them. Until that moment I thought I would never be able to escape my shadows of guilt, never truly be free of what I had done in the war. In that moment I believed I might do so after all.

And so it has proved.

I shall stop here, Cassie. I think I've answered your question. Besides, my attention has been snared by the sight of a woman with thick, stockinged legs being helped into Beryl's chair. She has declined the offer of Beryl's blanket and is now raising her hand to me in greeting as a sailor might acknowledge a passing ship. I shall wave back, of course. Just as soon as I put down the pen. Although it feels too soon for somebody else to occupy Beryl's place, life always rolls on – swiftly and relentlessly and oblivious to our desire for an occasional pause. Besides, the newcomer is probably entirely unaware of the significance of her sitting spot and can hardly be blamed for hoping to make the acquaintance of the woman on the other side of the room. These days any kind of human interaction is as rare and precious as a blackbird's song.

Write soon, my dear New Best Friend. That sad and bitter letter you so badly want to send can wait another decade or so.

Ruby

Letter Cassie to Stuart

7 May 2020

Stuart

You want to know why I'm ignoring your calls? I shall tell you. But on my own terms in a letter. Where I have the space and time to express myself properly, and if that means you've had to wait for the explanation, well, I'm afraid I don't much care.

The reason, in a nutshell, is a policeman. A very nice policeman who looks about twelve and goes by the name of Alfie Lane (I suppose I should refer to him as PC Lane, only Alfie suits him so well it's hard to call him anything else). He visited the caravan about a week ago to tell me some locals had complained about Noah and me being there, and we needed to go home. That all seems to have died down now – when we ran into Alfie in town yesterday, he gave Noah a tiny metal torch with a light so strong I'm sure the beam could drill a hole. Although Alfie insisted the torch was a spare, I think it was his way of saying sorry. My point, however, is that when he came to the caravan, for about ten minutes, I honestly believed that Noah and I would have to leave. After

Alfie told us about the complaints, he couldn't look at either of us. He flicked his gaze from floor to ceiling as if the caravan was too hot for his eyes to rest in any one place and in that long silence, I had the strangest sensation, like I could practically see the next chunk of the future unravelling in front of me. As if Alfie had knocked a domino and set in chain a line of other dominos falling into each other, ping... ping... ping. There we were, Noah and I, after Alfie had gone, emptying out all the nooks and cupboards of the caravan, unpinning the photos of Ned and the Farmer's Monthly Task Sheet, tipping the sand out of our shoes, leaving the bucket and spade and the Cloud Collector's Handbook neatly on the table for Austin. Then would come the long drive back to London, Noah asleep in the back and the traffic thickening like cream. Eventually we would pull up outside the house in Barnsbury – *your* house in Barnsbury – which would look exactly as it did when we left; your racing bike double-chained to the fence, the black bin already on the pavement, the sign that says, 'Beware of the Dog', although there's not and never has been a dog. Noah would wake, shifting from zero to a hundred miles an hour in a split second. He would be out of the car and running up the path, while I would follow slowly, trying to carry too many bags at once and dropping socks and packets of tea into the flowerbed. Then abruptly the pictures stopped. As if a connection had broken or one of those old-fashioned film reels had jammed and the tape started to spill off the side. At this point Alfie Lane shifted uncomfortably. He *was* looking at me now, staring really. As if he was worried, I might be about to shout at him or worse, start crying. In fact, I was still in Barnsbury, trying to make myself close the front door behind me and call out to you, but the images had become blurry and seemed a very long distance away.

All at once I knew why.

I didn't want to see this bit of the future. Not the part that involved you. I didn't want to know what it told me: that my unexpected arrival wouldn't be good news, that you wouldn't be pleased to see me. Now I *could* see you uncurling from the sofa, putting down your gin and tonic with a tiny but noticeable hesitation as if you actually had to think about whether it was worth pausing your drink to give me a hug. I could see in your expression a suppressed sort of panic. I could feel your lips press briefly on mine (surprisingly briefly) and the notion struck me like a brick falling into my lap that all the times you claim to have been with Trevor you were plainly not with *Trevor* at all. I remembered you saying all Trevor wanted to talk about were the articles he'd read in *The Dentist*, that he always had an excuse for not doing his share of overtime and how you almost came to blows over the last of the coleslaw at a barbecue last summer. *Of course*, you haven't suddenly become best mates. Lockdown has made us lonely, but not lonely enough to want to hang out with someone whose idea of fun is discussing root canals.

Who is she, Stu? The pretty dental nurse who only left school last year and was all over you at the Christmas party? A middle-aged mum who fancied a bit more than a cosmetic whitener? You know what, Stu. Don't bother to tell me because I honestly don't care.

Cassie

Postcard Mr Stanley Ross to Cassie

Postmarked 25 April 2020 received 7 May 2020

Voila, a picture of three ruins! Mayan ones, not your old dad (haha)! Hope the caravan is holding up better than my little camper van. Rain here makes the English version seem like drizzle for softies and turns out my roof has a couple of weak spots. Poor old Penelope Anne was sleeping right under the leak and got woken up at 2am by what she thought was a hose in her face! She's booked herself a hotel for tonight, but I'm confident she'll soon see the funny side and be back in the van. Life is like that: sometimes rain, sometimes sun, but once you've got the taste for adventure there's no going back. Besides, we can't hang around – next stop the Great Pyramid of Cholula!

As the Peruvian proverb says, *Little by little, one walks far...*

Love

Dad (& PA in absentia)

Letter Cassie to Ruby

8 May 2020

Dear New Best Friend

I'm sorry to hear about Beryl. I sat for a moment and imagined what it must have been like to realise her chair was empty, and then see someone else sitting there so soon after you heard she had died. I felt empty too – though not nearly as empty as you must have done. I'm also very curious and incredibly impressed. What medicine did you discover?

By the way, your advice was too late. I'd already sent my

sad and bitter letter yesterday. And guess what? It turns out that I don't feel sad or even particularly bitter.

I feel free.

Cassie

Letter Mrs Rosemary Ross to Cassie

8 May 2020

Dear Cassandra

Don't be cross. Or worried. And for heaven's sake please don't fuss, but I think your Aunty Dora and I have contracted this bloody virus. Goodness knows how because the only place we've been in living memory is the supermarket and we spray our hands and faces with my little bottle of sanitiser every time we get in and out of the car. Despite all our precautions, Dora started coughing three days ago and has barely stopped since. This morning I joined the chorus. Apart from sounding like I have a hairdryer in my throat, my only other symptom has been fatigue. I can't remember ever having felt as tired, not even when you were a baby and only slept when you were bored of gazing at the world through those earnest blue eyes (which wasn't terribly often). Although it's four o'clock in the afternoon I'm writing to you in bed, and I've already had to put the pen down twice to have a rest. If I manage to finish *and* walk downstairs, I'll leave the letter on the doorstep. Arthur from three doors down is dropping off some groceries and I'm sure he'll go to the post for me – the man can always wear a glove if he's worried about germs on the envelope. Now, for heaven's sake, don't call. One of us is bound to be asleep and by the time we locate the phone, you'll probably have hung up and be ready to dispatch an ambulance. And to be honest, Cassie, I haven't got the energy for conversation. What I *would* like is a letter from you in reply. One I can read at my leisure as many times as I like. I seem to remember asking you about Austin, and I don't believe you've told me very much. A nice long reply explaining *exactly* who that man is would be perfect.

Lots of love

Mum

PS I repeat: DON'T WORRY. By the time you're reading this Dora and I are bound to be through the worst of it.

PPS Yesterday, I had the strangest postcard from Penelope Anne. On the front was a photograph of a Mexican hotel with seven swimming pools and a kids club – not your father's scene at all, however deserted the place might be at the moment. On the back all she wrote was, 'I made the wrong choice!' What does that mean? Is she talking about hotels or your father? Or begonias? And why did she send it to me? Being in the same gardening club is hardly a reason to contact your boyfriend's ex-wife. The letters were so big and loopy, I can only think she'd been drinking and meant to write to someone else altogether.

Letter Cassie to Mrs Rosemary Ross

10 May 2020

Dear Mum

Of course, I worry about you having Covid. Both you and Dora ill and not a text or phone call to let me know! By the time I got your letter, you could have been feeling wretched, and without being macabre or melodramatic the situation might have been even worse than that. The only reason I know you're actually getting better is because I tracked down Arthur's phone number and he told me you were well enough this morning to shout down your grocery order from the bedroom window. Since he said you asked for steaks and a bottle of Merlot, I reckon you must be on the mend – unless Aunt Dora's cat is living the life of Riley.

Austin then.... I'm not sure what there is to say because I've actually never met him. I booked the caravan on Airbnb back in February, when I was looking for somewhere to take Noah as a treat for finishing his treatment. Once the lock-down happened, I assumed the booking would be cancelled. Instead, after I explained Noah's situation on the phone, Austin went quiet and after about a minute of silence told me he would leave the key where we'd agreed and leave it to me to decide whether to come to Norfolk or not.

I used to imagine him about sixty years old and (for some inexplicable reason) with a white handlebar moustache. However, he must be younger than that because he has a nephew and niece who are Noah's age so I've also stopped visualising the moustache (most of the time, anyway). Initially I mistook his steadiness for slowness and imagined that only someone about to start drawing a pension could like living in the countryside or find lambs and clouds and fields more than momentarily appealing. However, now that I'm beginning to love being here too, I've realised Austin's steadiness is nothing to do with age and all to do with being happy with what he has. Although he lives on his own (apart from Badger and

Ned – sorry, that's a dog and a lamb) he never complains and whenever he writes about his farm the page glows with a quiet sort of contentment. I imagine his perfect day out would probably be an afternoon on a grassy spot that's high enough to have a view of the coastline, a rug dappled with sunlight, a cooler of beers and a picnic of bread, ham, and strawberries. Did I tell you he brought a bucket and spade over to the caravan for Noah to use? I would have seen him – at least from a distance – but Noah and I were out shell hunting. He's also given Noah photos of Ned, who Austin had to rear by hand because his mother rejected him (Ned, that is, not Austin), lots of information about crop rotation, and picture of farm machines that Noah finds enthralling. The last thing he sent us was a book called the Cloud Collector's Handbook, which Noah and I wrestle over every morning before we rush out to examine the sky. Writing this, I've just realised I've never given Austin anything in return. I did offer him free haircuts for life, however that was a bribe for not taking Ned to the slaughterhouse and probably doesn't count. (I don't actually believe Austin would have done any such thing, but I wanted to be one hundred per cent sure.)

I'd better stop now and check Noah is really doing his maths homework. He's positioned the textbook suspiciously upright on the table and I suspect the Cloud Collector's Handbook or the Farmer's Monthly Planner is tucked on the inside.

Make sure you rest, Mum. Don't do too much too soon or else the virus could return like Jaws and bite you on the bottom.

Love

Cassie

PS I nearly forgot – Penelope Anne! 'I made the wrong choice'?!? Maybe Dad is the problem and not the leaky camper van. Perhaps she'd rather be having adventures with you!

PPS Areas you need to sanitise: your hands, your phone, the shopping trolley, the car door handle and possibly the steering wheel. Areas you DON'T need to sanitise: YOUR FACE (doesn't the stuff get into your mouth and taste awful?)

Letter Austin to Cassie

10 May 2020

Dear Cassie

Although your comment about my letters being like lights made me happy, it also made writing this one difficult because everything I started to say didn't seem nearly good enough to make you want to keep reading, let alone to brighten your day. In the end I decided to tell you what I did yesterday. Most people wouldn't be interested, and you probably won't be either, but I may as well be honest about the things that are important to me because I can't pretend to be someone I'm not, even if that means you find this letter (and me) dull and a bit of a disappointment.

Yesterday I made a pond.

It would be better to say, I rediscovered a pond. An old pond, a ghost pond, one that has been hidden underneath a field for nearly sixty years. I knew about the pond, and several more like them, because of an old Ordnance Survey map of the farm my dad kept in a drawer. Despite the date on the map being 1884 the person who did the drawing must have known a thing or two about map-making, because everything is correct and marked very carefully. Most of the landmarks are the same: the big flint barn on the brow of the meadow, the river that runs through a bed of rushes on the east boundary and the ruins of a chapel so old the dark inside is squashed with memories thick as water. Holding the map is a strange feeling, suddenly a hundred and forty years seems very short indeed and the time I shall be around to farm the land even shorter. One thing that has changed though, are the ponds which have been filled in to make the growing area bigger. You can work out where they were because the ground has sunk to make pond-shaped depressions and the seeds of all the plants that used to grow in the water are still there, waiting patiently for the chance to come to life. To peel back the years all you have to do is remove the soil dumped on top of the pond and find the layer of sediment containing the seeds.

That was how I spent yesterday.

In the digger, scooping up dirt from a pond-shaped dip in the corner of the sheep field with Badger beside me keeping a close eye on the sheep. I'd send you a photograph, only you'd take one look at the great big pit and mounds of mud and think I was a madman. Soon though, the hole will fill from rain and groundwater and as the seeds feel light and warmth on them for the first time in fifty years they'll think 'here we go' and in less than two years all sorts of plants will spring into life. Listen to the names, Cassie: Ragged Robin, Frogbit and Water Soldiers, Marsh Marigolds – which the dragonflies like – and Hornwort for the tadpoles. I shall have to move the sheep into a different field, otherwise, being sheep, they'll fall straight into the water, but it's a small price for bringing back a bit of the past.

That's all the news I have. I expect you're relieved there's no more talk about ponds, even if you've managed to read this far. Tell Noah this morning I saw the formation called Castellanus. He'll know what kind of cloud that is and what it means.

Austin

PS The government has said that later this week we can meet up with another person to exercise outside. Badger is desperate for a run on the beach. Would you like to join us and go for a walk? I could come over on Sunday.

Letter Mrs Rosemary Ross to Cassie

11 May 2020

Dear Cassandra

What a shame you weren't able to tell me more about Austin. I can see you hardly know him at all.

Dora and I are continuing to mend. Unfortunately, we couldn't taste the steaks, however the Merlot went down a treat and I've asked Arthur to pick us up a vindaloo tonight. That should give our Covid-impaired taste buds a run for their money.

Love

Mum

PS Of course I know how to use sanitiser. I was merely being figurative. (Though it does indeed taste awful. I once made the mistake of licking my finger after spraying my hands.)

PPS Your comment about Penelope Anne is ridiculous and doesn't deserve a response.

Letter Cassie to Austin

11 May 2020

Austin

Your letter wasn't dull at all. Dragonflies and Hornwort sound like characters in Harry Potter. I'm already visualising a zoo of tiny magical beasts in their own little oasis, only I doubt the water in the pond will be quite the same shade of brilliant blue as I imagine.

I would very much like to meet for a walk on Sunday. What time suits you best? I'll be the one in the bright green caravan with very short hair and a small boy by my side staring at the clouds.

Cassie

PS What *do* Castellanus clouds signify?

Letter Austin to Cassie

12 May 2020

Dear Cassie

An oasis for tiny magical beasts is by far the best description of a pond I've ever heard. Would eleven o'clock on Sunday suit you?

Austin

PS Castellanus is a sign the weather's about to change.

Letter Cassie to Austin

13 May 2020

It's a date!

Letter Cassie to Austin

13 May 2020

Dear Austin

I didn't mean a *date*, date. I must be over-excited about the prospect of an actual social engagement.

Yours sincerely

Cassie

Letter Stuart to Cassie

13 May 2020

Dear Cass

I've never been much good with words, but I want you to know I'm sitting alone at the kitchen table with a bottle of whisky trying to find a way to tell you how sorry I am. You're right. There has been somebody else. But only for a while, and only because you were so preoccupied with Noah. Honestly, Cass, this business with Noah was grim for me too. Even when you came back from the hospital, you weren't really there. Noah was all you ever talked about; all you could think about. Sex was out of the question. Most days *dinner* was out of the question. The fridge stayed empty and you never bothered to wash your hair or wore anything other than joggers. It was lonely, Cass, to be honest. Noah isn't mine, remember, so it's not really surprising I felt left-out and neglected, is it? I would have finished with *her*. I *did* finish with her, but then you disappeared to the back of beyond and I was on my own again. Properly, on my own. I couldn't even meet friends at the pub or go to the footy. That's not normal, is it? I just needed someone to be close to, to fill the gap while you weren't there. But it's over now, Cass, really over. I've decided I only want you and I promise I'll make it up to you. As soon as this bloody pandemic is over, I'll take us all on holiday somewhere you could never afford yourself. A resort with a swim-up bar and a twenty-four-hour kids club for Noah. You can strut about all day in a bikini and at night we'll make up for lost time.

Love ?

Stuart

Letter Cassie to Stuart

14 May 2020

Dear Stuart

Thank you for your letter. It made everything so much clearer.

Goodbye

Cassie

Letter Mandy to Cassie

14 May 2020

Hey Cass,

Stuart tells me you've got into letter writing so I thought I'd write you one myself. Besides, if I put 'sorry I slept with your boyfriend' in a WhatsApp, I'd see the exact moment you read the message, which would feel really weird even though I'm guessing Stuart has told you about us already.

I'm sorry.

I never meant for anything to happen, but while you were in hospital, I started dropping meals in for him and then one evening, when Ben was out, Stuart asked if I wanted to eat with him. We had a couple of bottles of wine, and one thing led to another. You know how these things happen... It was only supposed to be that one time, but you kept being away and Ben was busy too – to be honest, the two of you kind of pushed Stuart and me together so much we hardly had any choice. Of course, we never planned to carry on after Noah came out of hospital, yet somehow the opportunities kept presenting themselves. I even convinced myself I was doing you a favour by keeping Stuart *occupied* (if you know what I mean). When you asked me on Bonfire Night if I was having an affair, I couldn't believe it. I'd never thought of Stuart and me as having an actual affair. It was just sex, a bit of fun, while you were so engrossed with Noah. After that conversation, I felt awful for a while – even though you had no idea the guy was Stuart. We did stop then. I told him the sex wasn't worth the guilt trip. Ben was still suspicious, though. He must have realised something was up and then you went and told him I'd cheated on him! Although I was furious, I was also kind of relieved – I had the perfect excuse not to speak to you, and when Stuart invited me over after you went to Norfolk... well to be honest, Cass, I no longer felt guilty saying yes.

We're finished now, me and Stuart. Stuart says he wants to be with you. You won't want advice from me, nevertheless I'm going to give you some anyway. As if we were still friends. As if we were sitting in the White Hart. Don't take him back. You can do better than Stuart, Cass. At least I feel bad about what happened. The only time Stuart feels bad is when he doesn't get what he wants. Perhaps one day we really will laugh about it all over a bottle of Chardonnay. I hope so.

Love

Mandy

Letter Cassie to Mandy

16 May 2020

Dear Mandy

Thank you for your letter. It made everything so much clearer.

Goodbye

Cassie

Letter Stuart to Cassie

16 May 2020

Cass,

What do you mean *goodbye*? You obviously haven't understood a thing I've said and since you seem to have blocked my number I'm going to come and explain in person. We're now allowed to meet somebody else and I don't bloody care how far Norfolk is from London or what the Sunday traffic is like. This is an emergency.

Stuart

PS Don't try and stop me. By the time you open this letter, I'll be there already.

Letter Ruby to Cassie

17 May 2020

Dear Cassie

Rita, the new recruit, has arrived in Beryl's chair and we have just completed our little ritual of hand-waves and nods. Although Rita is most amenable with me, I get the impression she can be quite demanding with our carers. The curtains on that side of the room have been tweaked to keep out the sun, the radio is a notch or two quieter and yesterday I'm almost certain she rejected her supper of cottage pie. Having taken away the tray, Amy returned a few minutes later with an entirely different plate and for once she wasn't smiling at all.

So, my dear friend, you asked what medicine I discovered. First, I must stress the discovery wasn't only mine. I was merely one musician, blowing my trumpet as loudly and as bravely as I could, but it was only by playing as part of an orchestra that any of us could make music worth listening to. Together what we discovered was a drug, a compound able to treat acute childhood Leukaemia. Although our initial invention succeeded in stopping the cancer cells from replicating, it took time and patience to find a better drug, one that prevented the children from relapsing, and when we succeeded, the results were better than we had ever dared to dream. I've already told you about the day we received the news of those trials. The Tuesday that became a golden torch. The morning that shone forwards into the future and let me finally leave the past behind. From that moment onwards I woke every morning making the decision to love my life.

And I have done.

I'm enclosing the final tranche of my letters. After you've read them, I'll happily answer all of your questions. If, that is, you still want to write to me.

Love

Your New Best Friend

Ruby

PS I expect you're wondering if it's a coincidence Noah was ill with Acute Lymphoblastic Leukaemia. It isn't. I have to confess I knew all about Noah before you and I exchanged a single word.

PART SIX

Diary of Miss Ruby Summers

19 June 1940

Dear Diary

It was quiet today. The proverbial quiet before a storm. Or the stillness they say exists in the absolute centre of a whirlwind. At supper Mother and Father barely spoke at all, though I had the strong sense they had said an awful lot to each other before I sat down.

The one bright spark is we have been notified George will be discharged this weekend. Mother sounded less excited than I expected when she told me. She must still have been upset by Uncle Charles's visit. Apparently, George is in a London hospital called Moorfields. His injury is still a bit of a mystery as Mother said she had only been able to speak to someone in an office who didn't know a great deal. Father is going to collect George by car, even if it means using a whole month's worth of petrol coupons and we can't travel anywhere else for weeks. I'm trying very hard not to think about Edmondo or the pipe-cleaner man and to focus on looking forward to having my brother home again. We'll be able to read together and play cricket in the garden. As long as we don't listen to the news, it will almost be like things were before he went to university.

Letter Uncle Charles to Ruby

19 June 1940

My highly intelligent goddaughter

You must forgive my terrible manners. When I saw you yesterday my attention was so focused on the errant Brambillas I entirely neglected to ask how your studies are progressing. I imagine Latin is not the easiest subject to teach oneself, however comprehensive the available textbooks. As it happens, I know a young chap with a rather delicate state of health but an exceptionally strong grasp of the Classics. Since he was found unfit for the armed forces, he has moved to your part of the world in the hope the country air – when not spoiled by the prevalence of Messer-schmitts – will do him good. I am confi-dent he would be happy to give you lessons and similarly optimistic of persuading your parents to allow him to do so.

Assuming the idea of spending more time in the company of Latin grammar does not appal, I will make enquiries the moment my schedule permits.

Yours affectionately

Uncle Charles

PS If anything should come to mind as regards the whereabouts of the Brambillas, please let me know at once. In the heat of last Sunday's encounter information that might otherwise be at your fingertips may possibly have slipped your memory. It probably goes without saying that the sooner we find the Brambillas, the sooner I'll have time for matters such as Latin tutors.

Letter Mary Cartwright to Ruby

20 June 1940

Dear Ruby

I was very much hoping to see you at Ms Hodgkin's address on Tuesday afternoon. I hope the explanation for your absence is a dull one rather than a waning of your interest in Girton (or, heaven forbid, the sciences in general) being the cause. Trusting the former to be the case, I'm enclosing a copy of Ms

Hodgkin's paper for you to read at your leisure. I'm afraid without her marvellous explanations the essay might seem a little dry but I can assure you the presentation was every bit as exciting as a murder mystery. The level of attention in the room was palpable. All of us could feel the energy crackling about the lecture hall like the current from an electric generator, a remarkable sensation and worthy of a thesis all of its own.

Anyway, I must return to the demands of my own research. If you should be visiting Cambridge in the near future do make certain to let me know as I may be able to arrange afternoon tea in Girton. I'm certain Ms Wodehouse would be amenable to the idea; she appears to assume it's only a matter of time before you become a member of the college yourself.

Yours in friendship

Mary

Diary of Miss Ruby Summers

20 June 1940

Dear Diary

First there was the stick of the drawing room interrogation. Now Uncle Charles has sent me a big, fat, orange carrot in the form of a Latin tutor. Does he really believe I'm such a child that either one of them will make me do something I believe to be wrong? My own conscience is more persuasive than that. The problem is it persuades me of different outcomes depending on the hour. At midnight I'm certain I must protect Edmondo. By three in the morning Edmondo's father is in cahoots with Mussolini, while I am a traitor to my country. Yet by sunrise the Brambillas are innocent once more, I am exhausted, and the only person I want to talk with is the one person I may never see again.

Diary of Miss Ruby Summers

21 June 1940

Dear Diary

Could life get any more agonising? It's like standing on a floor that tile by tile, board by board, is being painted. Already I am cowering in the corner backed against the wall and soon – unless I learn to fly – there will be nowhere to go at all.

I overheard Mother and Father this evening. They were talking in the kitchen. I was halfway down the stairs when their half-hushed, urgent tones stopped me in my tracks.

'We should tell her.' That was my mother's voice. 'She ought to be made aware of what the police found.'

'She said she didn't know where the Brambillas had gone.'

'I know she did, but…' As my mother wrestled with her reluctance to think I might have lied to them, I grew so still my stillness seemed to be drawing me inwards, like a steel winch making me smaller and smaller.

My father didn't reply. There was the chink of crockery, the rough slide of the kitchen cabinets. It sounded as if my parents were drying up cooking utensils and putting them away.

Eventually my mother said, 'Are the police quite certain the Brambillas had a radio?'

'Charles said they believed the knob came from a radio set but they couldn't be entirely–'

'What's happened?' I seemed to have come unstuck and made my way down the stairs without even realising.

Mother folded a tea-towel onto the kitchen table. 'When the police searched the Brambillas' house they found a radio set in the wardrobe.'

'They found a wooden knob which they believe *may* have been part of a radio set.' My father gave her a sharp look. 'We mustn't exaggerate.'

I bit my bottom lip. 'Even if the knob did come from a radio set, that doesn't prove anything.'

'The Brambillas were not supposed to have a radio set,' my mother said. 'The government ordered all the Italians to hand their radios in to a police station weeks ago.'

'The radio might have been to speak with friends in Italy or to hear the Italian news. Wanting to have one doesn't mean they were helping Mussolini.'

'They have also disappeared, Ruby.' Father's tone seemed sad rather than angry. 'And without even a photograph of Mr Brambilla to pass between the police the chances of finding them to ask about the radio are very slim indeed.'

Mother gazed at me steadily. Seconds seem to pass. Minutes. A whole ocean of time. Then she said, 'What do you know, Ruby? Tell us what you know!'

'I've already told you. I don't know anything!'

I pivoted so quickly the linoleum squeaked under my heel and I ran from the kitchen. Upstairs I sat on my bed and waited for my parents to burst into my room and insist I hand over Edmondo's address. I even put my hands over my ears as if not hearing their questions would enable me to keep him safe a little longer. Nothing happened. At some point I opened my bedroom door and listened. I could hear Mother laying the table, music coming from the gramophone.

A short while later came the call supper was ready. Although I had no appetite, I made myself chew and swallow mouthful after mouthful of stew, hardly daring to lift my gaze. Mother and Father talked over my bent head as if the scene in the kitchen had never happened. I listened to them discussing the news, the awful fighting in Europe, the shortage of sugar, of tea – of most things in fact – the Allied losses at sea and the prospect of an imminent invasion, and I felt as if every sentence, every unhappy sentiment, was pushing me further and further away from them.

Letter Edmondo to Ruby

21 June 1940

Mia cara

Your letter was like the comforting beacon of a lighthouse.

Although we're safe and well for the moment, I don't know how much longer that can continue. My father is becoming increasingly anxious the authorities will discover our whereabouts and now my mother doesn't even dare visit the shops. Instead, when the larder is empty, my father disappears late in the evening and by the following morning we have enough provisions to prevent us from starving. If Fragolina or I dare to ask where the groceries came from, we're simply met with silence or the briefest shake of the head.

My father tells me all Italian men are being interned and that those suspected of belonging to the *fascio* are given the status 'category A', which means they face deportation as far away as Canada. I asked how this could possibly concern us, when the police have no reason to suspect my father of any such affiliations. He told me the problem is the thin, rather pale musician you met on our trip to the seaside. To my father's astonishment, this man turns out to be a supporter of Mussolini and my father is worried the police will suppose he and the musician are friends and assume bad things about my father too. Yet this so-called fascist friend doesn't even know where we lived! I only ever saw them together at the boarding house in Felixstowe where they merely enjoyed playing music and sharing a bottle of Disaronno. I can't believe my father was even aware of this man's political views or he would have terminated their association immediately.

Enough of sad things! There's one piece of good news. I've adopted a dog – or I should rather say I've been adopted *by* a dog. He's small and white and appeared in the garden one afternoon when I was reading. Judging by his ravenous appetite and filthy coat, I suspect he was abandoned by his previous owner. In any case, he shows no desire to leave. Every morning he's waiting for me on the kitchen step to spend the day chasing his tail or sleeping at my feet. Since he has no collar, I need to find a name for him myself.

Perhaps I should let you name him? Then whenever I call him, I'll hear your voice, see your eyes flame with laughter and your hair fall forward in a dark rush of water as you lean down to stroke his back.

Write again to me soon. Our letters are all that are keeping me sane.

I love you

Edmondo

PS I'm enclosing a very bad drawing of the dog! The way his head tilts to one side is how he always looks at me, as if a game is just about to start.

PPS You mentioned the police said they had found part of a wireless set on the floor of my parent's wardrobe. That must be a mistake. Our radio was kept in the kitchen and I know my father handed it in when we were ordered to do so because I accompanied him to the police station.

Diary of Miss Ruby Summers

22 June 1940

Dear Diary

I received a letter from Edmondo today and I haven't been able to sit still since. Edmondo believes the pipe-cleaner man hardly knows his father and has never been to their house when I'm quite certain the man was in their sitting room on the day of the birthday lunch talking to Edmondo's father. However often I tell myself that tall thin person may have been someone else, I know in my bones it was him. Another horrible problem is Edmondo seems to think that the only radio his parents had was one that he and his father handed in to the police, which means the wireless I saw inside the wardrobe must have been a second set that even he was unaware of.

What does this mean? I refuse to believe Edmondo's father supports Mussolini and wants to help Hitler to invade England. There simply has to be a perfectly innocent explanation – if only I could think of one.

Diary of Miss Ruby Summers

23 June 1940

Dear Diary

George came home today. I baked a cake, an insipid, rather leathery sponge with powdered egg, and made a banner from squares of paper – a coloured letter on each one – to drape across the hallway. The message spelled 'Welcome home, George!' Although rather childish, I thought the gesture might at least raise a smile and make his return feel like a proper celebration.

As it turns out my efforts were entirely pointless. The words could just have easily read 'no supper tonight', 'Hitler stinks' or 'I hate Latin' and it would have made no difference at all.

That's because George is blind.

George is blind.

George is blind.

George is blind.

If I keep putting the words down on paper perhaps the repetition will lessen the shock and make the awfulness more bearable. More bearable for me, I mean. How can such a catastrophe ever be more bearable for George? My clever, handsome, sweet, funny brother – who wanted to be a doctor – can no longer see anything out of his right eye and only the vaguest, murkiest shadows in his left, so I imagine it would take more than keeping a diary to help him to feel better. Even if he could write one, which of course he can't…

I stood at my bedroom window for nearly an hour, waiting for my parents to come home from the hospital. At last the Crossley turned into the driveway and with the June sunshine bouncing off the roof an unfamiliar sensation of excitement and anticipation bubbled in my throat. As soon as the car came to a halt, I expected the passenger door to fly open and George to come bounding into the house just as he used to do when he came back from Oxford. However, for a minute or two nobody seemed to move. Finally, Mother alighted from the back and as George climbed out of the front seat, she wrapped her arm around his waist in a way that seemed oddly practical rather than affectionate. They stood together in a stiff pocket of stillness before Father walked around to the boot and along with a battered kitbag, extracted a white walking stick which he placed into George's right hand. Even then my brain refused to process the different elements of the scene. Like separate puddles of oil and water none of the clues came together until the moment George tripped on the front step and nearly lost his balance, despite Mother's arm. Then as the door opened and I heard them all come into the hall the truth hit me with the force of a freight train.

I'm thoroughly ashamed to say my first thought was to hide away. To jump into bed and pretend I never saw them arrive, simply to have a few more minutes before I had to engage with the awfulness of the situation and George's pain and my parents' sadness became my pain and sadness too. Yet I knew the most important thing, the only thing, I should do was go downstairs immediately. At the top of the steps, I hesitated again. George was barely moving, tapping the wretched stick against the walls and across the black and white tiled floor before inching another foot forwards. His face was grotesquely visible too. All of the skin from the top of his forehead to the midpoint of his cheeks had a red, boiled looked to it, as if someone had painted half of his head as a practical joke.

All at once, something burst inside my chest. Without another thought I found myself flying down the stairs.

'George,' I cried, 'I'm so happy you're home!' I pressed myself against his chest and heard the clatter and roll of the stick falling to the floor as he wrapped his arms around me.

Much later, we had dinner. Mother had cooked steak and kidney pudding, probably because suet and the few pieces of meat didn't require any cutting up and could be eaten with a fork. All the same, she positioned herself close to George, pushing either his water glass or the salt pot into his hand whenever he groped across the table. Although George didn't say anything, I could tell how frustrated he was. I think he would rather have managed himself, even if it meant spilling his drink a few times and going without salt. Nobody knew what to speak about anyway. There was nothing to say, other than to ask George questions which he plainly didn't want to answer, or murmur how awful it must be for him (which would hardly have made him feel better), or take the other approach and say how lucky he was to be alive (in which case I would have forgiven him for throwing the salt pot across the room). As it was, we mumbled our way through the meal, in a clumsy mix of silence and half-sentences, with nobody eating much at all.

As soon as Mother began to clear the plates, George pushed back his chair. 'I'm going up to my room.'

Straight away Mother put the plates back down on the table. 'I'll give you a hand up the stairs, darling…'

'No.'

'Ruby then.' She sounded almost desperate. 'You don't mind helping your brother, do you dear?'

I shook my head before realising my mistake. 'Of course I don't mind,' I said instead. However, the words were rushed and unnecessarily loud.

'Sit down, Ruby.' The bitter voice sounded like that of a stranger speaking. 'I shall have to spend the rest of my life this way so the sooner I get used to it the better.' As George stood up, he knocked the edge of the table sending the crockery and glasses into spasms. Impatiently, he fumbled for the white stick hanging over the back of his chair before banging his way out of the dining room. Less than a minute later there was another crash, followed by an angry expletive.

Immediately Mother leapt for the door, but Father stopped her. 'Leave him be.

We have to trust him to tell us when he wants our help. George is right. He's got to learn to manage for the rest of his life.' He looked at her steadily. 'And we have to learn to let him.'

Silence descended, one that still rang with the clatters and bangs of George's departure. Father went to the sideboard and poured two large whiskies. Although Mother hardly ever drank, she finished the one Father gave her in three quick gulps, rubbed a hand across her cheek before gesturing at the plates. 'Bring these into the kitchen, for me please, Ruby. We'll let George settle in upstairs while we do the washing up.'

For a moment I couldn't seem to move. Then I gathered up the dirty crockery and did my best imitation of an ordinary evening. Not that ordinary exists anymore.

Diary of Miss Ruby Summers

24 June 1940

It's five past four in the morning, the start of another day, though still less than twenty-four hours since George came home which for now is the only measure of time that counts. I'm sitting on the window ledge in my bedroom. Although the sill is too narrow and cold to be comfortable, I'm watching the first cracks of light lift the edge of the sky like a drape pulling back to reveal a shiny new present. Today, I'm concentrating hard on each colour of the dawn and trying to appreciate every different shade of blue and gold. Since George can't see them for himself, I need to do the looking for both of us – even though this morning it's hard to believe there's anything good and beautiful left in the world, however magnificent the sky might be.

I woke up at about one o'clock, thinking I needed to use the lavatory. However, the moment I crept onto the landing, I became aware of a ragged, choking noise that seemed to be coming from George's room. As soon as I knocked, the sound stopped. Nevertheless, I eased open the door. A haze of smoke and nicotine hung in the air like muslin while moonlight spilled between the curtains, illuminating the floorboards scattered with trousers, a shirt and a pullover and the white stick nesting among them. George was perched on the edge of the bed, elbows on knees and the heels of his hands pressed into his eye sockets.

After a moment he lifted his head. 'Who's there?'

'It's me, Ruby.'

I picked my way over the clothes and half-pulled the curtains shut before sitting next to George. Without so much moonlight I could only see the vaguest shadow of his outline, but I was more aware of his presence than ever, the warmth of his arm against mine, the cotton-soap smell of his pyjamas and the rise and fall of his chest that caught, every so often, on a snag of emotion and tripped as if over a paving stone. I don't know how long we stayed like that – it seemed like hours but also no time at all. For the first few minutes I tried to come up with something comforting to say but however hard I concentrated I couldn't think of anything that might help so in the end I just kept still and waited.

At last, a calmness seemed to come over him. He sat up. 'Where's my kitbag?'

I groped for the handle and dragged the heavy canvas towards us. George extracted a packet of Woodbines from a side pocket together with a box of matches. Wordlessly, he held them out to me. I went to the window to strike a light before passing the cigarette back to George. My wrist was shaking as I did so, making the flame jump all over the place, but to my surprise George's hand was steady.

After a moment he said, almost conversationally, 'Frank didn't make it back.'

'Back from Dunkirk?'

George took two long drags on the cigarette and the tip glowed a deeper orange. 'Conditions were terrible, Ruby. Worse than anything you could possibly imagine. I may not be able to see you or my own bedroom, but I can still see the sand dunes full of men, the soldiers queuing into the sea.' He paused. 'I should probably start at the beginning, when we arrived at Dunkirk, if you want to hear the full story?'

I couldn't reply because my heart was beating too wildly, however it didn't seem to matter. George had acquired the odd, detached air of a newsreader reading out a bulletin. He leaned forward to knock ash onto the floor before turning to look at me directly with his new, empty gaze.

'The closer we got to Dunkirk, the worse the devastation. The roads were full of shattered buildings, corpses sticking out of rubble and lying in the dirt and a smell so bad we ripped off the ends of our shirts so we could cover our faces with pieces of fabric. Slowly we picked our way over the debris and made it to the seafront. The beaches were crammed with soldiers. Thousands of them, waiting. Praying for a miracle. To our west all we could see were plumes of black smoke billowing from burning oil tanks while the water was awash with bodies and the wreckage of small boats. No sooner had we arrived than we heard aircraft. Enemy planes, flying low to shoot us with machine guns. The noise was terrible, like a rainstorm on a tin roof that seemed to be happening on the inside of my head. Everyone dived into the sand, scrabbling desperately with their own hands to dig themselves under cover. Frank and I ran towards the dunes and tried to bury ourselves there, hoping the ridge would provide some shelter. Eventually, the planes flew away and instead of bullets the air was rent with men crying, screams for help and dreadful, pitiful whimpers.'

George paused and sucked on his cigarette. Although I longed to tell him to stop, that I couldn't bear to hear any more, I knew I had to listen. Even if I might never see the world the same way again, I owed it to him to have the courage to hear the truth. Besides, my tongue was so clamped to the roof of my mouth and my mind in such a state of shock I felt practically struck dumb.

'The attacks carried on for the rest of the day,' George said at last. 'Twice Frank and I ran into the sea but too many men were already waiting in the water for us to stand a chance of being picked up by a boat so we decided to find another way. Towards dusk, we spotted a small steamer heading towards a jetty. Although the landing stage was on fire and broken, we decided to take our chances. At one point we had to climb into the sea and swim between the bombed-out gaps, swinging from the girders like gibbons, until we managed to clamber onto the part still standing. Eventually we reached the end of the pier and willing arms tugged our water-logged jackets to pull us aboard. That should have been it, Ruby. That should have been us, safe. Only it wasn't.' George grasped hold of the bed, as if the frame had started to shake. 'Seconds later the Germans came back. A Messer-schmidt dived at us low and fast, aiming for the steamer. There was a tremendous roar, and a flash of yellow, like an exploding sun – it was the last thing I ever saw, that sun, and the last thing I remember until I woke up in hospital with my face covered in bandages and Frank… and Frank not there.'

He stopped. Leaning forward, he ground out the cigarette on a saucer beside his foot with an ease that made me think he had carried out the same gesture many times already. The silence seemed still to be absorbing his words, as if the meaning of them needed time to catch up with their sound.

After a few moments he fumbled for my

forearm. 'Right, I'm going to sleep now.' His voice had the same strange, mechanical pitch but then his grip on my arm suddenly tightened and he shouted in my ear, 'We need to win! We need to win this bloody war! The Hun are bastards, Ruby, utter bastards. We have to stop them taking our country too.' A second later he lay down, pulled up the bedcovers, and in less than a minute his breathing acquired a heavy, regular rhythm.

I started to shiver and soon I found I was shivering so hard the bed was actually shaking. In the end I must have stood up and made my way back to my own room, because that's where I am now, crouched on the windowsill, my diary propped against my knees and the weight of the most awful decision of my life pressing on my shoulders.

Letter Uncle Charles to Ruby

25 June 1940

My dear Ruby

You wrote to ask me what is happening to those Italians the government decide fall into category A. To be frank, my dear, many are being deported. We can hardly allow fascists to remain living amongst us when they would happily take up arms to support Mr Hitler the very moment that he should set foot on English soil. Nevertheless, I understand the government has decided to send abroad those whom they believe to be our enemy only once they've had an opportunity to state their case before a tribunal. In the circumstances I'm sure you'll agree it's an extraordinarily fair system. Besides, as regards the Brambillas, I'm told the authorities only wish to ask Mr Brambilla about his acquaintance with the dubious person whom you call the pipe-cleaner man and have no interest in Edmondo whatsoever. So Ruby, the upshot is, if you do know anything, anything at all, about their whereabouts you really must tell me or your parents without any further delay.

How is your brother, by the way? Blindness is a tremendously difficult affliction for any young man to come to terms with, but at least he escaped France with his life. A lot of our boys weren't even as fortunate as that.

Yours affectionately, and in anticipation

Uncle Charles

Diary of Miss Ruby Summers

26 June 1940

Dear Diary,

I did it.

I've done it all.

An hour ago, I gave Edmondo's address to my father, as well as the old programme he sent me with the photograph of *Marco and Anastasia Brambilla* on the front so the local police have some idea what Edmondo's father looks like. I even showed Father Edmondo's sketch of the Essex house. I expected Father to be angry I hadn't told him before. Instead, he simply said, 'Thank you, Ruby' and tried to give me a hug. I wouldn't let him though. I turned and ran up the stairs and have stayed in my bedroom ever since. A short while ago, Mother tapped on the door. 'Ruby? Are you there?' To my surprise, she didn't sound cross either. 'There's a piece of raisin cake and a glass of milk out here for you. I've left them on a tray.' Although I could sense her waiting, willing me to appear, I didn't reply and after a few seconds I heard her footsteps retreating slowly.

I couldn't possibly drink milk or eat cake. I feel sick enough as it is. I imagine Mr Brambilla has probably been caught already. Or perhaps the police are striding up the driveway and hammering on his door this very second, locking his wrists into handcuffs as Edmondo tries his best to comfort Fragolina and Mrs Brambilla all the while wondering if I, Ruby, the girl he loves, can possibly be the reason his father is being arrested…

Isn't doing the right thing supposed to make you feel marvellous? Well, Diary, I feel wretched so maybe that means I've done the wrong thing. And the worst thing of all is I will probably never know.

Letter Dr Rupert Godwin to Ruby

26 June 1940

Dear Ms Summers

I have been passed your name and address by Mr Charles Whittaker, whom I believe is your godfather.

I apologise for this unsolicited correspondence but Mr Whittaker has given me to understand you may require a Latin tutor? My expertise is in the Classics, both Greek and Latin, and I would be delighted to assist where I can. Since I am currently engaged at a boy's preparatory school in London (temporarily relocated to Essex) my suggestion would be a weekly itinerary of learning and assignments conducted by post, however I can also make myself available to travel to your home every other weekend if that should be required.

As regards the question of remuneration, you will be pleased to know that Mr Whittaker has asked me to say he regards the furtherment of your education part of his duties as your godfather and instructed me to send my invoices to him.

At the risk of being over-presumptive, I am including with this letter a number of worksheets directed to some basic grammar and vocabulary. Once you have completed these exercises, I will be better able to assess the height of the hurdle ahead of us.

Labor omnia vincit!

Yours truly,

Dr Rupert Godwin, MA (Cantab); PhD

Diary of Miss Ruby Summers

27 June 1940

Dear Diary

Labor omnia vincit: hard work conquers all! Unfortunately, I only know the translation because I consulted a Latin dictionary which makes crystal clear the amount of work I have ahead of me during the next few months even to sit the Cambridge entrance exams. If Mr Godwin had any idea at all, he would give me up as a lost cause.

I'm trying to convince myself the challenge is a good thing – what with learning Latin and my school certificate examinations I should have no spare time to sit and brood, even if that's all I seem to have done today. (At school my mind was so muddled two of my teachers enquired if I had a head cold.) Yesterday I wrote to Uncle Charles imploring him for news of the Brambillas the moment he hears back from the police and I have done the same again this evening (in case my first letter should be delayed in the post).

Letter Dr Rupert Godwin to Ruby

28 June 1940

Dear Miss Summers

I'm enclosing a list of one hundred essential Latin verbs. In my experience there's no substitute for simply starting at the top and working through them one by one.

Yours sincerely

Dr Rupert Godwin, MA (Cantab); PhD

Diary of Miss Ruby Summers

28 June 1940

Dear Diary

No news from Uncle Charles though he surely must know *something* by now. I'm quite certain the police would have acted the moment they had the Brambillas' address.

And why hasn't Edmondo written to me?

Letter Clem to Ruby

28 June 1940

Darling sister

What on earth makes you think Mr Brambilla has been arrested? You sounded so very upset in your letter, but I couldn't quite understand why you believed the police had found him or even why they might be searching him out. Never mind! I understand how awful it must be not to hear from Edmondo, whatever the reason for his disappearance. However, I must confess that while I'm truly sorry to learn of your unhappiness, I can't help feeling this latest turn of events might be for the best. Since Mussolini is now blatantly on Hitler's side, a relationship with an Italian is hardly feasible, is it? And with poor George so terribly injured and Mother at her wit's end we couldn't possibly be any clearer as to where our loyalties and energies must lie at the moment – *with our families and our country*, darling, in case I need to spell it out, which I'm quite certain I don't!

On a happier note, I hear that Mother and Father have come around to you applying for a place at Cambridge. Mother told me on the telephone that some chap that Uncle Charles knows is going to give you Latin lessons. When I asked why, she replied that Latin was a compulsory part of the Girton College entrance examination, as if the notion of you going to university was the most natural thing in the world. How on earth did you swing the parental mind? I suppose Charles must have said something, though I still can't imagine how even he managed to bring about such a change of heart. You must fill me in when I next see you.

Your loving sister

Clem

Diary of Miss Ruby Summers

29 June 1940

Dear Diary

Still no word from Edmondo. My pulse leapt this morning when an envelope addressed to me in Uncle Charles's handwriting landed on the mat. However, the letter inside was the briefest of notes enquiring whether my lessons with Mr Greenwood had started satisfactorily and made no mention of the Brambillas at all. Anyone reading it would never guess my every second of the last three days has been spent agonising over the probable arrest of my beau's father, terrified he will soon be deported because of *my* treachery.

I've been bought, haven't I, Diary? Just like a packet of soap powder, or chocolate, or tea, or any of the other commodities the Brambillas used to sell in their shop.

Diary of Miss Ruby Summers

29 June 1940

Dear Diary

There is no way to approach the events of today other than to record what happened as simply as possible. If I begin to think too much, I fear my composure will crumble and I won't be able to do anything except go to bed and pull the covers over my head for good.

I was studying in my bedroom (Latin verb declensions) when the doorbell rang. I didn't think anything of it until a moment later when Mother called up the stairs in an unnecessarily loud voice, 'Ruby you'd better come here.'

It suddenly struck me the visitor might have news of Edmondo, might even possibly *be* Edmondo, so I literally belted down to the hall without so much as combing my hair only to slide to a halt when I saw the person on the doorstep was an older, greyer version of

Mother wearing a stout-looking skirt and twinset.

Mother and the grey woman glanced at each other as if both were hoping the other might speak first. Finally, it was Mother who cleared her throat. 'Did you realise Edmondo had recently acquired a dog, Ruby?'

I blinked at her. 'A dog?' I wasn't even sure whether I could admit in front of a stranger that Edmondo and I had been writing to each other.

'Yes, a dog.' She sounded impatient. 'This very kind lady has got the dog in the car.'

I nearly said, 'In her car?' but stopped myself just in time. Instead, I said, 'What's happened to Edmondo?'

There was another pause. This time the grey woman spoke. 'I imagine you mean the Italian boy. All I know is that the police took him away about a week ago.'

I must have squeaked or gasped or something because the grey lady began to speak more quickly, as if to get what she had to say over and done with. 'I was walking my own dog at about six o'clock in the evening when I came across quite a commotion on the outskirts of the village. A policeman was escorting an older gentleman and young lad out of a house, while a woman – their wife and mother, I assume – stood on the doorstep clinging hold of a younger girl for dear life. All of them were crying and shouting to one another in what sounded to me like Italian.'

I felt Mother's hand on my arm.

'There was a dog as well, adding to the hubbub. Running in circles, barking, and by the looks of it trying to nip the policeman's heels. When the boy got into the back of the car the dog jumped inside too and the policeman was not at all amused. He asked if I would take the dog back to the house and of course, I was happy to help. Just as I was scooping the dog up, the boy gave me the most desperate look, a look that tugged straight at my heartstrings despite him plainly being a foreigner. 'Please' he said, 'would you take the dog to my friend, Ruby Summers. She lives in Bucklesham, Suffolk.' I was too surprised to ask any questions and before I could gather my wits the policeman intervened and made me step away from the car. I didn't know what to do. I thought I should take the dog back to the house, but as soon as the police car drove away the front door closed and, given the rather harrowing circumstances, I decided it might be better to wait a while before disturbing them. I went back the following day, and several times since, but nobody answered my knocking and now I'm quite certain the house is empty. Goodness knows where the mother and daughter have gone. Anyway,' the woman took a breath, 'there was nothing for it but to come here and try to find you, Ruby Summers. I must have driven around the village for twenty minutes until I found someone who knew where you lived–'

'–What did he say?' My voice was hoarse. 'What exactly did Edmondo say?'

'The boy? I think I've already told you what he said.' The grey lady hesitated then closed her eyes as if trying to squeeze out her last drops of memory. 'He said, please would I take the dog to Ruby – to you – in case he wasn't released.'

'So, Edmondo was being arrested too. He wasn't just accompanying his father?'

The lady opened her eyes. 'I don't think so, dear.' She gazed straight at me. 'It appeared very much to me as though he was going with the police because he had no choice in the matter.'

I couldn't speak. Although the path and the front garden were swimming out of focus, I didn't want to rub my eyes and make it obvious I was crying. In the end I simply stared along our driveway towards the field opposite, while the lady walked back to her car and opened the boot. A few seconds later, something wet and cold brushed against my calf and made me jump. A scruffy white dog with short legs and a long tail was pressing his nose against my legs as if examining their smell. I imagined him missing Edmondo, feeling abandoned and searching everywhere for the familiar scent he loved. Immediately I wanted to bury my face in his shaggy coat.

The grey woman turned her attention to Mother. 'I ought to be heading home now. I'll leave him with you if I may?'

'I don't suppose I have any option.' Mother sounded resigned. 'At least he seems a sweet little thing. Does he have a name?'

The woman was already turning to leave. There was a sudden briskness to her demeanour that made me think she might have been a schoolteacher or a nurse. 'Not that anyone told me. You'll have to give him a new one.'

As we went inside, Mother said, 'We'll need to keep the dog under control, Ruby. No going upstairs and no getting under George's feet and tripping him up.' Her voice faded abruptly as we both realised the dog was *already* upstairs and by the time I reached the landing, I could hear a low crooning coming from George's room. I peered around his half-open door. George was sitting on the floor fondling the dog's ears, while the dog sat as still as a statue.

'You've made friends rather quickly!'

George smiled and for an instant he almost looked like my brother again.

'Where has he come from? He seems a splendid little chap. What's his name?'

I ignored the first question. 'Whatever we want it to be.'

George's hands roved between the dog's ears and his torso, feeling all over as if learning the shape of his head and belly. Still the dog didn't move. 'Felix. Let's call him Felix. The boat that pulled me out of the water in France was called the *Felix* and in Latin, felix means—

'Lucky,' I supplied. I could see the word blazing in lights from one of Dr Greenwood's vocabulary lists. 'Felix means happy or lucky.' However rather than feeling satisfied or pleased the knowledge filled me with guilt, as if I'd been caught handling the spoils of a crime.

I'm back in my own room now. Felix is with George and Mother seems to have forgotten her rule about him not going upstairs already. I'm about to write to Uncle Charles (again). He promised me Edmondo would be safe, that the police were only interested in Edmondo's father. Now I know Uncle Charles lied. Or, at the very least he made a promise he couldn't keep. Sitting here, imagining Edmondo in an internment camp or a prison cell and worrying if I shall ever see him again, the two possibilities don't feel very different.

Letter Edmondo to Ruby

30 June 1940

OPENED BY THE CENSOR

Dearest Ruby

I wonder if this letter will reach you, and if so, how much of it will remain. You'll be able to tell by the number of blacked out passages...

They came for us three days ago. I'm guessing a neighbour or passer-by must have seen us or heard our Italian voices and tipped off the authorities. My father and I were allowed to bring only one suitcase each. My mother packed for us while my father tried to persuade the policeman to leave me behind – his pleas met with a wall of stone.

We spent that first night in the police station before we were taken to what they called a collecting station where fifty or sixty other Italians were already imprisoned. The place must once have been a racecourse because a track curled all the way round the encampment like a wide green ribbon only now fenced by barbed wire and with armed guards patrolling the perimeter. For two nights my father and I slept on palliasses inside a horsebox filled with the stench of manure and mouldy hay. During the day the guards allowed us a little exercise (so long as we stayed within sight) but once it became dark the same soldiers banged on the side of the horsebox and shouted, 'No talking, Mussolini!' if they heard so much as a whisper. Very early yesterday morning we were put on a train. When I asked a guard where we were going, he seemed reluctant to tell me. 'The north,' he said eventually. 'Lancashire.' And I believe that's where we are now. Living in an old factory building called Wharf Mills.

When we first arrived, the conditions didn't seem too bad. There was enough space, enough beds, to go round. However, all of the day and evening more Italians kept arriving – in police cars, in ordinary cars and even in double-decker buses that had names like 'Preston' and 'Blackburn' on the front of them. I've never heard so much Italian being spoken yet felt more of a foreigner. There must be three thousand men here now, residing with many tens of thousands of mice and rats. My father and I have quarters on the second of three floors. The men who came today aren't so lucky, they're sleeping in tents which cover the whole of two adjoining fields. Or perhaps they are the lucky ones. Already the stink inside the building is worse than the one in the horsebox. Men are smelly creatures, especially when we're forced to exist on top of each other. Last night I queued for nearly two hours to wash my face and hands and already the latrines are so insufferable some have even resorted to doing their needs in a corner!

On a happier note, I think the food will be alright. A lot of the Italians here used to work in restaurants and say they will enjoy the challenge of creating meals from the supplies. Yesterday evening my stew was served to me by Cesare Bianchi, former head chef at the Café Royal! We're also allowed to write home – wherever we now consider home to be. Our letters must be left on a desk outside the guards' office and I imagine every sentence will be censored vigorously.

To pass the time today, I used a broom and a wheelbarrow to clean up as best I could. The floor is layered in broken glass, mice droppings and discarded pieces of machinery, all coated in dust from the old cotton mills. Aside from that there's not much to do – other than worry. My father is driven to distraction about my mother and Fragolina. I'm anxious for them as well, but the person I miss the most, is you. You're my reason for keeping strong. You're my home.

Write to me here, Ruby. We're allowed to receive letters, and even some parcels. I don't know how long we'll be staying but for now this is the only address I have.

Mia amo

Edmondo

PS It's later now. Almost midnight. I'm scratching out these words by the stub of candle in a silence that shifts and settles like a restless child. At supper, word passed from man to man the morning will bring a big announcement. As soon as breakfast has been cleared away, we must assemble in the field behind the factory and await instructions. Rumour has it the announcement is deportation. That they will tell us who is no longer allowed to remain in England. I fear very much the list will include my father. After hearing the news he went to his bed and has not spoken since. His association with the musician we met in Felixstowe is the problem. I cannot, will not, believe my father is a fascist, however he has had no opportunity to prove his innocence and if he is deported our family will be scattered to the winds. No wonder then the darkness tonight feels like shadows cast by storm clouds. I'm taking this letter to the post room now in case tomorrow the storm breaks and there's no more time.

Letter Dr Rupert Godwin to Ruby

30 June 1930

Dear Miss Summers

I am enclosing three sets of exercises along with a short translation from Latin into English. Better to await further progress before attempting the task the other way around – changing English to Latin dents the confidence of even the most able scholars. Nevertheless, I can admit to being pleasantly surprised by the standard of your first assignment and told your uncle as much yesterday when we had luncheon together. You are evidently blessed with both a quick brain and a remarkable memory and I am optimistic our combined sustained effort may yet bring the Cambridge entrance examinations within your grasp.

Laborare!

Rupert Godwin MA(Cantab); PhD

Letter Uncle Charles to Ruby

1 July 1940

My dear goddaughter,

My apologies for the short delay in replying to your four letters; the fall of France, the regrouping of the English armed forces and the threat of invasion is keeping me more than a little occupied. I was, of course, sorry to hear the police have arrested and interned Edmondo and can assure you that particular turn of events was unexpected (by me, at least). However, given the evidence I understand exists in relation to his father, perhaps the authorities believed the boy must know, perhaps even sympathise with, his father's political persuasion? If there has been a mistake, I'm confident your friend will be allowed back to his mother and sister soon.

As regards your questions regarding deportation, the government has now decided the national interest requires the country to rid itself of those Italians who pose the biggest threat immediately and without the delay that hearings before a tribunal would necessarily entail. The reasoning is self-evident and requires no further explanation or justification from me. I believe a cruise ship, the Arandora Star, has been requisitioned to take the deportees to Canada and that she will sail from the Liverpool docks within a day or two. As soon as a spare moment presents itself, I will make enquiries and attempt to ascertain whether Edmondo's father is on the list of passengers.

Yours affectionately

Uncle Charles

PS I was extremely pleased to hear of your positive start in Latin. Doctor Godwin was most impressed – as I knew he would be.

Letter Clem to Ruby

2 July 1940

Dearest sister,

John has joined the army. I pleaded with him not to, begged him to think of me and the children – even of the boys in his class who will be almost as wretched as his own family to see him go – but he wouldn't listen. It all came to a head yesterday evening. As soon as Greg and Tabby were in bed, he said he had something to tell me. I knew what the 'something' was since we'd talked about nothing else for days.

'You've done it, haven't you?' I said. 'You've gone and signed up.' He didn't reply. I turned away to pick up my knitting so that he couldn't see how wet my eyes were and when he took hold of my arm, I shook off his hand.

'Clem?' he said. I still daren't look at him.

'There's nothing left to say, is there? You've made up your mind and it's too late to back out now.'

'I don't want to back out. I want you to understand.'

'You're in a reserved occupation! You're one of the lucky ones! Except now you're volunteering to go and get yourself killed and leave me a widow and the children fatherless!'

'I'm not much good as a husband or a father if I can't look myself in a mirror,' he said. 'And I can't do that at the moment, because I don't like what I see. In every newspaper and on the wireless there's nothing but struggle and sacrifice, struggle against a dreadful, evil tyranny and the sacrifice of ordinary men like me trying to save our country. And now I see soldiers returning from France injured and traumatised, or hear of friends who will never come back–'

'–And that makes you want to go?' I couldn't stop the bitterness, or the incredulity.

'Of course, I don't *want* to go, Clem, but neither do I want to be someone who didn't step forward when the time came. Well, the time *has* come.' He paused. 'And I don't want to discover that I'm a coward.'

There was a long silence. From upstairs Greggie coughed, it was such a gentle, childish sound it nearly broke my heart. John must have felt the same way because when I glanced up, tears were streaming down his face too. I dropped the knitting and wrapped my arms around him, my cheek pressed against his pullover. I wanted to hold on to that feeling, Ruby, I wanted to hold onto him for ever, but a moment later Greggie appeared in the doorway asking for a glass of water. Now it's already the following morning and in less than a week – perhaps by the time you're reading these words – John will have gone and I may never see him again.

So, my darling, though I was sad to learn the police have arrested Edmondo and his father, you must realise there is a war on, that they are Italian and we have to do everything we possibly can to stop Hitler and Mussolini. I now rather think if that means moving suspect aliens out of the country, so be it and as soon as possible! Surely if I can bear John joining the army you can forget about Edmondo, forget *all* the Brambillas in fact. Concentrate instead on your marvellous future. I know that one day you're going to make us very proud.

Your loving sister

Clem

Letter Anonymous to Ruby

2 July 1940

Dear Ms Summers

I write to offer my formal and unreserved apology. How foolish of me to fail to appreciate the reason behind your continued friendship with the Italian boy was to infiltrate the enemy camp! Now that he and his errant family have been found – I assume with your assistance – I can only thank you for your service to our country and beg you to forgive my earlier, unfounded, correspondence. As the war progresses, we must all hope that more young people are prepared to play their part like you, willing to put our country's interest above their own and act with whatever cunning the circumstances may require.

Yours in gratitude

Anonymous

Letter Mr Wilfred Frost to Ruby

3 July 1940

Chin up, young Ruby. The torch of hope burns in the darkest hours.

Daily Telegraph

4 July 1940

Mad Panic As Arandora Star Went Down: Survivors' Grim Stories Of Mad Scramble For Lifeboats

The British Luxury Cruiser Arandora Star (15,501 tons) has been torpedoed and sunk without warning by a German U-

Boat. Savage scenes of panic broke out among 1,500 German and Italian internees bound for Canada. Martin Verinder, of Romford, 18-year old steward aboard the Arandora Star, told a reporter today that but for attempts to keep the Germans and Italians under control hardly anybody would have escaped. Pale from his ordeal and with memories he will never forget, Verinder said bitterly, 'And if they had not panicked so completely, many, many more would have escaped. I was just up when the explosion occurred. Had I still been asleep I should not have been here today. All at once there was a crashing of glass, the lights went out and the ship shuddered and listed. We were led up two decks and through the saloons by a second steward. We had to find our way through the inky black with the aid of a few matches, stumbling across fallen and sliding tables, chairs and other furniture. In the old ball-room mirrors had fallen down on the Italian internees who had been moved there the previous day. Shards and splinters were strewn across the floor and some of the Italians had terrible injuries. On reaching the decks, we lost the second steward. There were amazing scenes of panic among the internees, all scrambling amongst the barbed wire that had been placed around the lifeboats to stop escapees. On the bridge, the captain was alone, giving orders to the soldiers and crew to throw everything floatable over the side. He coolly asked one man to fetch him a glass of water, and the same man brought him a coat as well. I knew as I watched him standing there that he would never get away.

'There were a dozen lifeboats for nearly 2,000 people so you can imagine the scramble which took place, especially since two of the lifeboats had been hit by the torpedo but we strove to lower the others over the side. One of them was carried away by the current. Another was weighted down with hundreds trying to get in it and smashed to pieces with the davits rolling down on top of them. Many hesitated to jump

overboard and caused terrible injuries to themselves by sliding down ropes into the ocean. Some of the Italians tried to take large suitcases with them and did not seem to understand that there wasn't enough room, soldiers even had to cut the handles off their cases to make them drop them. About 200 internees were still below, they must have gone down with the ship.

'The lifeboat in which I escaped was crammed with over 100 men. In the water men were clinging to every conceivable floating object and many hung onto the ship. I don't think some could swim, having come from mountain areas in Italy, though many seemed as British as we were, having lived in England all their lives. As we watched, the ship's guns were ripped off their moorings and a length of barbed wire trailing from the fixings hooked further victims into the Atlantic. Then the funnels that gave life to the engines broke from their rivets and crashed into the sea and the ship's boilers exploded. It was clear the ship was about to sink. I saw the captain walk to the side rails where many Italians were still refusing to leave. A moment later the vessel flipped up and sank stern first almost immediately so that those men still on board the ship must have been trapped as she came over.

'Afterwards everything was suddenly quiet. An eerie, very uncanny quiet. There was just the early morning sky and water to see. It was as though the Arandora Star had never existed; the few lifeboats that had been successfully launched were already far apart from each other in their own solitary sea.'

Letter Ruby to Edmondo

5 July 1940

Dearest, dearest Edmondo

What's the news of your father? Was he deported? Was he sailing on the *Arandora Star*? Although I don't usually pray for anything I've been awake all night, praying your father is safe, that you are both still together at the Wharf Mills factory, or even better have been released back to your mother and Fragolina.

To begin with I couldn't bear even to look at the newspaper reports, but eventually I read them all from beginning to end. You see, I owe it both to you and myself to face up to what I did, even if I cannot yet bring myself to explain what I mean. At least, not in writing, when I cannot see your eyes, touch your face, cannot make you understand how this thing that *I cannot tell you*, came about.

As I write I realise you might not know whether or not your father was aboard the *Arandora Star* either. Perhaps you are frantic for news yourself, with rumours doubling and trebling every hour? I swear I will do everything in my power to help, Edmondo. My godfather has a position in the War Office, and I posted him a letter yesterday pressing him to find out what has happened to your father with the utmost urgency. If I do not receive a reply by tomorrow, I will send a telegram and the very second that I hear anything at all, I will write again. In the meantime, every time that the postman knocks I shall live in hope of good news.

Mia amo

Ruby

ENVELOPE STAMPED: LETTER RETURNED TO SENDER: RECIPIENT UNKNOWN

Letter Ruby to Edmondo

12 July 1940

Dearest Edmondo

A week has gone by since I last wrote, the slowest week of my life. The weather has been beautiful, the hues of the sky and grass so vivid the blue and green seem to be competing to out-dazzle each other. This morning I told Mother and Father I would study outside and set up a table and chair under the oldest, biggest horse chestnut at the end of the garden. The truth is that behind the trunk I am invisible to anyone in the house, so nobody could see me lying on the ground, gazing up into the tree's canopy until all the lines and shapes lost their sense of meaning and simply became a pattern of colour.

Did you know that the blooms of the horse chestnut resemble ice-cream? They do if you stare at them long enough. The creamy petals come to look exactly like the white vanilla blocks your father used to sell for a penny at the village fete. I was remembering the fete, and the children who used to crowd around Prince, how your father gave them sugar lumps to feed him – 'Keep your palm straight,' he would say, 'even if he tickles' – holding flat the fingers of the youngest ones, when all at once I felt something tickling *me* and opened my eyes to find Felix sniffing my legs. I knew then George must be nearby as they have become inseparable. From the moment Felix first ran upstairs he adopted my brother and while he is polite to me, it's perfectly clear where his heart lies. Indeed, he's so careful not to trip up George I think he must have been a guide dog in an earlier life. I hope you can forgive Felix for choosing another. George has cheered up so much that I don't mind at all – except for the times when I wonder if the reason Felix prefers George is because he can tell what I did and why he came to be here, as if betrayal has a smell all its own.

Anyhow, as I predicted, a moment after Felix appeared, George's shadow fell across my face and a moment after that he sat down. He felt for my arm and shoulder. 'What are you doing?'

'Lying down,' I said. 'Having a rest.'

'Aren't you supposed to be studying? Your school certificate exams are next week.'

I rolled away from him and balanced on my side. The summer green scent of the grass was so strong I could practically taste it. 'I can't work all the time.'

'You didn't study yesterday, or the day before that.'

'For someone who can't see anything, you seem to know an awful lot!' Of course, I regretted my temper immediately. I wanted to apologise but a dreadful ache had filled my throat and if I had opened my mouth a howl would have burst out. Felix sat beside my head. He was panting happily in the heat, his tongue lolling sideways over his jaw in a way that would have seemed quite comical had I been in a mood to find anything funny. Instead of speaking I wound his coat between my fingers.

'There's something wrong, isn't there, Ruby?' I shook my head – pointlessly, of course. As the seconds ticked by, I became very aware of the different sounds, the ragged engine of Felix's chest, the drone of several bees, and my brother shifting his position somewhere behind my shoulder.

Eventually, he said, 'You can tell me, Ruby. You can tell me anything.'

I didn't reply and kept my eyes on the ground. I found I couldn't look at George, even though he couldn't see me.

I was aware of Felix moving first, his coat twisting out of my grip the instant before George began to walk slowly back up the garden, his white stick prodding the earth like an extension of his own arm.

It's the afternoon now and I'm sitting on my bed. While we were having lunch, George said very little and stopped eating each time I spoke as if to catch every nuance in my voice. Still, he won't have learned anything because I kept the conversation firmly focused on Mother's volunteer work with the women's service, which was not terribly difficult because she can talk for a surprising amount of time about knitting blanket squares and gas mask checks. A few minutes ago, just as I was settling down with this pen and notepaper, I heard the floorboards creak outside my door. There was a pause in which I could practically feel the wood preparing itself for the knock before the footsteps went away again. I'm certain that was George and I'm very relieved he decided against disturbing me because I wouldn't have told him the truth. The first person I must tell is you, that's the least I can do to start to make things right.

So here is the truth, Edmondo – and I'm going to write this very quickly – before the sensible part of my brain can stop me. The reason you are in a factory, separate from your mother and sister, the reason your father is being deported, the reason he may be dead – drowned at sea, or burned in an explosion, or crushed by a falling lifeboat – is me, not an observant neighbour. It's all because of me.

Soon after you left Uncle Charles asked me if I had your address. Of course, I said I didn't, but I could see he didn't believe me and insisted I had a patriotic duty to disclose your whereabouts because of your father's friendship with that thin musician. He seemed so very certain about your father that when George came home so terribly wounded, I found I couldn't resist telling him any longer. Can you forgive me? Can you ever understand? I don't suppose you can for a second. I imagine you know your father to be a loyal supporter of the Allies and I think in my heart I know that too, which is why I feel so wretched. Yet it's a funny kind of knowledge, like a shadow that keeps changing depending on the light, and I can find myself thinking very different things with barely any space between.

I've stopped and reread from the start and although I so badly want to tear the page up and write about something else instead, I'm making myself continue. Because there's something more. So far, I've told you the truth, but I haven't yet told you the whole truth – not the way they make you promise in court – there's a tiny part that's missing, a part that might not be important or might be what makes my soul as black as night.

You see, when Uncle Charles pressed me for information, he didn't only use the stick of patriotic duty, he also dangled a carrot. A big, fat juicy carrot right in front of my nose that goes by the unlikely name of Professor Rupert Godwin. The Professor is a Latin teacher. And Uncle Charles as good as offered him to me in exchange for your address. I've lain awake for hours, searching the very depths of myself, to work out if being taught Latin and a chance at the Cambridge entrance examination was a part, even a small part, of the reason why I gave you up.

I don't believe it was, Edmondo. I sincerely don't believe that carrot had any share in the decision, but the truth is that I will never be certain for the rest of my life. I want to be a scientist and science depends on facts. The only fact that matters here is that it was me who told the authorities where to find you. Me. The woman you trusted. The woman you love. Even if you should somehow manage to forgive me, I shall never forgive myself.

There, I've said it. I must run to the postbox right this minute before I give in and cross out all the paragraphs above.

Ruby

ENVELOPE STAMPED: LETTER RETURNED TO SENDER: RECIPIENT UNKNOWN

Letter Uncle Charles to Ruby

13 July 1940

My dear goddaughter

My apologies for the tardiness of this response. As the situation is a little hazy at the moment (to say the least) I thought it best to wait until I had reliable information rather than raise your hopes prematurely. However, I am now reasonably confident Edmondo's father was not aboard the *Arandora Star*.

The passenger list of that sad vessel, the list of survivors and the lengthier list of known fatalities have all been checked by sources I trust and I have been told the name *Marco Brambilla* appears on none of them. I am also informed the government made a last-minute decision to exempt from deportation married men with children, even those most strongly suspected of fascist sympathies. Since Mr Brambilla has a wife and two children there is good reason to suppose he would not have been on the *Arandora Star*, or any other cruiser bound for Canada. I will endeavour to find out whether he and Edmondo have been moved from Wharf Mills to another location.

Your ever affectionate

Uncle Charles

Diary of Miss Ruby Summers

15 July 1940

Dear Diary

I'm back.

Writing this diary is like holding up a mirror to the inside of my head and recently I haven't been able to look there too closely. Tonight, while there's still no news of Edmondo or his father, Uncle Charles's letter was a tremendous relief and I'm trying my very best to be patient and positive. Patient, positive *and* productive. This morning I studied for three hours at my desk without so much as venturing downstairs for a glass of water. Although the weather remains glorious, and I would far rather have resumed my position underneath the horse chestnut trees, the combination of soft green light and summer heat would not have been conducive to serious work. At least this afternoon I could go outside with satisfaction of having completed all of Professor Greenwood's assignments. I actually became so engrossed in The Aeneid I translated more pages than he asked me to: It turns out that when Aeneas abandoned Dido, the Queen of Carthage, to fulfil his destiny and found Rome, she was so distraught she built a funeral pyre and threw herself onto the flames. Aeneas could see the enormous fire from his ship, even far out at sea. I wonder what he thought as he watched all that billowing smoke. Whether he realised what Dido had done and if the feeling of guilt ever went away…

Stop.

I must think of other things besides Edmondo and my own worries. It's bound to be only a matter of time before I hear that he and his father are safe and well. And perhaps, in time, Edmondo will understand what I did and forgive me. Unlike Dido and Aeneas, as soon as the war is over (which hopefully will be a year or two at most) Edmondo and I can be together again.

There's a lot of news these days about air attacks. We've fallen into the habit of sitting around the wireless before supper, all four of us. Five if you include Felix, who jumps onto George's knee the moment Big Ben chimes the six o'clock hour, as if doing his best to alleviate the gloom. What I find worst, however, is not so much the news itself but what they're *not* telling us. Last night the reporter said over seventy German planes had been shot down compared to only a few of ours. I couldn't help thinking that sounded rather too good to be true which made me wonder, who actually writes the news? Who decides whether to tell us the truth and how do they know what to say for the best? What if the real numbers of British planes shot down would make us panic? We might give up and surrender to Germany because of lost morale whereas if we believe things are going well, we might carry on and eventually win the war. All these thoughts were still swirling around my head after the news finished. I was going to ask Father about them, but I suddenly felt so tired and befuddled I decided to have a bath instead.

On my way to my room, I saw George sitting on the edge of his bed staring at nothing and felt even worse. I've been horrible to him recently, when his woes are so much worse than mine, so I asked if he would like me to read to him. I thought he would refuse but he nodded and gestured towards his bookcase.

'Pick anything from there.'

Most of the shelves were crammed with files of notes and medical texts but the bottom one contained a stack of novels from years ago. We sat with backs against the headboard while I read out loud from *Biggles Flies Again* until the light outside the window deepened to indigo. Felix was curled up beside us with his chin on my thigh as if rewarding me for finally getting something right. After nearly an hour I closed the book and told George I would finish the story the following evening.

At first George just nodded, but then as I swung my legs off the bed, he said, suddenly and loudly, 'Whatever happened, Ruby, it's not your fault.'

I froze. 'What do you mean?'

'I overheard Mother speaking to Uncle Charles on the telephone. About the *Arandora Star*.'

I relaxed slightly. 'Oh that. For a while I was worried Mr Brambilla might have been on the ship, but Uncle Charles made enquires and–'

George interrupted me. 'You mustn't blame yourself, Ruby. It's Mr Brambilla's fault. What happened, happened because of what he did, not because of what you did, or what' – he paused – 'or what you might have told anyone.'

At that point I slid off the counterpane as if George had pushed me. Although he wasn't making much sense, I couldn't bear for him to know I had betrayed Edmondo.

'I didn't tell anyone anything…' The lie made me swallow. I started again. 'And anyway, Mr Brambilla wasn't on the ship. Uncle Charles wrote to tell me and his letter arrived yesterday.' My voice sounded high and tight, giddy even. At the doorway I inhaled to steady myself. It took an effort to get the air into my lungs and once I had done the breath seemed to stick in my chest. I left immediately and have been here in my bedroom for the last hour watching the moon climb over the trees and thinking about the strange things George said. I've reached the conclusion he must have been confused by what he overheard. He could only have listened to Mother's part of the conversation and I can't believe Uncle Charles would have written what he did in his letter if he wasn't as certain as he could be that Mr Brambilla was not a passenger on the *Arandora Star*. I must be patient and positive…

Next week I have my school certificate. I shall work like a beaver for those examinations and afterwards, Diary, turn my attention back to Latin and the Cambridge entrance papers.

***

Letter Marco Brambilla to Ruby

30 August 1940

Dear Ruby

What is your reaction, I wonder, on seeing that the writer of this letter, this longed-for letter, is not Edmondo but his father? I imagine you pulled out the paper the instant you lifted the envelope from the door mat, and are now walking, slowly, slowly, with your head bent over the page, perhaps up the staircase to your bedroom, perhaps to the end of the garden, to a secret spot where nobody will disturb you.

Where am I? My home is now the Isle of Man, a small green land between the coasts of England and Ireland. We – my fellow Italians and I – crossed the sea at night on a ferry that had room for only half the number of men on board. Shoulder to shoulder, we struggled to keep our feet – and the contents of our stomachs – as the boat heaved through the waves and the sea air did little to mask the smell of unwashed bodies. When at last we arrived, the locals were waiting. Not to welcome us, of course, but to spit and throw things – rocks, litter, handfuls of dirt – anything they could find, shouting, 'Mussolini! Mussolini! Go to hell, Mussolini!' We had to walk through the barrage of bricks and stones, until we reached here: the Palace Camp.

I wonder sometimes if the name is a joke. An example of English humour. The camp is simply rows of boarding houses that are surrounded by double coils of barbed wire and sentries armed with guns. Still, living here is not as bad as I expected. Like any other community we have organised a structure: first a home supervisor, above him a street supervisor, and at the very top the camp supervisor. Men who used to work in hotels and restaurants have volunteered to be in charge of the canteen while the priests give classes to educate the younger boys. During the last two weeks the guards have started to allow us to send and receive letters and even to work outside the camp. I provide labour to the Agricultural Board for one shilling a day. Mostly I dig potatoes and cabbages but sometimes I tend the horses and their warm breath and stamping hooves remind me of dear Prince.

I'm getting ahead of myself. I doubt my days on the farm or our little hierarchy of superiors are of any interest to you. What you want to know is why I'm here. Rather, what you most want to know is why this letter is from me and not from Edmondo. To answer that question, we must go back to the very early morning of 1 July.

By dawn that day all the prisoners were gathered outside the camp, waiting for an announcement and frightened into silence by the rumours of banishment to Canada that had already spread like fire through the night. A tall army captain pushed his way to the front and climbed a flight of steps up to a storeroom. At the top, he waved a piece of paper. 'Listen here! I'm going to read out a list of names and if you hear your name, you must move immediately – without any fuss or delay – over to the parking area beside the road.' He gestured towards the site entrance where three empty trucks had just arrived. More of them were queuing in the lane beyond.

As a ripple of shock passed through the crowd I reached for Edmondo's shoulder.

The army captain called out the first name. 'Vito Maestranzi!' Nobody moved but everyone could tell where the man was standing by the cry that rose like a distress flare.

'Vito Maestranzi!' the captain shouted. 'Get moving Maestranzi! This list has five hundred names!'

As the sun climbed higher in the sky, the number of men by the gates grew. Soon the first truck was full and drove away. Then the second, after that the third. My grip on Edmondo tightened. I knew what was coming. Even so when I heard my name – *Marco Brambilla* – my first reaction was disbelief. I gazed at my fellow Italians. Perhaps there was another Marco Brambilla who would move instead of me? A second later reality bit its teeth. I turned to the man on my right. He was old, with a face like leather and kind eyes. 'Look after my boy,' I said.

'I will,' he promised.

I embraced Edmondo. I inhaled his

smell. I met his gaze for the briefest of moments then forced my path to the waiting truck.

For the first part of the journey I refused to open my eyes. It was enough to feel the speed of the wheels, taking me further and further away from my son. I couldn't bear to watch the road stretching behind us too. The other Italians were also quiet. At some point later, probably much later, I noticed a sign telling us Liverpool was only forty miles away.

'I hope our ship is an ocean liner,' I said out loud. 'That they take us to Canada in style!' Although I spoke in Italian the man next to me replied in English and his accent was from London. 'We ain't going to Canada, mate. We're headed for the Isle of Man. It's the lot back at the factory who've got a bloody ocean to cross!'

It felt like Prince had jumped onto my chest. 'That can't be right!' I searched the other faces in desperation. 'My son was left behind and I'm the one the government wanted. There must be a mistake!'

The London man shifted in his seat. He looked uncomfortable 'Maybe he's in another truck, mate. One that's behind ours.'

I twisted around and gazed at the convoy. I was finding it hard to speak or even breathe. The line of lorries extended as far as I could see. Edmondo had to be in one of them. Surely, he was on his way to the Isle of Man as well?

I made myself believe those things, Ruby. That Edmondo and I would soon be reunited. For the rest of the truck journey, on the night crossing and during our arrival through the gates of Palace Camp, I kept hoping. I strained my ears and eyes for the briefest snatch of his voice, a glimpse of him in the distance.

There was nothing.

Just a few days later whispers began of another story. A story that at first was too terrible to understand. The big ship carrying the Italians to Canada had been torpedoed by the Germans. The ship had sunk. Many were drowned. Or burned. Or unaccounted for. The whispers grew louder, became questions and shouting and men running back and forth every hour of the day and night.

Shall I spare you the details of my wait? The number of times I sat outside the sentries' office while inside telephone calls were made to London. After days like this, many, many days, an officer with pale skin and a moustache the colour of wet sand came to my room. This man told me my son had been put on the boat to Canada. He was aboard the *Arandora Star*, and his name had not been found in any list of hospital patients or in any English internment camp. And if Edmondo was not in England – the officer held out his hand but would not meet my eyes – the only reasonable conclusion was that Edmondo had drowned. I thought the officer was about to pat my shoulder. Instead, after a moment of hesitation, he turned and walked away.

So, in answer to your question, the question you have been asking all these long, long weeks: where is Edmondo? Edmondo is nowhere, Ruby. Edmondo is lost to us all.

My letter is nearly finished but there's one last question I want to ask you. Which of us is to blame, do you think? It's a matter I've thought about a lot.

I know you were writing to Edmondo while we were in hiding, so you must have had our address. I suspect you saw the thin musician, the same man you met in Felixstowe, at my birthday celebration when you came inside the house. Were you told by the government he is a fascist? Perhaps they convinced you I must be a fascist too. Did you believe them, Ruby? Enough, it seems, for you to give my family away to the police. What they did not tell you is this thin man is my oldest friend and the son, as it happens, of my father's oldest friend. It's true he's a fascist. However, nobody understands that I am the only person alive who might have been able to change his way of thinking, to persuade him to take a different view. And he is the same to me. That's the reason – the only reason – we continued to meet each other.

Will you believe me? It matters not. I have already paid the heaviest price for not turning my thin friend in to the police and now very little matters at all.

I have come to the end. There's nothing more to say. I cannot forgive you, but somewhat to my surprise I find I do not blame you either.

What else can we do but what we think is right?

Marco Brambilla

PART SEVEN

Text Cassie to Austin 14.52

17 May 2020

Hi Austin, thanks so much for getting the shopping. Sorry to miss you just now. We're back at the caravan if you're still up for a picnic.

Text Cassie to Austin 15.31

17 May 2020

Hi Austin, I want to say... actually I'm not sure what I want to say, but could you possibly come back? Or give me a call. Whenever works for you – Noah and I aren't going anywhere! Anyway, really hoping to hear from you soon. Cassie

Text Cassie to Austin 17.11

17 May 2020

Hi Austin, just wondering if you saw my earlier messages? I'm so sorry about what happened today. It's hard to know what to write, when I don't know what you were thinking before and I don't know what you're thinking now. Of course, you might not be thinking about me at all. Maybe you went home because you had work to do, and not because you're upset or angry. And that would be fine. Honestly. But could you let me know. Please. Cassie

Text Cassie to Austin 17.16

17 May 2020

Are you upset or angry?

Text Cassie to Austin 18.15

17 May 2020

I'm guessing yes.

Text Cassie to Austin 19.22

17 May 2020

Me again. I've realised I haven't paid rent for weeks. What with that and how today turned out you must be really fed up with us. Fed up with me, anyway. If you'd like us to vacate the caravan, just say the word and I'll start to pack...

Text Cassie to Austin 21.30

17 May 2020

Austin?

Text Cassie to Austin 22.15

17 May 2020

Hey Austin, last message from me. I've decided as soon as Noah wakes in the morning, we're going to pack up and leave. Let me know how much rent I owe you and I'll make sure to pay without delay. Sorry things worked out like this. Cassie

Email Cassie to Austin 22.30

17 May 2020

Dear Austin,

Since you're not responding to my texts, I'm wondering if you've blocked my number? I'm sending you an email, just in case. I wanted to let you know Noah and I will be off in the morning. At least tell me how much rent to pay. You've been very kind to us and I'll always be grateful for that.

Cassie

PS What you might have seen, wasn't what it looked like. I really wish I'd had the chance to explain that to you.

Letter Cassie to Ruby

17 May 2020

Dear New Best Friend

Although it's your turn to write to me I'm going to take things out of order. Perhaps your next letter is winging its way in the post this very moment? If so, I'll probably never even see it because Noah and I are leaving here in the morning.

Life sucks. (I know, I've said that before.)

I was so looking forward to today, Ruby. Stupidly I'd got the idea into my head today was going to be the start of something. Between me and Austin, I mean. How crazy was that when all we'd done was write a few letters to each other? My mind must have been turned soft by lockdown. Or Covid. Maybe I've had the virus and not realised. Either way, I can't have been thinking straight because when he asked me to go for a walk, I treated the invitation like a date! I even got up early to wash my hair before spending an hour deciding what to wear. That's quite an achievement when my entire Norfolk wardrobe fits into a cupboard the size of a shoebox.

It all started so well. We'd arranged a time of eleven o'clock and on the actual dot of the hour a battered old Land Rover turned into the caravan park. As soon as the door opened, Badger (that's the name of a dog by the way, not an actual badger) made a beeline for Noah who dropped onto his knees and let himself be smothered with doggy kisses. Austin got out more slowly and came around the far side of the truck.

I recognised him straight away. I suppose the man *could*

only be Austin, but he seemed so familiar that for a second I thought we must have met somewhere else (which is odd because when Stuart then arrived, he looked like a stranger rather than someone I ever lived with). At least the Covid rules forbade Austin and I from touching or getting too close because they were probably the only reasons I didn't actually run towards him, and now I would die remembering any such thing. As it was, we just stood and stared at each other. He was taller than I expected. Stockier too, dressed in jeans and a faded cream and green checked shirt with a sweater slung over his shoulders. His hair was bleached the colour of straw and long and thick like an old-fashioned pop star. The way he stood reminded me of a soldier, strong and upright, yet he was holding a farmer's cap in his hands, twisting the peak subconsciously, and the green of his shirt was the exact same shade as his sweater (which can't have been coincidental, can it?) I almost admitted I used to imagine him being an old man with a handlebar moustache but the notion already seemed so ridiculous I didn't bother, and by the time I had gathered my thoughts he was crouching down to Noah's level, showing Noah how to pet Badger and make him sit for a biscuit.

We set off for the beach immediately. I can't remember what we talked about but once we started, we didn't seem to stop. Noah and Badger chased each other in huge circles and sometimes Austin would break off mid-sentence to race after them, making Badger bark and Noah laugh so much I thought he might trip over his own feet! After what must have been ages Austin asked whether we'd gone too far and all at once I realised the distance we'd come and how difficult Noah might find the long walk back. I needn't have worried. When Noah began to tire, Austin said that if I didn't mind bending the Covid rules a little, Noah could sit on his shoulders. After all they wouldn't be breathing towards each other, or even using the same level of air. Noah loved the ride! He was shining with happiness. I probably was as well because the rest of the walk seemed to pass so quickly.

Too quickly.

As we reached the caravan Austin lifted Noah down from his shoulders and Noah grabbed my arm with a hundred questions. 'I'm hungry! Can we have a picnic? Can Austin and Badger stay for lunch?'

'Yes, of course,' I started to say, and stopped. The only potential picnic items in our fridge were cheesy strings, a few squidgy tomatoes, and a couple of Mister Men yoghurts. I really wished I'd thought about picnics the day before.

Austin must have noticed me hesitate. 'I have to go to the supermarket today. Why don't I do that now and pick up some bread and ham and a bit of fruit while I'm at it?' He looked straight into my eyes. 'If that's alright with you?'

My eyes must have said yes because Austin smiled and turned to Noah. 'Is that alright with you too, young man?'

Noah was beaming. 'And crisps. You need to get crisps.'

Austin inclined his head. 'Bread, ham, fruit and *crisps*.' He whistled to Badger then kept whistling while he headed towards his truck. As he opened the passenger door for Badger I recognised the tune drifting over the grass ('Good Life' by One Republic) and for some reason that made the day feel even brighter. 'Come on,' I said to Noah, 'you find plates and I'll fetch a blanket to use as a picnic rug.'

Noah was counting out plates (four – one for Badger, of course) when I heard an engine. *That was quick*, I thought. Then I put down the makeshift picnic blanket. It was far too quick; Austin couldn't possibly have got to the shops and back already.

Outside, a figure was standing near the entrance barrier into the park and they began to wave manically the moment they saw me.

'Cassie! Cass! I'm over here!'

The earlier brightness seemed suddenly to dim and my brain stop working both at the same time.

'It's Stuart,' Noah said, helpfully. I wondered if he would run over to say hello. Instead, he took hold of my hand and neither one of us stirred a muscle.

After a moment Stuart ducked under the barrier and began to walk towards us. He was dressed casually, but *careful* casual if you know what I mean? Ironed jeans, a T-shirt bearing a Ralph Lauran logo, and trainers so brilliant white they must have been fresh out of the box that morning.

'Hi Cass.'

I still didn't move.

'Didn't you get my letter? I wrote to you yesterday and said I would drive up today. *Five hours* it's taken because of road closures. And I brought you these.' One hand thrust a potted orchid towards me, the other a box of truffles trussed with a huge yellow ribbon.

'It's Sunday,' I said flatly. 'There isn't a post today. Why didn't you send me a message or an email this morning?'

'I thought you'd blocked my number. And anyway... I didn't want you to tell me to stay away.'

For that split second, he sounded nervous, almost vulnerable, but he spoiled things immediately by nodding towards the caravan.

'Have you really been staying in that hideous green thing the whole time?'

'I like it, she's an example—'

'—an example of an early Avondale, yeah you told me!' He smiled at me, head on one side like he was indulging a toddler. 'Come on, Cass, time to head home now.'

'Home?'

'Back to London with me. I cleared out the boot of my car for extra space. We can have you packed up in no time and all of us home by six.'

Noah squeezed my fingers. 'What about the picnic? What about Austin?'

Stuart frowned. 'Who's Austin?'

'The owner of the caravan. The farmer who saved the lamb. I've told you about him before.'

'Oh.' I could practically see the cogs in Stuart's head processing the possibility of Austin posing some kind of threat before dismissing the notion out of hand. His reaction made me feel angry. Angry, but also a hopeless kind of inevitability.

I sent Noah to the caravan to fetch a sweater, then turned to Stuart. 'You had an affair,' I hissed, '*with my best friend!* How can you think I would go back to London with you?'

'And I am sorry, Cass. Truly sorry. But I've explained the circumstances – the highly unusual circumstances, what a difficult time it was for me...'

'A difficult time for *you*!'

'For all of us, of course. For *all* of us. Look'– he made another poking movement with his hands – 'a vanilla orchid and Belgian chocolates! What do you say we draw a line and start again?'

'I don't want an orchid. Or your wretched chocolates!'

'Cass!' Stuart gazed at me with a wounded expression, before putting both the plant and the box on the ground with exaggerated care and pulling something out from inside the orchid's cellophane wrapping. 'A letter arrived from the school. Surely you want to see that?'

I took the envelope – I could hardly throw *that* back in his face – and as he seemed to be waiting, pulled out the paper and scanned the page quickly. 'It's about the pen-pal scheme. The school is arranging a visit to the care home.'

Stuart ignored me. 'Look, Cass, why don't we go for a walk on the beach, and have a chat?' He rotated to Noah who had just reappeared. 'You'd like that, wouldn't you? A walk on the beach.'

'We've just been for a walk.' Noah sounded confused.

Stuart glowered at him. 'Then we can go for a second one. A short one.' Another hurt grimace. 'I've come a long way to see you. I think you at least owe me that.'

It was like trying to stand stationary in the sea while the tide is going out. Somehow, I felt myself bundled back towards the pines and flight of the steps over the dunes. Stuart was holding my hand, tugging me forwards, while Noah trotted a few paces behind. When we reached the shade of the woods Stuart came to a halt.

'Cass,' he ran his forefinger from the ends of my recently cropped hair down the length of my neck, 'this new look of yours is really growing on me.'

Although I knew what was coming, a tree trunk stopped me from moving and it felt too late to tell him to stop. As if he'd already decided for both of us what would happen. He pressed his mouth onto mine and the taste was immediately familiar. Not in a good way, though. Not in a good way at all. Stale and dry like yesterday's leftovers. Coming to my senses, I pushed him off with both hands, harder than I meant to in fact, and he staggered backwards, tripped on a root, and fell over.

'What the hell, Cass!'

'I'm not interested, Stuart. It's finished. You slept with my best friend and what's worse than that is I don't even care that much. Not about you anyway. I think she must have mattered to me more than you did!'

There was a long reproachful silence.

Eventually, he stood up and brushed his trousers. Silently, Noah held out Stuart's mobile which had fallen out of his pocket and he took it without looking at either of us before starting to limp towards the holiday park. After a few paces he paused and exclaimed to nobody in particular. 'I've got fucking sand in my shoes!'

Noah and I followed behind. I could tell Noah was happy because he was swinging my arm but I daren't glance at his face in case we started to giggle. I expected Stuart to stop beside his car but instead he made straight for my caravan and when we caught up, he was peering under the step with the plant pot in one arm. After a minute he straightened and began to search behind the caravan instead. He still seemed to be hobbling. I was determined not to say anything, but Noah plucked the back of Stuart's shirt.

'What are you doing?'

Stuart swung around and glared at him. 'Looking for my chocolates.' His gaze hardened. 'Have you got them?'

'Don't be ridiculous!' I said. 'How could Noah have them? He's been with us.' As I was speaking, I became aware of another car arriving and the engine switching off.

'Well, they've disappeared so somebody's taken them. Your dodgy farmer probably stole them to flog them on eBay or something.'

'For God's sake Stuart, of course he hasn't! Besides, it's only a box of chocolates.' Despite myself I peered under the caravan chassis.

'They were bloody expensive.'

'Well show this to the policeman then. Ask him to interview the local foxes.' I pulled out a yellow ribbon from under the front tyre. Half a yellow ribbon to be exact.

'What policeman?'

I pointed over the barrier, where a policeman called Alfie Lane was standing behind Stuart's Golf with a notebook and pen. 'The one that's writing down your number plate.'

'Fuck!' Stuart sprinted towards his car. His limp appeared to have gone.

A few moments later I heard snatches of Alfie saying

something about Covid rules, and local journeys and Stuart muttering something about a sick granny and an emergency before suddenly shouting much more loudly 'You can't fucking fine me for visiting my own girlfriend!'

Alfie ripped a page out of his notebook and tucked it behind one of the windscreen wipers. 'Actually, I can.' He glanced at me then back at Stuart before adding in a loud, friendly tone, 'Besides, mate, she doesn't look to me like she's your girlfriend.'

For a second Stuart was seemingly transfixed. Next, there was a swirl of noise: a car door slammed, an engine roared, tyres slewed across the tarmac, before all at once peace descended with the abruptness of someone elbowing their way to the front of a crowd and I realised that Stuart had gone.

I wondered if Alfie might say something about me still being in the caravan, or even fine me too. Instead, he simply waved before getting into his own car and driving slowly away.

'Well,' I said to Noah. 'I bet you're hungry now! Austin will be back soon and we can have our picnic.' Even I could hear the lightness in my voice.

To my surprise, Noah shook his head.

'What's the matter? Don't you want a picnic anymore?'

'Austin already came back. He's left the shopping in the caravan.'

'What do you mean? When was he here?' I was already hurrying up the step. A Co-Op bag with packets of ham, cheese, grapes and strawberries was visible just inside the door.

'I don't know,' Noah said miserably. 'I didn't see him.'

'But why didn't he wait? Why did he go away again?' I probably sounded about the same age as Noah.

Noah didn't reply. He didn't have to. We were both thinking the same thing. Austin *might* have thought Noah and I had popped out again. Perhaps though, he saw me walking hand-in-hand to the beach with Stuart, canoodling under the pine trees. Maybe he even saw me *kissing* Stuart. I groaned. 'I'll message Austin now,' I told Noah. 'I'm sure he'll come back.'

But Austin didn't come back, Ruby. And he hasn't replied to my messages either. Not to any of them. As soon as it gets light, I'm going to start packing.

As I say, life sucks.

Cassie

Letter from Ms Margaret Flemming MA, MoE (Leadership) to Year 6 parents

14 May 2020

Dear Parent

Dear New Best Friend initiative

I hear marvellous things from Miss Gibbs regarding your children and their *New Best Friends*. What a wonderful opportunity for our young people to hear from those with a lifetime of learning in the classroom that matters most! To enrich the experience even further I have arranged for any child who lives in the vicinity of Shirley House to pay their pen pal a visit. (Not inside of course!) Between two and four o'clock on Sunday, 31 May, the children will be permitted to walk through the Shirley House gardens at a minimum distance of two metres from the (closed) windows. Each child will be given a slot of precisely ten minutes to allow for arrival, departure and their own personal 'walk', and I must ask everyone to observe the timetable most rigorously to ensure minimal pupil interaction. How thrilling, nevertheless, to put a face to their *New Best Friend's* name and witness the enthusiasm of their correspondents! Eager waving will be encouraged on both sides!

Your child must already have the address of Shirley House (otherwise sending letters will have proved tricky!) but I repeat it here to avoid any confusion: 9 Nightingale Place, Barnsbury, London N1 8YD. Although the parking area has two entrances, I understand a strict 'in' and 'out' policy is in operation. Let's make sure we adhere to the signs!

I'm hoping for a tremendous turnout so please email me by Monday, 25 May – or better still write a letter! – to confirm your young person's attendance. Everyone will be notified of their time slot during the following week.

Yours sincerely

Margaret E. Flemming (Headmistress)

Text Mrs Rosemary Ross to Cassie 07.05

18 May 2020

I've just picked up your voicemail (left on my phone at 2am – Cassandra, what is going on?) Of course, you and Noah can come and stay, but why are you leaving that lovely caravan?

You sounded so happy there. Never mind. Explain when you get here. If the police stop you, just tell them you're going home.

Postcard Mr Stanley Ross to Cassie

Postmarked 5 May 2020 received 18 May 2020

Travelling solo again! PA says she's going back to England at the first opportunity. She's missing a friend from gardening club, apparently! Not to worry, me and the old camper van get along by ourselves just fine. Now tossing up whether to head for Guatemala or Belize! How's your own adventure shaping up? Remember, Cassie, as the old Maori proverb says, *Turn your face towards the sun and the shadows fall behind you!*

Love

Dad

Letter Cassie to Ruby

18 May 2020

Dear Ruby,

I'm sitting on the caravan step again. Surrounded by boxes and suitcases (how can we have twice as many bags as when we arrived?). We were supposed to leave hours ago. Three hours ago. The trouble is I decided to check the mailbox one last time in case Austin had left me a note. He hadn't. Instead, I found a postcard from my father and your latest letter with all the enclosures and since then I've barely lifted my head from the page.

Where do I begin, Ruby? I suppose the starting place must be Edmondo. I can't imagine how dreadful you must have felt to lose him, believing you were the one to blame. That feeling has never completely gone away, has it? Didn't you say to me, *guilt is the most enduring of all the emotions...*? However, if Edmondo is who I think he is, I might be able to help. I'll need some answers from you first, though.

How did you join the pen-pal scheme, Ruby? And find out about Noah being ill?

I know you're not a resident of Shirley House because I discovered yesterday that Shirley House is near Noah's school in London and not in Suffolk at all, which means all this time I must have been writing to an entirely different home. That's why you told me to send my letters care of the Manager's Office, isn't it? Now I think about it, I realise the address you gave me only refers to the building number and not to the name. I can't believe I never noticed that before. Anyway, although I could fill page after page with questions I'm going to stop here and wait for your reply.

Your New Best Friend (I think)

Cassie

PS From tomorrow, Noah and I will be staying with my mother so please write to: Mariner's Rest, Turnpike Lane, Gunwalloe, Cornwall.

London Evening Standard

22 April 2019

Fifty haircuts in eighteen hours!

Cassie Ross, hairdresser, and mum from North London, has raised over £5,000 for Great Ormond Street Hospital by doing a sponsored marathon haircut and fleecing the locks of fifty willing recipients in an exhausting 18 hours of continuous cutting. Ms Ross wanted to thank the hospital in a practical way for treating her son, Noah aged five, for Acute Lymphoblastic Leukaemia and sepsis. With luck, he has every chance of making a full recovery. First, in the chair was Ms Ross's mother, Mrs Rosemary Ross, followed by Ms Ross's grandmother, Mrs Carmella Hayward. Mrs Hayward, aged ninety-two, said she had only asked for a trim because she didn't want to tire out her granddaughter so early into the marathon! The three women are pictured below with Noah, a pupil at St Cuthbert's Primary School, Barnsbury. Ms Ross said she was grateful to every single person who has sponsored her or volunteered to have their hair cut, adding it still wasn't too late to donate via her JustGiving page The Big Chop.

Letter Ruby to Cassie

19 May 2020

Dear Cassie

I'm sending this letter and the newspaper clipping from last April to the holiday park as I'm quite confident you'll still be living in your bright green caravan and not at your mother's. I have every faith in Austin. He's not a man to be deterred from a good thing as easily as you seem to think – and you're a good thing. A very good thing.

The clipping was sent to me by a friend in London who knows that even at my age – *particularly* at my age – I love to read of children recovering from Leukaemia and relive that special Tuesday morning all over again. On this occasion, however, her kindness rekindled rather different memories. I recognised your grandmother immediately. Although I never knew she married – or indeed what happened to any of the Brambilla family – I was certain the Mrs Carmella Hayward staring back at me from the page was Edmondo's sister, and a magnifying glass (supplied with a smile by Amy) together with an old photograph (supplied in the war by Edmondo), soon confirmed my belief. *Dear Fragolina.* How wonderful to see that sweet face again and realise the young scientist I once was had played a part in saving the life of her great grandchild.

It won't surprise you to know I kept that cutting, tucked carefully inside my box of letters, until a morning not so very long ago caused me to read the caption again. One afternoon, shortly after Amy had switched to Radio Four, the head-mistress of St Cuthbert's came on the radio, practically bursting with enthusiasm about her pupils becoming pen pals with the residents of a care home called Shirley House. The more she talked the more the name of her school sounded familiar and the instant I checked the cutting and realised that Noah went to St Cuthbert's I began to envy his would-be pen pal and wish I had the chance to write to him myself.

Then I realised I could.

After all, who would know the names of the Shirley

House residents? Almost certainly not Mrs Flemming. All that I had to do was contact the school and request them to pair me with Noah. Nobody was likely to check where I lived and I could simply give my real address to Noah as the one he should write back to. I was so excited I wrote to Noah immediately. The rest, as they say, is history.

Though not, perhaps, the history you were expecting.

Will you forgive me? For making you correspond with an old lady under false pretences. For telling you the truth behind your family's wartime tragedy. I have waited all my life for the chance to explain myself so when Mrs Flemming surged into the day lounge with Noah and her pen-pal scheme, I'm sorry to say the temptation was too much to resist. At ninety-six I knew such an opportunity would never come again.

Dear New Best Friend, how your wonderful letters exceeded my hopes! Every envelope put a smile on my face to rival Amy's and threw a blanket of light around these last dark weeks. Now I ask nothing more. Unless you choose otherwise, this will be the last you hear from me.

Your New Best Friend

Ruby

PS I have sent you only the caption from the newspaper cutting. I'm afraid the photograph itself is too precious to give away – even to you.

Letter Mrs Rosemary Ross to Cassie

23 May 2020

Dear Cassandra

What an extraordinary message to find on my answerphone. Your grandmother was very reluctant to talk about the war because her father had been a fascist and brought great shame on them all. However, I do know that Edmondo definitely didn't drown on the *Arandora Star*. As I remember the tale he drifted on an upturned table until a lifeboat came into view, swam for his life and was taken back to Scotland with the rest of the survivors. Unfortunately, less than a week later, some of those poor souls were deported again – this time to Australia (on a ship called the *Dunera*, if I remember correctly). Edmondo spent the rest of the war in an Australian internment camp and was only able to trace your grandmother and his parents once the fighting was over. By that time his father's guilt must have become too much to bear because he'd admitted his dreadful part in the business and moved to Ireland. What else do I know? Edmondo settled in Italy, married – briefly, I believe – and has a daughter. How strange you should be corresponding with his childhood sweetheart! I've found a Milan address amongst your grandmother's papers, but I've no idea whether Edmondo is living there now or even whether he's survived the pandemic and is still alive. I've copied out the address on the back of the paper, but don't get your hopes up, Cassandra, it was an awfully long time ago and I imagine he'll have forgotten all about your Ruby Summers by now.

A big hug to you and Noah

Mum

PS Your message wasn't the only one on the answerphone. Penelope Anne said she wanted to come and see me! I messaged back immediately and told her she couldn't do any such thing because it would be contrary to the Covid rules. (At long last those blasted rules have come in useful for something!)

Flyer Cassie to residents of Wells-next-the Sea

29 May 2020

CALLING ALL RESIDENTS OF WELLS-NEXT-THE SEA

FREE HAIRCUTS 1 JUNE 2020!

Is your hair driving you mad? Are you desperate to visit a hair salon or barber? I am Cassie Ross, an experienced hairdresser, and this Monday I will be cutting hair in the outside space of the caravan park from 8am until 4pm – for FREE!! All welcome, including children.

NB Please wear masks and observe social distancing when queuing.

Letter Cassie to Ruby

2 June 2020

Dear Ruby

Your letter didn't come as a surprise. By the time I finished reading about you and Edmondo, I had guessed there must be some connection between you and my Italian grandmother and I'm glad you wrote to me. Getting to know you has been the best thing about lockdown. Or the joint best thing if I'm totally honest. You were right about Austin (I'm not at my mother's!) but more of that in a minute. First, I have to tell you some sad news. My grandmother Carmella passed away from a stroke last year, shortly after the photograph in the newspaper was published. She was just as lovely and sweet as you remember, and never at all bitter about the war, so I'm sure she would have forgiven you. Besides, Ruby, it turns out you weren't the person who needs forgiving, someone else was to blame and not you at all. I promise you'll know more about that soon. And as for the amazing life you led afterwards.... well, every night I hug Noah and say a prayer of thanks to you and all the other scientists whose discoveries mean my little boy is alive today, squirming in my arms and complaining about how tightly I'm squeezing him. Although Noah has a follow-up appointment in two weeks' time, I'm not even worried because I can see for myself how healthy he looks.

To Austin then... can you picture my huge smile?! After I'd finished writing to you, sitting amongst my packing and the bags overflowing with shoes and packets of food, Noah took the letter to the holiday park postbox while I began to heave the cases into the boot of the car. I was so preoccupied I didn't hear an engine until a vehicle swung far too fast into the entrance and stopped with a screech on the far side of the barrier. For a split second I worried Stuart had come back, then Austin leapt out of the driver's seat clasping his phone and sprinted toward me.

'Cassie!' He slid to a halt beside the caravan step.

I froze. I was holding a cardboard box full of Noah's cars

with a toy elephant perched on top and could barely see over the top.

'Cassie,' Austin was panting, 'I'm so sorry I disappeared.' He took another breath. 'It was Badger.'

'Badger?'

'While I was putting the shopping inside the caravan, he found a box of chocolates and raced off before I could grab him. By the time I caught him up he'd scoffed the lot as well as a yellow ribbon. The chocolate made him dreadfully sick and the vet had to operate because the ribbon was tangled up inside his stomach. I nearly lost him, Cassie. If we hadn't gone straight to the vet's, it would have been too late.' He inhaled like someone who had just sprinted the hundred metres. 'I would have called you from the car but...' he hesitated and this time not to get his breath '... but you looked a bit busy when I left.'

Behind the soft ears of Elephant, I blushed. 'I did message you,' I stammered. 'I messaged you lots of times.'

'I didn't try to check my messages until later. When I was waiting at the vets while Badger had his operation and by then my phone had died. It was only when I went home this morning for a shower and got my charger that I saw your texts...'

'And email.'

'And email. I'm sorry, Cassie. Do you really want to leave?'

I swallowed. 'I don't know.' At that precise second, I didn't know. And I didn't know what to say about Stuart or what Austin had seen me do with Stuart. And I didn't know how to get back to that lovely feeling on the beach when Noah was riding on Austin's shoulders and the thought of us all having a picnic together was the most perfect idea imaginable.

'How is Badger now?' I said instead. My arms were aching from the weight of the box.

'The vet says he'll be OK. I haven't seen him yet this morning because I came straight here. I never even had my shower.' He gave an unhappy smile. 'As soon as I saw your messages, I jumped back in the Land Rover.'

I realised how tired he looked. His face was as rumpled as his shirt, the same faded green one he had been wearing the day before. I imagined not seeing that face or that shirt ever again and it felt as if my heart was being emptied out with an ice-cream scoop.

'I've still got the supermarket food you bought,' I said after a moment. 'We could have that picnic today instead?'

'What about all this?' He gestured at the sea of belongings scattered around the caravan.

'I'll put them back in the caravan, while you visit Badger. We'll eat when you get back.'

'You're not leaving then?'

I shook my head. 'Not unless you want to evict me for rent arrears.'

So, Ruby, we had our picnic after all. In fact, Austin has been to the caravan every day since, either for a meal, or a walk on the beach, or simply to sit beneath the stars and talk. The other evening, I told him about you and my great uncle, Edmondo, and how you recognised Fragolina from the newspaper article. Explaining the story gave me an idea. I decided to do another haircutting session in the caravan park. Not sponsored this time, or to earn money, but free for the local residents. Everyone would be safe in the open air and the gesture would be a kind of thank you for me being here during lockdown.

Austin printed off fifty flyers back at his farm and we stuck one in the window of the supermarket and left the others beside the tills. I still wasn't sure that anyone would read them, or they would be bothered to come to the caravan park to get their hair cut by someone they didn't know. But they did! By eight o'clock in the morning the line stretched halfway along the sea wall. Everyone was standing at a respectful distance wearing masks, asking their neighbour what they thought about different styles and lengths. Some people had even bought magazine pictures which they were holding up to the queue for advice! PC Alfie Lane was one of the first in the chair. He said long hair wasn't right for a policeman and also itched under his helmet. Others were simply desperate to feel like themselves again – or sometimes the new person they had become during lockdown.

The very last person to sit down was Austin. By that time my hands were so tired they were beginning to shake. I was hoping he didn't want to change his appearance much for other reasons too. To me, his long hair was part of him and I didn't want him to suddenly look like a stranger. I needn't have worried. When I picked up the scissors, he shook his head.

'I just wanted to see you, Cassie.' He looked directly into my eyes. 'Whatever I'm doing it seems I always want to see you.'

From inside the caravan, I could hear one of Noah's teachers describing how to make a papier-mâché angel on Zoom – *Take a piece of cardboard, like the side of a cereal packet, and ask your mum or dad to draw the shape of a wing.* I strongly suspected Noah had no interest in papier-mâché angels and was probably studying his farmer's chart again. I knew I ought to go inside and help.

Instead, I leaned over the chair until our mouths were nearly touching. The voice of the teacher melted away. I swallowed. 'I always want to see you too,' I said.

That was yesterday, Ruby, so now you're up to date. But that can't be the end, can it? You can't possibly think I'm going to let you stop writing to me because of who you are. As soon as it's safe I want to meet you and I want you to meet Noah and watch him running around with Badger and turning cartwheels and behaving like any other six-year-old. Until then we'll have to make do with letters. Only don't send them to the caravan because we won't be staying here much longer. Use this address instead (I'm sure you can guess whose it is): Goose Farm, Blackwater Lane, Little Burnham, Norfolk.

With love

Your New Best Friend

Cassie

PS I'm sorry it took me so long to reply. I was waiting for something. You'll find out about that something shortly.

Letter Austin to Cassie

3 June 2020

Dearest Cassie

I suppose this might be the last letter I ever write you. In many ways I hope so, because that would mean you never live anywhere except with me. However, a part of me is a little sad about that. You never save text messages or emails, but you do keep letters. At least I do, and I know I'll always have the ones you sent me from the caravan. Whenever you're away and I want to hear your voice all I'll have to do is unfold a piece of paper and you'll be standing next to me. It's the closest thing I can think of to magic. That's why I wanted to write to you one more time. In case you're ever without me, read this and know I'll be missing you from wherever I am, counting the seconds until we're together again, just as much as I miss you today.

I'm counting already.

Love

Austin

Letter Edmondo to Ruby

4 June 2020

Mia Ruby,

I see your fingers tremble as they open an envelope with an Italian postmark. Your eyes scanning the page in astonishment. Once. Twice. Perhaps even three times. Yes, mia cara, it is me, Edmondo. We may be in different countries but at this moment are we not standing beside each other, breathing in the lilacs and the scent of grass while the sun dips over the meadow behind your house? Did you even know I am alive? That I survived the sinking of the Arandora Star and was deported to Australia? I believe dear Cassie wanted to be certain neither old age nor the virus had taken me before raising your hopes. If so, I am happy for you to hear the news from me. After all, this is our story.

I've seen the letters and diaries you sent to Cassie. You've blamed yourself over the years when the blame should have been mine – and my father's. I asked you to keep an impossible secret, to put my interests above those of your country in a time of war. How could you have not done what your family wanted without other consequences, other regrets? Who among us would have chosen differently? And – though it still hurts me to say it – you made the right decision. You see, it turns out my father was indeed a fascist. I like to believe he became corrupted by talking to his musician friend but for all I know the truth might be the other way round. In any case, the cloud he cast over our family is the reason I never came to you after the war. By then you were a scientist with an extraordinary future ahead whereas I was an Italian, and now the son of a traitor. How could I have come back into your life after six years of silence and put your position and all you might achieve at risk? It would have been impossible. Instead, I made a home for myself in Milan, comforted by the knowledge you were doing the work I had always understood you were meant to do.

Mia Cara, we did not spend our lives together, but we have still lived well. If I find myself wishing things could have been different, I will think of Noah playing on a beach and the countless children your work has saved. Of the happiness my own child has brought me. There are many kinds of lives to lead, all of them wonderful in different ways.

The great advantage of old age is that some memories fade to dust while others retain such colour that they continue to brighten every day. Now, I barely remember the war. You, on the other hand, I could never forget. Besides, we may be nearing the end of our lives but they are not yet over. Forgive me for daring to dream of one last adventure, one last chance to hold your hand.

Your old best friend

Edmondo

PS I'm enclosing a menu from the Felixstowe Grand. For our cake and champagne, when this new war is over. After all, if it's our story, we have the right, don't we, to choose our own ending?

A LETTER FROM SARAH

Dear reader,

I want to say a huge thank you for choosing to read *Letters to a Stranger*. If you did enjoy it and want to keep up to date with all my latest releases, just sign up at the following link. Your email address will never be shared and you can unsubscribe at any time.

www.bookouture.com/sarah-mitchell

The book was inspired by an article I read in the news magazine, *The Week,* describing how the Head of a primary school had encouraged the children to become penfriends with the residents of a care home during the pandemic. I owe that Head a huge debt of gratitude. I also can't help but wonder what tales their lovely initiative uncovered – the fact there must be so many untold stories hidden within the lounges of care homes and day-care centres everywhere makes the Head's idea a very special one.

I think the article in *The Week* resonated with me so much with me because of my own great affection for letters. I'm old enough to have a box of them myself. Letters that were written to me many years ago from relatives – particularly my mother, who always made the ordinary effortlessly entertaining – and friends. Every time I consider clearing them out, I end up sitting on my bedroom floor surrounded by paper and transported back to the past. Needless to say, I never manage to throw away a single page. In all honesty, I agree with Austin – letters *are* the closest thing to magic, and in some ways this book is really a love letter to them.

If you enjoyed *Letters to a Stranger*, I would be very grateful if you could write a review. I really appreciate hearing what my readers think, and it makes such a difference helping new readers to discover one of my books for the first time. Also, I love to hear from my readers – you can get in touch through Twitter – whether you have any comments or thoughts about the book or would just like to say hello. It means a great deal to know that I am not writing in isolation and that there are readers out there actually reading and enjoying my work.

And, if the book inspires you to write a letter of your own to someone, I shall be delighted.

With thanks,

Sarah Mitchell

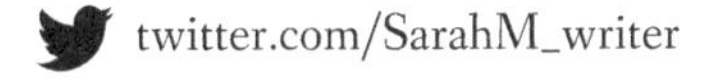

ACKNOWLEDGMENTS

As always, I would like to thank my wonderful agent, Veronique Baxter, for her constant support and advice, and my thanks too, to my lovely editor Isobel Akenhead, whose expert guidance helped the book to become the best version of itself. For research purposes, the book, *Missing Presumed Drowned*, a true story of the internment of Italians resident in Britain during the Second World War, by Stefano Paolini, was an invaluable source of information and inspiration. It contains first-hand accounts of Italians living in Britain during the Second World War, as well as newspaper articles and contemporaneous documents, and truly brings home the sense of fear and isolation that must have been felt by those who suddenly found themselves living in a country that regarded them as an enemy. I should mention that the dates of the letters quoting certain articles do not always exactly tally with the date a particular article first appeared in a newspaper, though any discrepancy is only a matter of days. Thanks are due too, to the iconic Troxy in London, for the kind permission to use their letter headed "Sunshine in November". Closer to home my friend Clare Barter not only provided fabulous feedback but did so by way of a (now much cherished) handwritten letter, while my husband, Peter – aka plot consultant – dealt with my stream of seemingly random questions and small disasters with his usual patience, imagination, and good humour.

CPSIA information can be obtained
at www.ICGtesting.com
Printed in the USA
BVHW032208270223
659375BV00002B/17

9 781803 149547